Where Memories Lie

WHERE
MEMORIES
Lie

Where Memories Lie
The Inheritance Duology
Book 1

Irene Lee

STEEL THORN
PRESS

Published by Steel Thorn Press

ISBN: 979-8-9931398-1-4

Cover design by Frina Art

First Edition

Printed in the United States of America

For my husband, who passionately hates fantasy novels, but encouraged me to write one anyway.

Memory is the treasury and guardian of all things
—*Cicero*

Introduction

Magic has always existed.
But it hasn't always coexisted peacefully with the mundane world. For centuries, unregulated magic surfaced unpredictably, often with dangerous results.

Roughly a quarter of the population have magical abilities. Many are healers, illusionists, or elemental users. A rare few possess powerful magic, most notably the memory specialists, who can trace psychic imprints, read emotional residue, and recall event memories.

Since the early 20th century, magic has been regulated and woven into infrastructure. The system was designed to protect both magical and mundane citizens. Most people trust it because it works.

Regulation isn't perfect. Some magic users push the limits of the law. Others reject oversight entirely, arguing that it violates personal freedom and that the gifted should not be bound by ordinary laws.

In recent years, those voices have grown louder.

Magic is a gift, but people are not inherently good. And when regulation fails, the consequences ripple through every part of society. What comes next will test whether the system can adapt—or whether the very gifts meant to protect the world will be the force that fractures it.

1
What's Past Is Prologue

Whereof what's past is prologue; what to come,
In yours and my discharge.
—*William Shakespeare, The Tempest*

Gravel shifted beneath Elias' knees as he adjusted beside the loading dock. Cold pressed through the tactical pants into his legs. Alex stayed crouched beside him while Elias focused on the warehouse.

"Reading anything?" Alex asked.

Elias let his focus settle. He willed his awareness forward, pushing his magic through the abandoned warehouse until shapes brightened where people moved. "Multiple people inside. Seven individuals, maybe eight. They're positioned defensively but not expecting contact. I'm not sensing fear or any anxiety. It's kind of odd."

"Weapons?"

"The trace sharpens around metal. Standard firearms, some kind of explosive device in the northeast corner. Nothing we can't handle if we move fast. They're using the main floor for planning meetings and the upper level for equipment storage."

Alex studied the building's exterior. Elias could feel the silver combat magic waiting at the edge of Alex's presence, ready for the moment they moved. Their magic had worked seamlessly since the FBI Academy. Elias's memory magic searched the field, and Alex always acted as his anchor whenever the traces pulled too deep. Something in their magic reached for the other on its own, drawn together by a bond neither of them could explain.

"Which entry looks better?" Alex asked.

"Southwest loading dock gives the cleanest approach. The targets are clustered in the center, clear fields of fire and several exits." Elias concentrated. "Standard takedown protocols should be sufficient."

Alex nodded to Agent Morrison, who keyed the final approach. Seven FBI agents plus Alex and Elias made nine. It was more than enough if the intel held.

The loading dock stood unlocked, just as Elias had said. Alex moved the team through the building quickly but carefully. Silver gathered at Alex's hands, shimmering in Elias's peripheral vision. Elias flowed behind him, feeding positions into comms.

"Targets maintaining position in central area," Elias reported. "No indication they're aware of our presence."

"Explosive device status?" Alex asked.

"Still in the northeast corner. No change in the signature." The green threads tightened around the device on Elias's mental map. He kept his report simple. Alex trusted him, so he didn't need to provide extra details.

They moved through the lower level room by room, the way they always did. Agents checked their sectors while weapons tracked downrange. Elias's mental map matched the room perfectly. The men were where he'd seen them and the guns were where he'd marked them.

Still, something felt off. The details came sharper than they should have. Elias felt a flicker of something odd in his mind. He opened his mouth to speak but stopped.

Alex reached the central area and stepped toward the device. Elias saw him stiffen. The silver magic around Alex's hands flared with sudden, violent intensity.

"Everyone out now. The device is active," Alex shouted over the comms.

Gunfire erupted from concealed positions as the terrorists realized the trap had been found. Elias saw the device through a gap in the crates. A small screen was lit up, the timer reading five seconds.

He tried to move, but the world turned white. The blast tore through brick and shredded steel. Before the heat could reach him, Alex was there, throwing his weight over Elias to pin him to the floor. A shell of silver light erupted around them, vibrating with the force of the impact. Elias watched through the shimmering barrier as the building turned into chaos. Brick and metal flew outward while smoke filled the air.

Alex's jaw was set tight as he forced the barrier to hold against the hammering fragments. Then, Alex's eyes rolled back. As the silver shield flickered, Elias caught Alex's collapsing weight. He screamed Alex's name, reaching through the dust and blood for the partner who had just saved his life.

University of Chicago Medical Center Three Days Later

Elias sat in the stiff hospital chair he'd slept in every day since the explosion, watching Alex under sedation that kept the worst pain at bay. The doctors said Alex would recover completely, though the shrapnel scar across his back would be a permanent reminder of how close they'd come to losing everything.

Seven agents were dead. Seven good people who would never come home because Elias had read the situation wrong, had been so confident in his abilities that he'd led them into a trap someone with his training should have seen. He had been sure of his read. He'd been wrong.

Alex stirred under the drugs and silver light flickered at his hands in small reflexive patterns. Each movement tightened the guilt in Elias' chest. His partner had nearly died protecting him from the consequences of that failure.

The door opened quietly as Dr. John Dixon came in for evening rounds and checked the monitors. "Any change?" he asked, consulting Alex's charts.

"No. Still unconscious." Elias' voice sounded hollow. "When will he wake up?"

"Soon. His brain activity shows normal patterns, and the swelling has reduced significantly. Probably within the next day or two," Dr. Dixon said. "He's going to make a full recovery, Agent Sinclair. You were both incredibly lucky."

Lucky. Seven agents were dead because Elias had been overconfident in abilities that had failed catastrophically when it mattered most. That wasn't luck. That was incompetence.

Elias stayed at the bedside through the night and into the next morning. He turned the sequence over in his head, accepting his part in it. His memory magic hadn't lied before. Somehow, he'd misread the room.

He went to his apartment for a shower and a change of clothes. He brought a coffee and the newspaper back out of habit, but he froze in the corridor when voices reached him. Dr. Dixon's tone was measured. Then came Alex's voice, steady and awake. Elias leaned against the wall, the tension in his chest finally easing. Alex was going to recover.

He stared at the hospital door, imagining the questions

Alex would ask. *Was anyone else hurt? You said the device was inert. Why were you wrong?*

The weight of it pressed on him. Alex wouldn't have confidence in his assessments again. The partnership and the trust that had made them the Bureau's most effective team felt like a glass floor that had finally shattered. He'd been overconfident in his magic, and it had failed when lives depended on it.

He turned and walked away from the room. He couldn't face the disappointment he knew would be waiting in Alex's eyes. Alex would heal, but Elias didn't see a way to repair the rest. Some things just stayed broken.

2
Severed Connections

No man is an island entire of itself
—John Donne

Eighteen Months Later

FBI Chicago Division—November 15

"Alex!"

The shout cut across the afternoon hum of the FBI Chicago Counterterrorism unit. Agent Alexander Sutton looked up. Blue eyes narrowed as Cross approached.

Cross was still adjusting to the pace of high stakes cases. He'd been assigned as Alex's partner three months ago, and he'd already lasted longer than the previous two agents. Alex didn't want a partner. Not really.

Cross was competent, respectful, and quiet. He waited for Alex to take the lead, never in step and never closing the gaps before they opened. Alex had stopped expecting anyone to.

Elias had transferred out eighteen months ago. He'd

requested it without talking to Alex, and Alex had accepted the reassignment without asking for an explanation. Since then, no partner had filled the space Elias left behind.

Alex cut off that line of thinking. "What is it, Cross?"

Cross tapped his tablet. The analytical magic infused into the database highlighted passages as he read. "CTA elevated train, inbound Red Line. Conductor's dead. Passengers reported unusual circumstances before the crash."

Alex closed his file. "Unusual how?"

"Witnesses say the conductor started screaming about fifteen minutes before impact. He was clawing at the air, acting like he was fighting something they couldn't see." Cross's face tightened. "Train veered at Fullerton Station. It could've been worse, but emergency magical systems engaged and cushioned the impact."

Alex recognized the signs. "Magic at play?"

"That's what Transit thinks. Their ward systems detected an anomaly in the conductor's cab, but the readings were inconsistent." Cross frowned at his tablet. "Local magical response teams are on scene, but they've requested Bureau consultation."

Alex gathered his jacket and weapon. He noted the way Cross waited for him to take the lead. It was a professional courtesy to a senior agent that felt wrong, like walking beside someone who was always just out of step. Elias had never needed to wait for instructions. He'd never required coordination beyond subtle magical cues. They'd developed an efficiency that made other teams look clumsy. Two different magical specialties had flowed together with a precision that exceeded the sum of their individual parts.

"Transit Authority sending a liaison?" Alex asked as they headed toward the elevator.

"Detective Sarah Kim, Chicago PD. She'll meet us at the crash site." Cross activated privacy wards around the elevator as they descended. The air shimmered briefly as protective enchantments prevented their conversation from being overheard.

"Preliminary report suggests the conductor lost consciousness before the train left the elevated track. Emergency systems engaged, but response time wasn't sufficient to prevent derailment."

Alex handled the driving while Cross reviewed the case. The screen displayed magical enhancements that cross referenced incident reports with pattern analysis. Chicago traffic moved through its usual morning congestion. The city's magical infrastructure was visible to anyone with magical sight. Intersection management systems coordinated conventional signals with transit priority spells. Emergency vehicles used dedicated magical transit lanes, their passage marked by the brief shimmer effects most drivers ignored.

Kinetic tram lines sparked midair between buildings, their amber energy creating transportation networks that supplemented conventional rapid transit. Wards hummed across rooftops in patterns that most citizens never noticed, protective spells maintaining security zones around sensitive facilities.

It was a magnificent system, the result of decades of careful integration between magical and mundane technology. It was also increasingly fragile. Too many small failures, too much strain on systems designed for lighter loads.

"You think this is connected to the recent infrastructure problems?" Cross asked, following Alex's gaze toward the city.

"Everything's connected to the infrastructure problems," Alex replied. "Question is whether this represents normal system failure or something more deliberate."

The crash site was visible from three blocks away, emergency response vehicles creating a perimeter around the elevated track where the Red Line train hung partially over the street. Magical support pillars had been conjured to prevent complete collapse, their crystalline structure glowing with stabilization spells that would hold until conventional repairs could be implemented.

Cross parked behind the Transit Authority command vehicle, where personnel coordinated with Chicago PD and emergency medical services. The air buzzed with communication spells and detection magic, Bureau and local authorities working to process a scene that exceeded normal incident response protocols.

Detective Sarah Kim approached. "Agent Sutton," she said. "I'm the Chicago PD. Thank you for coming so quickly."

Alex shook her hand. "What's the situation?"

"Conductor Michael Rodriguez, twenty-three years with CTA, excellent safety record, no history of medical or psychological problems." Detective Kim led them toward the elevated platform where the derailed train cars sat at an angle that defied normal physics. "Passengers report he became agitated around seven-fifteen this morning, approximately fifteen minutes before impact."

"Agitated how?" Cross asked, pulling out his notepad.

"Screaming, clawing at the air in the conductor's cab, acting like he was fighting off invisible attackers. Several passengers attempted to get his attention, but he didn't respond to external stimuli. Just kept fighting something they couldn't see."

Alex studied the train's position, noting the way emergency magical systems had engaged to prevent catastrophic collapse. The elevated track showed scorch marks where the train had left the rails, but the damage patterns suggested controlled failure rather than random accident.

"Magical signatures?" Alex asked.

"That's where it gets interesting," Kim replied. "Our ward systems detected an anomaly in the conductor's cab, but the readings were unlike anything in our database. Not a conventional magical discharge, not equipment malfunction. Something else entirely."

They climbed to the elevated platform with the aid of stairs conjured by the Transit Authority's maintenance specialists. Alex steadied himself on the narrow steps, his six-foot athletic frame balanced against the sway of the damaged platform. From that viewpoint Alex could see how the emergency response had transformed Fullerton Station into a technological command center. Paramedics worked alongside licensed magical healing specialists to treat injured passengers, their coordination demonstrating the integration that had made Chicago a model for magical emergency services. Transit warders moved between the derailed cars with detection equipment, their abilities focused on assessing enchantment interference that might explain the conductor's behavior.

"Registration records show the conductor had no magical abilities," Detective Kim reported as they approached the train. "Standard background check, no immediately obvious connections to extremist organizations, no recent changes in personal circumstances that might explain erratic behavior."

The crash site reeked of burnt copper. Alex tasted it before he saw it and as he reached out with his magical senses he immediately withdrew. It felt old and dangerous.

"Cross, start with passenger interviews. Get me timeline, behavior, anything out of place." His gaze never left the residue, its rhythms beating in time with something that didn't belong here.

"Detective Kim, I need access to the conductor's cab."

The forward car of the train hung over the edge of the elevated platform at an angle that required careful navigation to reach the conductor's position. Magical safety lines provided security against falling, but the entire structure groaned with stress that made every movement feel potentially hazardous.

"Emergency systems engaged approximately thirty seconds before impact," Kim explained as they climbed toward the cab. "Cushioning spells and structural reinforcement prevented catastrophic damage, but response time wasn't sufficient to prevent derailment."

Inside the cab, a thermos had rolled across the control panel, dripping cold coffee onto scattered forms. Michael Rodriguez sat slumped in his chair, eyes wide, mouth frozen mid-scream.

"Medical examiner's preliminary assessment?" Alex asked, studying the body without touching anything.

"No obvious cause of death. No trauma, no indication of poisoning or medical emergency. He appears to have suddenly died. But his expression suggests he was experiencing something horrifying when it happened."

Alex opened his senses again. The echo hit harder here, the same strange pattern only sharper. It pushed back against him as if alive. His magic faltered under it. He didn't have memory magic, so he couldn't trace where it came from.

"Agent Sutton? What are you detecting?"

"I don't know," Alex said, his voice grim as he began to slowly circle the conductor's cab.

"A magical signature unlike anything I've ever encountered," Alex observed, his eyes scanning the cab.

"It's not any form of magic I recognize, not a system fault. Something else entirely."

As he traced the spread of the foreign energy, the pattern pointed to sustained exposure, not a single burst. It was as if the conductor had been trapped in it for minutes before it killed him.

"How long was he acting strangely?" Alex asked.

"Based on passenger statements, approximately fifteen minutes from initial behavioral changes to final collapse," Kim replied. "But he remained conscious and responsive to train operations through most of that period."

"He was fighting it," Alex observed, noting the way the magical residue clustered around areas where the conductor would have been struggling against whatever was affecting him.

"Something was trying to override his consciousness, and he resisted until his system couldn't maintain the effort."

If someone had the power to target human consciousness itself through magic, it meant that kind of attack could be used deliberately and on a larger scale.

Alex stepped back from the conductor's cab, his magical senses still stinging. "Officer Kim, I need your ward system logs for the entire morning. And I want passenger manifests cross-referenced with the magical registration database."

"You think this was deliberate?" Kim asked.

"I don't know for sure," Alex replied. "But someone needs to explain how this energy got into a secure transit system."

"Passenger statements are consistent," Cross reported, consulting his notepad while standing safely away from the conductor's cab.

"Rodriguez appeared normal until approximately seven-fifteen, then became agitated and began exhibiting behavior suggesting he was fighting off invisible attackers."

"Fighting how?" Alex asked, his attention split between Cross's report and continued analysis of the magical residue that seemed to pulse with malevolent intelligence.

"Witnesses said he was clawing at the air, shouting for something to leave him alone." Cross's expression tightened as he continued.

"But through all of it, he kept the train on course. Professional protocols held, even while he was clearly under extreme psychological distress."

"No visible trauma, no drug use, and no medical conditions that explain a sudden breakdown," Officer Kim said. "Rodriguez was healthy, no sign of mental instability."

The magical residue told a different story. Alex traced the layered patterns with his senses and they felt too deliberate.

"This wasn't designed to kill him," Alex said. "I think the magic was trying to override his consciousness. Keep him functional but compliant. He probably died from the effort of resisting whatever was trying to control him."

"Control him to do what?" Cross asked.

"I don't know. But whoever did this wanted him alive and under their influence for a while."

Before Alex could say anything else, a sharp voice cut in over Officer Kim's comms. "Control, we have a situation at Fullerton Station. An individual fleeing the scene, refusing to stop for questioning, displaying magical abilities."

Alex and Cross exchanged glances, both recognizing the timing that suggested a connection to their investigation.

"Description?" Alex asked Detective Kim who immediately relayed the question into her radio.

The officer on the other end responded, "Male, approximately thirty years old, dark clothing, moving south from the station platform. Officers are in pursuit but subject is using magical illusions to evade capture."

Alex and Cross descended from the crash site to find Chicago PD coordinating with backup units. Security footage showed the suspect avoiding direct camera angles.

"He was watching our investigation," Alex said.

"Last known position was Red Line tunnels heading south toward downtown. Subject appears to be using service access routes to avoid main transit areas." Detective Kim said.

Alex and Cross took off at a run toward their suspect. The chase took them into Chicago's hidden infrastructure, service tunnels and maintenance areas that most citizens never knew existed. Emergency lights threw hard shadows across concrete walls crowded with pipes and cables.

"Movement ahead," Cross called, pointing toward a section of tunnel where emergency illumination spells had been disrupted, creating pools of darkness that suggested recent magical interference.

Silver coiled at Alex's hands. He readied himself for whatever waited in the tunnel. The underground environment favored magical combat over conventional weapons, enclosed spaces where energy discharge could be controlled and directed with precision.

They rounded a corner. The suspect was fifty yards ahead, walking quickly. The man turned and looked at Alex. His reaction was immediate and precise. He didn't look panicked as he chose paths that kept him out of sight.

The man dove toward a veiled stairwell and sent a pulse through the tunnel's ambient magic. Enchantment rippled and collapsed. Alex felt his power wobble as the interference hit. The silver dimmed and tightened, and he stumbled. In that second the suspect melted into concealment beyond ordinary invisibility.

"Where did he go?" Cross shouted, scanning with his lesser senses.

"The signature's the same as the crash site," Alex said, bringing silver light back to his palms. "Whoever killed the conductor is tied to this man."

Cross lunged forward, sweeping his hands through the stale air as if he could peel the layers back. His face was white with effort. "Illusion magic, but on steroids. No illusionist has this level of concealment ability," he panted.

They surfaced into morning crowds. Alex spotted the man across the street, standing and watching with a small, mocking smile.

They pushed through commuters and vendors. Just as

Alex thought they had him boxed, the suspect stopped and turned. Alex shouted, "Stop. FBI."

The man only smiled and palmed something in his jacket. The interference flared with brutal intensity and the world skewed. Alex's senses fractured. He forced through the disorientation and sent a kinetic pulse. The strike missed by inches. The suspect slipped away on practiced footing.

Cross tried to close, but the disruption crippled his perception too. Less than thirty seconds later the man vanished into a camouflage so complete he left no trace of sight or sense. When the field cleared, the street was empty.

"Son of a bitch," Cross muttered.

Alex crouched and read the residue left in the air. "He can't be working alone. This was planned. It's part of something larger."

Back at headquarters, two hours of paperwork waited. Alex sat at his desk replaying the chase.

"They were testing our response," he said.

Cross looked up from his notes. "For what?"

"I don't know. Today was a run to see what our systems do." Alex saved the report and closed his laptop. Afternoon light slanted across the office.

"And now they know more about our capabilities than we know about theirs," he added, running a hand through his hair.

"Want to grab dinner?" Cross asked. "There's a new Mexican restaurant down the street."

"Thanks, Marcus, but I'm good," Alex said.

Cross nodded. "See you tomorrow then."

That evening Alex microwaved leftover Chinese food, still in the container. Three days old. He hadn't cooked in months. He ate standing at the counter, thinking about the partnership he'd lost eighteen months ago. Elias would've traced the foreign magic back to its source by now. Memory magic could follow psychic echoes in ways Alex's combat magic couldn't. Elias would've known who cast it, maybe even why.

Together, they'd been legendary within the Bureau. With Elias at his side, the work had always come easier. The conductor's death would have made more sense and their suspect harder to lose. But that partnership was gone, destroyed by circumstances that neither of them had fully understood at the time.

Alex set down the chopsticks and picked up his phone, then put it back down. He wanted to call Elias. Tell him about the strange magic he'd encountered. Ask him for his help. But he knew Elias wouldn't welcome a call. The polite nods in the hallway said enough. Distant and guarded, like they'd never been partners or best friends.

Elias had asked for space and Alex intended to give it to him. For as long as he needed.

3
Memory's Edge

Memory is deceptive because it is colored by today's events
—Albert Einstein

The call came through while Elias Sinclair was staring at the same financial report for the third time in an hour, the numbers blurring together. Two days of Chicago's gray November drizzle had streaked the FBI building's windows, and his third cup of coffee wasn't helping his concentration any more than the first two had.

Major Crimes ASAC Timothy Livingston stepped out of his office and walked to Elias' desk. "Sinclair, Rivera, ASAC Lindsey in Counterterrorism is asking for help."

He handed Rivera the preliminary incident summary. "Lindsey has agents on the derailment. The rest of her team is tied up. Sinclair, you have CT experience. Go. Report back to Lindsey." He retreated, muttering about staffing.

A moment later, Agent Nicole Rivera appeared at his desk

with her coat already on and car keys jingling. "Dead body. And it looks like your kind of weird."

Elias glanced up, dark hair falling across his forehead, his green eyes meeting Rivera's with tired sharpness. At thirty, she was everything the Bureau wanted in a modern agent. Smart, educated, ambitious, and completely lacking in patience for partners who couldn't keep up with her energy. She'd been his partner for seventeen months, since he requested reassignment away from the counterterrorism unit.

"What kind of weird?" he asked, saving his work and reaching for his jacket with movements that felt heavier than they should. He was just two years younger than Rivera, but sometimes he felt like he was twice her age.

"Infrastructure specialist found dead at her office. No signs of forced entry, no struggle, no obvious cause of death." Rivera paused, flicking the page with her finger. "But the responding officers swore the place felt wrong. Magically wrong."

The past eighteen months taught him that his magic was unreliable and the insights he once trusted could be disastrously wrong. He had requested a transfer away from counterterrorism, yet now he was being asked to help with a case. He felt a headache starting.

"Any details on the victim?" Elias asked as they walked toward the elevator. Rivera moved with the confident stride she always had, never second-guessing herself.

"Dr. Michelle Torres, forty-seven years old, Lead Systems Coordinator for the Chicago Department of Transportation. Infrastructure integration, magical and mundane systems coordination. She worked on the projects that keep the city's transportation hubs synchronized with conventional transit, making sure the kinetic rail spells don't interfere with electrical grids. Technical side of keeping Chicago functional."

The elevator descended past the floors of analysts and administrators. Elias watched the numbers count down and pushed aside the familiar weight of self-doubt that had settled since the warehouse incident.

"Convenient timing," Elias observed. "A suspicious train derailment a couple hours ago and now we have a dead systems coordinator."

Outside, the morning air was cold and damp. Rivera drove like a Chicago native, aggressive and confident, weaving between buses and delivery trucks while maintaining a steady stream of commentary about the case.

"Building's got standard wards, nothing fancy but they were still active. Whatever happened, it was fast and quiet."

"Estimated time of death?"

"The medical examiner thinks she's been dead for a few hours. Scheduled to run diagnostics before dawn, never logged her results. Maintenance flagged it when she didn't check in."

Elias processed the timeline. It aligned with the derailment that morning. "So she died just before or at the same time as the train accident. That's a big coincidence."

"The question is whether she was murdered because she was a loose end or because she discovered something."

The address led them to an infrastructure station tucked into a strip of municipal buildings in Albany Park. From the outside, it looked like any other city office. Holiday lights strung across neighboring windows were visible through the frosted glass doors, their cheerful glow a sharp contrast to the scene inside. Elias had seen it before, the way death intruded on ordinary life without warning.

Detective Brianna Lee met them inside, her coat still buttoned against the cold. "Control room," Lee said, leading them down the narrow hall. "No alarms tripped. Staff arrived this morning and found her slumped at her station. No signs of forced entry. System was still running when they got here."

The control room stretched before them, walls lined with consoles and monitors tracking grids of water, transit, and power. A schematic was frozen mid-update. A mug sat on the desk, a dark ring staining the scattered papers beneath it. Engineering logs lay open, a pen dropped mid-sentence, the line trailing off as though someone had been interrupted mid-thought.

Dr. Torres sat slumped in her chair, posture too natural for someone dead. Jeans, boots, fleece jacket half-zipped. One hand still rested on the console. Her face was relaxed, almost peaceful, but the stillness in the room had a wrongness about it.

"Any witnesses?" Rivera asked.

Lee shook her head. "The building is quiet after midnight. The janitor said that around five she got this strange feeling. Like the air shifted. She couldn't explain it, just said something felt wrong. Spent the next hour looking over her shoulder as she cleaned, but never saw anything."

"Psychic spillover?" Rivera asked.

Elias nodded. "Depends on what kind of magic was being used, and how powerful the user was."

It was the workplace of someone who understood how complex systems fit together, someone who had built a career around keeping Chicago's veins of power, water, and transit running. And now she was another casualty in a war most of the city didn't even know about.

"No obvious trauma, no signs of poisoning, no indication of a medical emergency," Lee said, checking her notes. "Blood work is pending."

"But the scene feels wrong," Elias said. The unease clung to the room the way it always did when harmful magic had been used.

Lee nodded. "That's what the responding officers said. Nothing they could put their finger on, but something about the scene made their skin crawl."

Lee nodded toward the monitors, their frozen displays still showing transit schematics. "The system shows manual overrides into the speed regulators around the time she died. They pushed the settings past normal tolerance."

"On purpose?" Rivera asked.

"Doesn't look like procedure." Lee's tone was flat. "It looks like she jammed the acceleration through every safeguard the city had in place."

Rivera shook her head. "Why the hell would she do that?"

Elias stared at Torres' body. She looked peaceful, except for the fact that she was dead, her face relaxed in a way that suggested whatever had killed her had been quick and painless.

But unlike normal death scenes, this room hummed with magical residue that made Elias' abilities recoil. Traces of foreign energy signatures lingered in the air like invisible smoke, patterns that spoke of sophisticated magical manipulation designed to be overlooked by conventional investigation.

"What's your read?" Rivera asked, watching him with the mix of fascination and impatience she brought to all his magical work. She understood the basics behind magical abilities. What she couldn't do was use magic. Couldn't provide the grounding Alex used to give him.

And what she understood even less was why he'd become so hesitant about trusting the insights from his magic.

Elias approached the body slowly and let his magic open to the residue that lingers when a life ends. Usually he could read the echoes cleanly. Usually, death left traces he could read like words on a page. Fear, pain, anger, resignation, the emotional signatures of a life ending.

He watched Torres' final hours. Morning routine, reports pulled up, the slow slip of something through her wards like smoke. Torres sat at the console. Her thoughts ran one clear, insistent line: The train must be corrected, the settings must be fixed, do it now. Her fingers moved with urgent purpose. She believed she was saving the train. The sequence she followed bypassed safeguards and forced controls into ranges she never would have chosen under ordinary judgment. The control panel accepted entries that fit that false certainty. The conviction in her mind continued even as her body began to fail.

"She believed that she was preventing a catastrophe. I'm seeing the actions of someone convinced that she was doing something to save lives," Elias said.

"Why would she think that?" Rivera asked.

Elias moved closer to Torres. His magic was telling him something was wrong here, something that went beyond a simple death from natural causes. But after the warehouse incident, he'd learned to question every instinct, to second-guess every magical insight.

Still, he couldn't ignore what he was sensing. "There's something else. Something old." The magical signature felt ancient, far older than anything he'd encountered in modern cases. Not decades old, but centuries. The energy had weight that spoke of power accumulated over time, magic that had been worked and reworked until it became something dark and purposeful.

The energy patterns pulsed with rhythms that seemed almost alive, magic that had been shaped for a purpose he couldn't understand. But underneath the foreign signatures, he could sense the echo of Dr. Torres' final moments, confusion and growing terror as something invaded her consciousness.

"Someone was here," he said, extending his memory magic toward the residual traces. "Before she died. Someone with magic that's different."

Rivera stopped writing, her expression shifting from professional interest to something approaching alarm. "Different how?"

"It feels very old, and dark." Elias found himself leaning closer to the body, his professional curiosity overriding the warning signs his abilities were providing. "This isn't modern spell work. It's something much older, something that feels like it was designed for purposes that violate every principle of legal magical practice."

The ancient energy signature was unlike anything in his experience, but it called to his memory magic with the promise of secrets waiting to be uncovered. The professional investigator in him wanted to understand what had killed Dr. Torres, to trace the source of magic that could attack human consciousness so precisely.

"How old are we talking?" Rivera asked, her pen poised above her notepad.

"I'm not sure." Elias extended his abilities deeper into the magical residue, seeking the source and purpose of energy that predated modern magical regulation. "Whatever this is, it comes from a time when magic didn't have the safeguards we take for granted now."

The ancient magic pulsed around him like a living thing, patterns that seemed to recognize his investigation and respond with interest rather than concealment. The complexity drew him in.

Without Alex's combat magic to shield him during dangerous memory work, Elias should have been more cautious. Should have recognized the way the ancient energy was reaching toward his consciousness. Should have pulled back when his abilities detected hostile intelligence woven into the magical patterns.

Instead, he pushed deeper.

The memory trace revealed Dr. Torres' final hours in vivid detail. Her morning routine, reviewing infrastructure reports while preparing for the day's meetings. The gradual intrusion of something foreign into her apartment, magic that moved like smoke through her security wards without triggering conventional alarms.

Then the assault on her consciousness, ancient power

overwhelming her mental defenses with surgical precision. Not random violence, but targeted extraction of specific knowledge about Chicago's infrastructure vulnerabilities. Dr. Torres had died protecting information someone desperately wanted to steal.

But as Elias traced the memory deeper, seeking the identity of her killer, the ancient magic struck back.

Pain shot through his skull. The hostile energy recognized his probe and redirected itself at his unshielded consciousness. The ancient magic wasn't actively malevolent at first. It had been used to extract information, but now it seemed to want to show him something.

Elias gasped and staggered backward, blood running from his nose as the magical backlash overwhelmed his defenses. The ancient energy followed his retreat, pursuing him through psychic channels while attempting to establish a connection. It showed him a moment buried in history. A horrific scene from a time when magic was woven into power, not for balance, but for dominance.

"Elias!" Rivera's voice seemed to come from very far away as she rushed to his side.

Without Alex's magic to sever dangerous connections and shield him from hostile energy, Elias found himself fighting alone against power that exceeded anything he'd ever come across.

"What's happening?" Rivera demanded, her hands on his shoulders as he convulsed with pain from the magical assault.

Elias couldn't answer. The ancient energy suddenly became aggressive and pulled him into memories that couldn't possibly be real, of a place older than any person who had inhabited that office.

Through sheer force of will, he wrenched himself free from the hostile connection, severing the link between his abilities and the ancient energy with violence that left him gasping and disoriented. The malevolent magic released him reluctantly, its attention turning back toward concealing the evidence of Dr. Torres' murder.

"I need medical response at our location," Rivera said into her radio.

"No," Elias managed, wiping blood from his face while trying to steady himself against the wall. "I'm fine. Just give me a minute."

"You're not fine. You're bleeding and you nearly collapsed." Rivera's professional composure cracked as she saw the state he was in. "What the hell was that?"

"A magical trap, left behind to overwhelm anyone who investigated too deeply."

He wasn't telling her everything. The pattern had behaved as if it were aware of his probe, but there was so much more. So much that couldn't be real.

"Are you hurt? Should I call for backup?"

"I'll be okay. But we need to be careful with this scene."

"Is it dangerous?"

He thought about telling her what he had seen, but part of him wondered if he had imagined it. Memories had lied to him before, and he couldn't trust that what he saw was real.

"Whatever killed Dr. Torres is still actively dangerous to memory investigators. It's something older that possibly predates magical regulation."

Elias steadied himself against the wall, his head still pounding from the assault.

"The ancient magic could bypass modern wards," Elias said. He remembered the way the hostile energy had moved through Dr. Torres' workspace like smoke through screens. "Contemporary magical security wasn't designed to detect threats from historical magical traditions."

Rivera looked up from her evidence documentation. "So we're dealing with someone who has access to magical techniques that can defeat modern security?"

"Or someone who's found a way to replicate those techniques using contemporary methods," Elias replied.

As they prepared to leave the crime scene, Elias found himself taking one last look at the magical residue that clung to the room. The ancient energy signatures remained active, pulsing with hostile intent.

He wanted another look. He also wanted to stay conscious. With proper preparation and protective measures, he might be able to trace the ancient energy back to its source, identify the person responsible for Dr. Torres' death.

But Rivera was already heading toward the door, and the rational part of his mind recognized that further investigation would require magical support he no longer possessed. Without Alex's combat magic to shield him from dangerous memory work, attempting to engage the ancient energy again would be suicidal.

◇✧◇

The drive back to the FBI building was quiet. The ancient magical signature suggested someone with access to historical research or traditional knowledge, but the precision of the attack indicated contemporary training in how to apply that knowledge effectively.

"Preliminary report?" Rivera asked as they pulled into the Bureau garage.

"Infrastructure specialist killed by unknown magical assault, probably connected to her work on city systems integration." It sounded inadequate even as he said it. He rubbed his forehead. "Killer demonstrated capabilities that exceed normal magical ability."

"But you think there's more to it?" Rivera asked.

"We're dealing with someone who has access to archaic magical techniques that can defeat contemporary security systems and kill people without leaving physical evidence." Elias met Rivera's eyes. "This isn't a typical murder case."

Rivera nodded grimly. "I'll coordinate with the

infrastructure security teams, get them to review protocols for detecting historical magical threats."

The ancient energy signature remained vivid in his memory as Elias drove home through Chicago's evening traffic, hostile magic that offered answers and threatened anyone who dug too deep. A killer was still at large and Elias was left wondering whether his abilities would be sufficient for whatever came next.

4
Forced Convergence

The whole is greater than the sum of its parts
—Aristotle

FBI Chicago Division—November 16, 9:00 AM

Assistant Special Agent in Charge Corryn Lindsey stood at the windows of her corner office, watching Chicago wake to another gray November morning. Long light brown hair framed her face, softening the sharp focus in her expression without diminishing her authority.

Steam rose from the coffee cups carried by pedestrians seventeen floors below, and the first commuter trains of the day discharged their cargo of office workers into the downtown streets. The magical infrastructure had stabilized overnight, protective wards shimmering back to life around the towering buildings like heat mirages made visible. Street lamps glowed with renewed enchantments, and the traffic management spells at intersections pulsed with steady blue light as the city's magical safety net rewove itself.

She'd been running the FBI's Chicago counterterrorism division for eight years, long enough to recognize patterns that younger agents might miss. The infrastructure attack two days earlier had been sophisticated, professional, and deliberately restrained. Someone with extensive knowledge of magical systems had tested their defenses without causing permanent damage. Long enough to know when two of her best people were destroying themselves with stubborn pride.

The knock on her door came precisely at nine-fifteen. Alexander Sutton had always been punctual, a habit drummed into him by his military family and reinforced by the years he's spent in the Army. Lindsey turned from the window as he entered. He held himself carefully, slight tension in his shoulders.

"Alex. Thanks for coming in. Coffee?"

"I'm good, thanks." Alex settled into the chair across from her desk, his posture alert but controlled. Around him, the air held the faint shimmer that accompanied powerful magical abilities kept under tight control. "Your message said this was about the infrastructure case?"

Lindsey poured herself a large cup of coffee from the machine in the corner, buying time to organize her thoughts. Alex had been one of her most reliable agents for six years. First as part of the most effective magical crimes team the Bureau had ever assembled, then as a competent solo investigator who never missed deadlines and never caused administrative headaches. But reliability wasn't the same thing as effectiveness, and effectiveness wasn't the same thing as happiness.

"Partly," she said, returning to her desk. "I've been reviewing your preliminary report on the train derailment. Interesting. That ancient magical signature you detected–very unusual."

Alex's expression didn't change, but Lindsey caught the slight lift of his chin. "The energy patterns were unlike anything in Bureau databases. Hostile, intelligent, designed to attack human consciousness."

"Which brings me to why you're here." Lindsey opened the folder on her desk, revealing crime scene photos and forensic reports. The images showed Dr. Torres' peaceful workplace, so ordinary that it took trained eyes to recognize the subtle wrongness that indicated supernatural murder.

"We've had a murder that matches your magical signature exactly. Infrastructure specialist killed by the same ancient magical techniques you encountered at the train crash."

She watched Alex lean forward slightly, his interest engaged despite his neutral expression.

"I asked Major Crimes to assign Agent Sinclair since we were all tied up with the train derailment and the Augustus trafficking case. He and Agent Rivera worked the case together," Lindsey continued, studying Alex's face for any reaction to his former partner's name. She noticed the slight tightening around the eyes, a barely perceptible shift in posture. "Dr. Madison confirmed the magical signatures are identical. Same source, same techniques."

"You think they're connected."

"I do. You and Elias both reported sensing an old, unidentified magical signature. Same strange circumstances around the deaths." Lindsey leaned back in her chair, her own protective wards humming almost inaudibly as they responded to the tension in the room. "Someone's targeting people with knowledge of Chicago's infrastructure. Your conductor and Dr. Torres were both killed by an unknown magical assault."

"What do you need from me?" he asked finally.

Lindsey had been preparing for this moment for months, ever since she'd noticed the way Alex and Elias avoided each other in the halls, the polite nods that replaced what used to be an easy friendship. She'd watched two of her best agents wither into competent but isolated individuals, and she'd finally decided that enough was enough.

"I need you to work with Elias on this. I've borrowed him and Agent Rivera from Major Crimes." Her voice was quiet.

The change in Alex was immediate. His posture stiffened, and for a moment, genuine emotion broke through his professional mask. Silver light flickered around his hands before he forced it down.

"Ma'am, I don't think that's—"

"Alex." Lindsey held his gaze. "I've been patient with this situation for eighteen months. I respected Elias' request for separate assignments, and I've watched two of my most effective agents struggle with cases that you could have solved together in half the time."

"With respect, ma'am, Agent Cross and I have been handling our caseload—"

"Competently, yes." Lindsey pulled out another file, this one thick with commendation letters and case summaries. The pages glowed faintly with preservation charms, magical signatures that verified their authenticity and prevented tampering. "Do you remember the Al-Rashid cell investigation? The one where you and Elias uncovered that magical weapons smuggling operation running through the port?"

Silence stretched, his eyes on the wall instead of her face. "That was a long time ago."

"It was eighteen months ago. "Agent Cross is competent. Agent Rivera is thorough. But neither can coordinate magical ability the way you and Elias did."

"Those days are over," Alex said quietly.

"They don't have to be. "Alex, I've got two cases that appear to be connected by unknown magical techniques. I need my best people working together to stop whoever's behind this before it escalates further."

Alex's jaw tightened and he kept his gaze locked on the file.

Lindsey closed the file and leaned forward. She inhaled

deeply and said, "Alex, I need to tell you something about Elias."

He met her eyes with concern. "Ma'am?"

"Three weeks ago, ASAC Livingston had to pull him from an undercover assignment. He'd been working infiltration on a group suspected of funding organized crime activity. According to Livingston, he was taking unnecessary risks. Dangerous risks." Lindsey looked down at her folded hands, "He confronted suspects without backup, entered situations where his magical abilities were compromised, and overall just behaved recklessly. Not like Elias at all."

Alex was quiet, but Lindsey watched the conflict pass across his face. Concern warring with old hurt.

"His partner, Agent Rivera, has been asking for guidance on how to handle his reckless behavior. She's worried he's going to get himself killed. I'm worried about the same thing. Elias Sinclair used to be one of the most careful, methodical investigators I've ever worked with. Now he acts like he doesn't care whether he comes home at the end of the day."

"Why are you telling me this now?"

"Because eighteen months ago I lost my best team. Not to budget cuts or reassignments or career advancement. I lost them to pride and misunderstanding and whatever happened in that warehouse that you're both too stubborn to talk about."

Lindsey stood, moving back to the window where the city's magical infrastructure pulsed with renewed life.

"And because I think the only person who can help Elias is you. That partnership grounded him professionally and personally. And your friendship... Alex, you know you're the only family he has."

Silence stretched, his eyes on the wall instead of her face. When he spoke, his voice was measured. "He's the one who requested the transfer."

"He thought you'd blame him for what happened."

"I never—"

"I know. Just like he never blamed you for the decisions you made that day. You never had the talk, did you?"

"No." He looked away.

Lindsey could see the concern and personal pain playing out across his features.

"I'm not asking you to fix your relationship," she said gently. "I'm asking you to save lives." She thought to herself that one of those lives was Elias.

Alex was quiet for another moment, then nodded slowly. "When do you want us to start?"

"This morning. Conference room four has been set up with both case files and evidence. I've asked Elias to meet you there at ten-thirty." Lindsey returned to her desk. "Alex, I know this isn't easy. But I'm hoping that working together might help you both remember why you made such an effective team."

Alex stood up, straightening his jacket with sharp, precise movements. "Anything else, ma'am?"

"Just be patient with him. And maybe with yourself." Lindsey opened another file, signaling the end of the meeting. "What happened eighteen months ago, it doesn't have to define the rest of your lives."

After Alex left, Lindsey stood at her window again. The city pulsed with renewed strength, wards steady again after the grid failure. Somewhere, people were planning attacks that could cripple Chicago's magical grid. The two agents best equipped to stop that were about to sit in a room together for the first time in over a year, carrying eighteen months of hurt between them.

She'd done what she could. The rest was up to them.

◇✦◇

Conference Room 4 — November 17, 10:25 AM

Alex arrived at the conference room five minutes early, settling into the chair facing the door where he could see anyone entering while keeping his back to the wall. Someone from the evidence team had already arranged both case files across the surface. Crime scene photos and forensic reports spread out like pieces of a puzzle waiting to be solved. The room's built-in wards hummed softly, privacy enchantments that would prevent any surveillance or eavesdropping while they worked.

The infrastructure attack files were familiar territory. Alex had spent hours thinking about the strange magic he'd encountered. The look of fear on the train conductor's face.

The illusionist should never have escaped. Not from him.

Alex knew exactly how strong his combat magic was. He'd been tested, rated at the highest level the Bureau recorded. No one had ever beaten him in open magical combat. Not at Quantico, not in the field.

And then there was Elias. They'd been roommates at the Academy, where instructors noticed something strange whenever they worked together. Their magic didn't just complement each other. It wove together, merged in ways no one could fully explain. Elias was powerful. Too powerful at times and he held back out of fear of losing control. Or worse. That the government would reclassify him and force him to transfer into the military. Alex was the only one Elias trusted to pull him back. Or stop him, if it came to that.

The door opened at exactly ten-thirty. Elias Sinclair entered with the authority Alex remembered, but thinner now, dark circles under his green eyes. His charcoal suit hung a little loose.

"Alex." Elias' voice stayed neutral. He closed the door and took the chair across the table without meeting Alex's eyes.

"Elias." Alex kept his voice level, the mix of anger and concern under control. Eighteen months of silence weighed between them.

They bent over the files.

"Looks like the cases might be connected," Elias said.

"Looks that way." Alex gestured to the files spread between them. Elias' attention seemed slightly unfocused. "Same level of sophistication, same kind of advanced magical techniques."

Elias nodded, pulling the Torres file toward himself with hesitation. Alex watched his fingers hover over the images without touching them. The old Elias would have been talking about theories or proposing ideas by now.

"Magical assault using some form of ancient magic to hijack control. Professionally executed," Elias said after a moment, his voice quieter than before. "I've never felt anything like it. Not just memory manipulation. The kind of magic that was present predated modern regulation."

"Train derailment," Alex replied, pointing to his own files. "Testing our response protocols, measuring our capabilities. Also professionally executed. I sensed a strange, hostile magic."

They worked side by side for twenty minutes—Alex on tactical elements, Elias on psychological traces. It was a pale echo of their old partnership. Elias second-guessed himself. He hovered over images instead of talking through theories.

"The timing's not a coincidence," Alex said, spreading the infrastructure attack timeline across the table. The documents arranged themselves in chronological order, responding to minor levitation magic that made organization easier. "The train incident yesterday, Torres murdered the same morning."

Alex traced the sequence with his finger, leaving faint trails of silver light that highlighted the connection points. "Torres was the lead systems coordinator. She would have understood the transit authority's protocols and codes better than anyone else in the city."

Elias said, "They used her to sabotage the train. She believed she was preventing a catastrophe. They forced her to set the controls that caused the derailment."

Alex's brow furrowed. "How do you force someone like Torres to believe that? What kind of magic makes her act against everything she knew? What did your trace tell you about the killer?"

For a moment, something flickered across Elias' face. Uncertainty, maybe, or fear. His expression wavered before steadying again. "Dangerous old magic. No emotional connection to the victim. They knew exactly what they were looking for."

"Did you get anything else? Magical signature, psychological profile, any fragments?"

Elias was quiet for a moment too long, his attention turning inward. "Some. Not as much as I'd hoped. They laid a trap for anyone who tried to investigate too closely. I wasn't able to get past it."

Alex frowned. "Could this be a fae?"

Elias shook his head. "No. Fae magic feels different. This isn't them."

Alex felt a stab of frustration. The old Elias would have painted a detailed picture of the killer from the magical traces left at the crime scene. This Elias was holding something back, either from professional caution or personal doubt.

"Maybe we should bring Dr. Madison in," Alex suggested, silver light flickering around his hands as his own frustration affected his control. "Get her analysis of the magical techniques used in both cases."

"That's probably a good idea."

Another polite agreement. Alex missed the passionate debates they used to have, the way they would challenge each other's assumptions. That creative tension had made them both better investigators.

Now they were just two competent agents trying to solve connected cases without stepping on each other's feelings.

Alex was about to suggest they review the evidence timeline when Elias spoke up, his voice quieter than before.

"How have you been, Alex?"

The question caught Alex off guard. Personal, after thirty minutes of case-related conversation. He looked up to find Elias watching him with something that might have been concern, green eyes holding a warmth that had been absent from their interactions for months.

"Fine," Alex said automatically. "Busy. You?"

"Fine." Elias' smile was brief and didn't reach his eyes. "Rivera's a good partner. Very thorough."

"Cross is a good agent. Gets the job done."

They were talking around the real conversation, both aware of the distance between them. Alex found himself studying Elias more carefully, noting the strain he tried to hide —the set of his shoulders, the faint tremor in his hands when he thought no one noticed.

Lindsey had been right. Something was very wrong.

"Elias," Alex started, then stopped. The words he wanted to say felt too charged for this small room, too complicated for a professional meeting.

"We should probably focus on the case," Elias said quietly.

"Right. The case."

They spent another hour mapping connections between the train attack and the Torres murder, building a timeline that suggested coordination between different elements of the same operation. It was competent work, the kind of methodical analysis that would eventually produce results. But it felt thinner than it should have, lacking the spark their investigations once had.

When they finally closed the files, Alex felt a weight settling between them like a physical presence.

"I'll coordinate with Dr. Madison," he said, standing up and straightening his jacket. Silver light flickered briefly around his hands before he regained control. "Get her analysis of the magical techniques."

"I'll follow up on the other potential targets. People with

similar clearances." Elias gathered his files with precise movements. "We should probably meet again tomorrow. Compare notes."

"Tomorrow works."

They moved toward the door together, then stopped awkwardly when they reached it at the same time. For a moment, Alex could see the exhaustion Elias was trying to hide, the rigid way he held himself as though one wrong move might crack him.

For a brief second, the air shimmered like heat over asphalt. Something passed between them, too quick to name, but it left a resonance. Like a circuit that had almost closed.

"Alex," Elias said quietly. "About what Lindsey said. About working together. I know this isn't—"

"It's fine," Alex interrupted. "We're both professionals. We can handle this."

Elias nodded, but something in his expression suggested he didn't entirely believe it. He opened the door and stepped into the hallway, then looked back.

"It's good to see you," he said, so quietly Alex almost missed it.

Then he was gone, leaving Alex alone with the evidence files and the realization that seeing Elias again hadn't brought the clarity he expected. If anything, it had raised more questions. About what had really happened eighteen months ago, about why Elias had been taking dangerous risks, about whether the distance they'd maintained was protecting them, or slowly destroying them both.

Alex gathered his files and headed back to his desk, wondering if they could work together long enough to solve this case. The faint trace of their brief reunion lingered in the conference room air, silver and green energies slowly fading as the privacy wards settled.

But even as those traces disappeared, Alex could still feel the echo of Elias' presence, the familiar signature of an old partnership. Whether that connection could be rebuilt remained to be seen.

What mattered now was stopping whoever planned to turn Chicago's magical infrastructure into a weapon. Everything else would have to wait.

5

Academic Ties

A little learning is a dangerous thing
  —Alexander Pope

The call came in while Alex was reviewing Dr. Madison's preliminary analysis of the memory extraction signatures, her notes spread across his desk like fragments of a puzzle. The interference patterns found at both scenes were unlike anything in the Bureau's database. Precise, layered, and far too sophisticated for an independent actor.

With only two confirmed victims, Madison hadn't drawn firm conclusions. But she noted consistencies in the magical residue, subtle patterns in how the memory damage unfolded. If the same hand was behind both incidents, it wasn't random. Someone with deep, possibly ancient knowledge of memory manipulation was testing something. And it wasn't over.

Around the report, faint traces of analytical magic glowed in the margins where Dr. Madison had annotated her findings.

The enchanted text shifted and reorganized itself as Alex read, highlighting connections between different pieces of evidence and cross-referencing technical specifications with known magical signatures.

"We've got another body," Agent Rivera announced, appearing at Alex's desk. He'd never worked with her, but Elias seemed to like her. "University of Chicago. Retired Army Colonel in the Military History Department."

Alex looked up from the report summary that he'd been studying. "Same signature as the others?"

"No idea. The scene is still being processed." Rivera consulted her tablet, scrolling through preliminary reports. Colonel Joseph Cameron, fifty-five years old, recently retired from Aberdeen Proving Ground, now teaching military history. Found dead in his office this morning by a graduate student."

"Where's Elias?"

"Already en route. He said to tell you he'd meet you there."

Alex gathered his files and ballistic vest, noticing the way Rivera's expression remained carefully neutral when she mentioned the case assignment. As a result of ASAC Lindsey pairing Alex with Elias, Rivera was relegated to analysis and backup work. She never complained, but Alex caught the clipped tone when she mentioned new assignments. It was a clear step down from the high profile major crimes cases she'd been handling as Elias' partner. She hadn't said anything about the arrangement, but Alex could sense her frustration.

University of Chicago

The drive to the University of Chicago took twenty minutes through Chicago's morning traffic, giving Alex time to think through what they already knew about Colonel Cameron. Recently retired from Aberdeen Proving Ground suggested someone with access to classified military research, exactly the kind of expertise that terrorists might find valuable. If this was connected to the Torres murder, they were looking at a pattern of targeting people with specialized knowledge of Chicago's magical infrastructure and research capabilities.

The University of Chicago campus stretched across several city blocks in Hyde Park, its Gothic Revival architecture creating an atmosphere of academic gravitas that had attracted scholars and researchers for over a century. Students hurried between classes with hunched shoulders and buried faces, their scarves and coats barely helping against the lake effect winds that swept across the campus.

Magical heating spells warmed the air in invisible pockets around doorways and gathering spaces, small oases of comfort that students moved between. The campus wards hummed with protective energy, ancient enchantments layered with modern security systems to create one of the most magically defended academic institutions in the Midwest.

Alex parked near the Military History building, a newer structure that managed to blend seamlessly with the university's historic architecture, while housing some of the country's most advanced magical research facilities. The building's wards glowed faintly, tuned to contain dangerous experiments and block unauthorized entry. That those same wards had failed to protect Colonel Cameron suggested either an inside job or someone with extraordinary magical abilities.

Chicago PD had already established a perimeter around the building, their patrol cars creating a barrier between the crime scene and the growing crowd of curious students and faculty. Detective Lee met Alex at the main entrance, her weathered face tight.

"Third floor, Colonel Cameron's office," she reported, her breath visible in the cold air. Around her, the building's protective wards cast a faint blue glow that was visible to anyone with magical sight. "A graduate student found him around nine-thirty this morning when he didn't show up for a scheduled meeting. The door was locked and the office wards were active. No signs of forced entry, or indications of a struggle."

"Just like Torres," Alex observed. He adjusted his stance, hands brushing the air as the investigation wards resonated against his magic.

"Which is why we called you guys instead of treating this as a normal suspicious death." Detective Lee led him through the building's main lobby, past display cases filled with academic awards and research achievements. The walls themselves glowed faintly with preservation spells, enchantments that protected centuries of academic history from fire, flood, and the passage of time. "Your partner's already upstairs, working the scene with the magical forensics team."

The elevator carried them up through floors dedicated to different aspects of magical research. Theoretical applications on the second floor, practical development on the third, classified government contracts on the fourth. Professor Cameron's office was located in the practical development section, appropriate for someone whose work bridged the gap between academic theory and real-world applications.

The hallway outside Cameron's office buzzed with controlled activity. Forensic photographers documented every detail while magical technicians swept for traces of supernatural evidence. The university's security chief, a nervous man in his forties who kept adjusting his glasses, provided a steady stream of information about building access, ward configurations, and Colonel Cameron's research schedule.

"Colonel Cameron arrived yesterday morning at his usual time," the security chief explained. "Signed in at 7:15 attended a faculty meeting at nine, worked in his office until approximately 6 p.m. Building security shows him leaving through the main entrance, ward access confirms he properly secured his office before departing."

"Any unusual activity overnight?" Alex asked, watching the magical forensics team work their investigation spells around the office doorway.

"Nothing. Building wards remained active, no unauthorized access, no emergency alerts. The graduate student who found him this morning used her own access card to enter the building, then discovered the door to Colonel Cameron's office unlocked."

Alex frowned, noting the contradiction. "I thought you said the door was locked when the body was discovered."

"It was. But the electronic access log shows the door being unlocked at approximately 9:28 a.m, three minutes before the graduate student called campus security."

That was interesting. Either someone had unlocked the door immediately before the body's discovery, or the locking mechanism had malfunctioned in a way that suggested magical interference. Alex made a mental note to have Dr. Madison examine the building's ward system for signs of tampering.

Colonel Cameron's office occupied a corner of the building with windows facing both the campus quadrangle and the city beyond. Bookshelves lined the walls, filled with academic journals and what appeared to be first editions of foundational texts on magical theory. A desk dominated one corner of the room, its surface covered with research papers and what looked like grant applications for government funding. Several photos showed Cameron smiling beside colleagues at conferences, awards clutched in hand, or relaxing at a faculty picnic with a woman who might be his wife.

Colonel Cameron's body sat behind the desk. He wore a dark suit and tie, reading glasses perched on his nose, a cup of coffee gone cold beside his computer keyboard. But unlike Torres, his expression wasn't peaceful. His features were set, his mouth drawn tight, suggesting he'd understood exactly what was happening to him when the magic struck.

Elias let the residue settle across his senses, cold and deliberate.

"This wasn't like Torres," he said quietly. "He knew someone was here to kill him."

Just like the Torres scene, this office hummed with magical residue. Traces of foreign magic lingered in the air like visible smoke, patterns that spoke of sophisticated magic and deliberate concealment. The academic wards that normally protected the office flickered weakly.

Elias stood near the windows, his hands hovering over a stack of papers without touching. His jaw tightened, eyes narrowing as the traces fought back against his reading.

Around Elias, the air shimmered faintly, green threads of memory magic coiling through the room. They stuttered, faltering as though Elias held them under tight restraint. Green energies swirled through the office space, following pathways invisible to normal sight as they traced the lingering impressions of recent events. But the patterns seemed hesitant and uncertain. Elias was holding back from the full depth of investigation his abilities could provide.

"Anything?" Alex asked quietly, noting the way his own magical abilities automatically synchronized with Elias'. Silver combat magic flowing to support the memory work.

Elias looked up, and for a moment, Alex saw frustration flash across his features. The magical patterns around him wavered briefly. "Same magical resonance as Torres. But there's something else."

"What kind of something else?"

"I'm not sure yet." Elias moved closer to Colonel Cameron's body, his concentration deepening. The energies around him strengthened, fed by Alex's unconscious support, and began to form coherent patterns in the air.

For a moment, the field between them hummed with

unnatural clarity. Like a half-finished circuit flickering to life. Brief, reflexive, and entirely untrained.

"The killer left behind more traces this time. Either they were in a hurry, or—"

He stopped, his entire body going rigid. Alex felt his own combat instincts sharpen, recognizing the signs of imminent danger even before his conscious mind identified the threat. The magical energies in the room shifted abruptly, hostile patterns emerging from beneath the surface of normal investigation traces.

"Elias, what is it?"

"Something else," Elias said quietly. His shoulders locked, and the green light threading the air shivered around his hands. "The magical signature feels ancient. Like the signature in Torres' control room."

"How ancient?"

"Centuries I think. This isn't modern magic.

The ancient magical resonance was exactly like the one that attacked him in Torres' control room. It called to his memory magic with the promise of secrets waiting to be uncovered. The professional investigator in him wanted to understand what this magic was. He wanted to experience the images again to prove to himself that he didn't imagine it.

The Colonel recognized what was happening to him," Elias said. Silver light pressed at the edges of his vision as Alex's magic wrapped close, forming a barrier between him and the desk. He extended his abilities deeper into the magical residue. "He had enough experience to know this wasn't natural magic being used against him."

"Recognized how?"

"He was trying to analyze the signature even as his memories were being extracted. Fighting back, gathering intelligence. Alex, Colonel Cameron was a memory specialist in the Army. He understood what was being done to him and tried to resist."

The ancient magic pulsed around them like a living thing, patterns that seemed to recognize Elias' investigation and respond with interest rather than concealment. It was seductive in its complexity, promising insights into magical traditions that had been lost to time.

"There's a magical trap embedded in the psychic traces. Anyone who tries to read them deeply enough to identify the killer will trigger it."

Alex stepped closer, his own magical abilities instinctively responding to the potential threat. Silver light began to flow around his hands, combat magic forming defensive barriers that could protect them both if the trap activated.

"What kind of trap?"

"Memory feedback loop. Designed to overload the mind of anyone using memory tracing." Elias' voice sounded calm, but Alex could see the tension in his shoulders, the way his defenses were struggling against whatever hostile enchantment had been left behind. I came across one at Torres' crime scene. It grabbed hold of me and didn't want to let go."

"So we document what we can and call in a specialist to disarm it."

Elias nodded, but his attention remained focused on the desk where Colonel Cameron had died. Alex could see him studying the arrangement of papers, the positioning of the coffee cup, the way the reading glasses had been placed with precise care. The scene had been staged to look natural, but someone with Elias' magic could read the subtle signs that revealed a more complex truth.

The magical trap was a web of hostile enchantments designed to attack anyone who dug too deeply into the crime scene. And beneath its surface, traces of the killer's presence lingered.

"Agent Sutton," Detective Lee called from the doorway. "Campus security wants to brief you on Colonel Cameron's recent research projects. They're waiting in the conference room down the hall."

Alex glanced at Elias, who was still studying the crime scene with the intense focus that had once made him the Bureau's most effective magical investigator.

"I'll be right back. Don't touch anything."

The conference room contained a half dozen university administrators and security personnel, all eager to provide information that might help solve the murder of one of their most prominent faculty members. Colonel Cameron had been working on classified research for the Department of Defense, analyzing historical military strategies and their applications to contemporary magical warfare. His security clearance gave him access to government databases and research networks that would be valuable to foreign intelligence services or terrorist organizations.

"Was he working on anything involving Chicago's magical infrastructure?" Alex asked, watching the administrators' reactions.

"No," the department chair replied. "He came to us from the Department of Defense where he worked on classified projects that he never spoke about. He was still working on contracts with the government at Aberdeen Proving Ground."

Alex wondered how Colonel Cameron's work at Aberdeen could possibly be connected to their infrastructure case. Every city in the country used magical systems and there was very little classified about them. Other than protocols and access codes. But this murder was clearly connected.

Alex spent twenty minutes gathering information about Colonel Cameron's research, his contacts with government agencies, and his recent consulting work. The pattern was becoming clearer with each detail. Both Torres and Cameron had possessed valuable knowledge and both had been killed by someone employing ancient magic techniques.

When Alex returned to Colonel Cameron's office, he

found Elias standing much closer to Cameron than he'd been before, his hands extended toward the Cameron's body preparing to touch him directly. The energies around him had intensified, swirling through the air as he pushed his abilities to their limits.

"Elias, what are you doing?"

Elias didn't look up from the papers, his concentration intensely focused. "I can get more information about the killer if I can read the traces more deeply. The trap is sophisticated, but I think I can work around it. I was able to break free last time."

"You just said it was designed to overload anyone with memory tracing abilities."

"I said anyone, not me specifically," Elias stated with confidence. But underneath it, Alex could sense something else. A determination that bordered on recklessness.

"I've been studying defensive techniques since the warehouse incident. I think I can push through the offensive attack without triggering the worst effects."

Alex felt alarm bells going off in his mind. This was exactly the kind of dangerous behavior that ASAC Lindsey had been worried about, the unnecessary risks that suggested Elias didn't care whether he came home at the end of the day. The magical trap pulsed with malevolent energy, clearly designed to cause permanent damage to anyone foolish enough to trigger it.

"Elias, step away from the desk."

"I can handle this, Alex. I just need to—"

"I said step away." Alex moved closer, crowding Elias and moving him away. He positioned himself between him and Cameron's body. Silver light flared around his hands, combat magic forming barriers that could contain the trap's effects if it activated. "We're not risking your life or your abilities on a trap that's specifically designed to target magical investigators."

Elias' eyes flared with green light, he started to speak but stopped himself. His shoulders sagged as he stepped back from the desk.

"Fine. But we're missing an opportunity to learn more about who killed him."

"We're avoiding the risk of losing our best investigator to a magical booby trap."

Alex kept his voice calm, but he could feel the tension between them, silver and green energies swirling through the air as their abilities responded to the confrontation between them. "There are other ways to gather intelligence without triggering whatever the killer left behind."

Elias nodded, lips pressed tight, his gaze fixed on the desk instead of Alex. The old Elias would have trusted Alex's judgment without question, confident that they could find other approaches to solving the case. This Elias seemed driven by a need to prove himself, to take risks that might validate his abilities—or punish him for past failures.

They spent the next hour documenting the crime scene and coordinating with the university security team. The magical forensics specialists confirmed Elias' assessment of the magical trap, identifying it as an advanced defensive measure designed to prevent detailed investigation of the killer's magical signature. Disarming it would require specialized equipment and at least six hours of careful work. Assuming they could find someone with the expertise to attempt it safely.

"We'll have Dr. Madison coordinate with the trap specialists," Alex decided, watching the hostile energies pulse around Colonel Cameron's desk. "She has the technical knowledge to oversee the disarmament process."

Elias agreed, but Alex could see the disappointment in his expression. The old partnership would have involved more discussion, more collaborative decision-making. Now Alex found himself making unilateral choices designed to protect Elias from his own reckless impulses.

◇✧◇

"Serial killings," Rivera said as they reviewed the evidence back at the FBI building. "But not a traditional serial killer. Someone who's targeting specific people for specific information. And there are no personal connections between them. Nothing else in common that I can find."

Alex replied, "Systematic targeting of people with knowledge that could be used to plan attacks on critical infrastructure and the yet unknown connection to Colonel Cameron."

"The question is whether we're looking at a lone operative or a larger organization," Elias added. He'd been quiet since arriving back at the office, processing what they'd learned about the killer's methods and motivations. "We need more information on what this ancient magic is and who is behind it."

Alex nodded, studying the crime scene photos spread across their conference table. Both Torres and Cameron had been chosen for their specific expertise, but there were other people in Chicago with similar knowledge. If the terrorists were systematically targeting everyone who understood the city's magical infrastructure, the body count could grow quickly.

"We need to identify other potential targets," Alex decided, watching the way Elias' attention brightened slightly at the mention of continued investigation. "People with the kind of knowledge that made Torres and Cameron worth killing for."

"I'll coordinate with both the city and the university," Rivera offered. "Get lists of personnel with similar clearances and expertise."

"And I'll work with Dr. Madison on analyzing the magical signatures," Elias added. "Even with the trap preventing detailed investigation, we might be able to identify patterns that tell us something about the killer's background or training."

They spent the rest of the afternoon building profiles of potential targets and coordinating protective measures with local law enforcement. It was methodical work, the kind of systematic analysis that might prevent future murders if they could identify the killer's next target in time. But Alex found himself watching Elias throughout the process. The careful way he held himself and a determination that was driving him toward increasingly dangerous choices.

The reckless behavior at the crime scene had been subtle, but it was exactly what ASAC Lindsey had been worried about. Elias was taking unnecessary risks, pushing himself toward dangerous situations trying to prove something. The old partnership had been built on mutual trust, a deep friendship, and teamwork. This new dynamic required Alex to make decisions that felt uncomfortably like supervision.

As evening approached and the office began to empty, Alex found himself alone with Elias in the conference room, crime scene photos and evidence reports spread between them like a barrier. The tension from their earlier disagreement in Cameron's office still lingered in the air.

"We should call it a day," Alex said finally, looking at his watch. "Pick this up tomorrow morning."

Elias nodded, but he didn't move to gather his files. Instead, he stared at the photographs of Colonel Cameron's office, his expression thoughtful and somehow distant.

"I could have read more from that trap," he said quietly.

"And I think you could have ended up with permanent brain damage," Alex replied sharply. "The trap was specifically designed to target magical investigators. There's no safe way to trigger it deliberately."

"Maybe. But we lost an opportunity to learn more about who we're chasing."

Alex studied Elias' profile, the stubborn set of his jaw and the way his hands remained clenched on the table. "Is that what this is about? Proving that your abilities still work?"

Elias was quiet for a moment. When he spoke, his words came clipped and even. "My magic failed eighteen months ago. Seven people died because I read a scene wrong and gave you bad intelligence. If there's a chance to prove that I can still do this job effectively, I have to take it."

"Your magic didn't fail," Alex said quietly, silver light beginning to flow around his hands as his protective instincts unconsciously responded to Elias' pain. "Something went wrong that day, but it wasn't because you couldn't do your job."

"It felt the same." Elias finally looked up from the photographs, meeting Alex's eyes directly for the first time. "And until I can prove that I can still be trusted with this kind of investigation, I'll keep feeling like I'm letting everyone down."

Alex felt old pain and current frustration rise. Elias was blaming himself for circumstances that neither of them fully understood. That self-doubt was driving him toward increasingly dangerous behavior. The distance they'd maintained was supposed to protect them both from difficult conversations, but it was also preventing the kind of honest communication that might help Elias understand what had really happened eighteen months ago.

"We'll figure this out, but not by taking unnecessary risks that could get you killed."

Elias nodded, gathering his files with movements that suggested the conversation was over. But as he stood and started to leave, he stopped and looked back at Alex with something that might have been gratitude or perhaps regret.

"Thanks for stopping me today. At the crime scene. I know I was about to do something stupid."

"Just be careful," Alex replied with concern.

After Elias left, Alex remained in the conference room, studying the evidence they'd collected. He found himself worrying about his former partner's increasingly reckless behavior. Elias was taking unnecessary risks that made him dangerous to himself and potentially to others. The magical trap in Colonel Cameron's office could have killed him, and he'd been willing to trigger it deliberately just to prove his abilities still worked.

Alex gathered his own files and headed toward the elevator, wondering if they could solve this case before the body count grew higher.

6

Under Fire

FBI Chicago Division—November 19

The breakthrough came from an encrypted flash drive hidden in Colonel Cameron's desk drawer, discovered only after Dr. Madison's team had spent three hours analyzing every piece of evidence from his office with equipment designed to detect magical concealment. The drive contained research collaboration files that showed academic networks being systematically infiltrated.

Alex and Elias sat at the conference table with ASAC Lindsey as Agent Rivera spoke. "Dr. Stephanie Panahi, Northwestern University Materials Science," Rivera reported, consulting the newly decrypted files that glowed briefly, indicating their security classification. "She's been collaborating with Colonel Cameron on classified projects through Aberdeen Proving Ground."

Alex studied the documents that showed years of correspondence between the two researchers.

"Her research involves advanced materials analysis for government applications," Elias observed. "The kind of work that could have strategic value."

"Which makes her the next logical target," Lindsey concluded, consulting tactical assessments that showed Dr. Panahi as extremely vulnerable to the same kind of attack that had killed Cameron. "If someone's systematically eliminating researchers who understand the classified project that Cameron was involved with, she's probably already on their list."

Rivera added,"Email analysis shows Dr. Panahi received multiple calls yesterday from numbers that don't exist. But more interesting, we found a series of email exchanges between her and Colonel Cameron from last month."

"What kind of exchanges?" Alex asked.

"They were discussing something called 'Avalon.' The emails suggest they were both concerned that it had been compromised," Rivera replied, consulting the decrypted correspondence.

"No details about what Avalon is, but the security classifications suggest something highly sensitive."

"Background check confirms Dr. Panahi worked at Aberdeen Proving Ground as a civilian researcher for three years before joining Northwestern," Rivera added.

"Same timeframe as Colonel Cameron's assignment there."

Lindsey, recognizing the immediate potential threat, made the decision to contact Dr. Panahi immediately. "Get to Northwestern immediately. Interview Dr. Panahi, assess her security situation, determine what protection she needs. If the pattern holds, they'll likely move against her within hours."

Alex and Elias gathered their files while Rivera coordinated with Northwestern campus security to ask them to locate Dr. Panahi and ensure she wasn't left alone. As they prepared to leave the office, Elias headed toward the motor pool parking area where Bureau vehicles were assigned to individual agents.

"I'll take my car, you take yours," Elias said as he put on his suit jacket and consulted directions to Northwestern's Materials Science building. "We can cover more ground if we arrive separately."

"Bad idea," Alex replied immediately, as he recognized tactical vulnerabilities in operating separately. "After what happened to Torres and Cameron, we stay together. Same car, coordinated approach, we work as a team."

"Alex, it's a routine academic interview. Dr. Panahi isn't under active threat yet. We're just gathering intelligence."

"Torres was in her home when someone killed her. Cameron was working in his office when they extracted his memories. Not to mention that they left two magical traps for us." Alex's tone grew more firm as he pressed his point. "We don't split up until we understand what we're dealing with."

Elias started to argue, then recognized the concern in his partner's expression. After eighteen months of essentially working alone, the idea of teaming up felt both reassuring and constraining. But Alex's instincts had always proven reliable during their previous cases and that was hard to ignore.

"Fine," Elias agreed, following Alex toward the Bureau vehicle assigned for their joint use. "But I'm driving."

"Actually, I'm driving," Alex said. "You can navigate and backseat drive."

"I don't backseat drive," he said with fake annoyance and a roll of his eyes. But he complied and got in on the passenger side of the vehicle.

The drive to Northwestern took thirty-minutes and gave them time to plan how to handle Dr. Panahi. And whether she was about to become the next name on the hit list. "So," Alex said as they merged onto Lake Shore Drive, the November sky gray with approaching storm clouds that made the afternoon feel later than it was. "Lindsey mentioned you got pulled from an undercover assignment a few weeks ago. What happened?"

Elias turned toward the window, watching the blur of traffic instead of meeting Alex's eyes. His hand flexed once against his thigh before going still. "It went fine. Standard assignment, routine stuff."

"Rivera said you were taking unnecessary risks. That they were worried about your safety." Alex kept his voice neutral, remembering that Elias' recent behavior had been concerning enough to warrant Lindsey's personal intervention. "What kind of risks?"

"Nothing unusual," Elias replied, his tone carrying the dismissive quality he brought to topics he didn't want to discuss. "Undercover work always involves calculated risks. Sometimes calculations are wrong."

Alex studied his partner's profile, noting the tension around his eyes and the way he held his shoulders with the defensive posture that suggested he was holding back.

"Elias, what happened during that assignment?"

"I said it was fine."

"And I'm saying that an ASAC doesn't pull agents from undercover operations unless something goes seriously wrong. Lindsey mentioned you were confronting suspects without backup, entering situations where your magical abilities were compromised." Alex spoke more carefully now, the concern in his tone no longer easy to hide. "That doesn't sound like routine undercover work."

Elias remained silent for several minutes, watching Chicago's urban landscape pass outside the passenger window while thinking about questions he'd been avoiding since Livingston had terminated his undercover assignment. The truth was that he had been taking increasingly dangerous risks, pushing himself into situations that rational tactical assessment would have avoided.

"I was investigating a group suspected of funding magical extremists," Elias said finally, his voice carrying reluctant honesty rather than the dismissive tone he'd used before. "Trying to gather intelligence about their financial networks and recruitment methods."

"And?"

"And I started questioning informants without letting anyone know, meeting contacts in locations where magical abilities could be detected and countered, pushing for information that put both me and my sources at risk." Elias' voice grew quieter as he admitted behavior that violated basic undercover protocols. "Lindsey said I was acting like I didn't care whether I came home."

Alex felt his concern deepen as he recognized patterns that suggested Elias had been struggling with more than just confidence issues. The reckless behavior sounded like someone who'd lost his sense of self-preservation, possibly as a result of guilt over the warehouse incident.

"Were you trying to prove something? About your abilities, about your effectiveness as an agent?" Alex asked carefully, noting the way Elias' magical energy had become more withdrawn during the conversation. Even after eighteen months he could still sense Elias' magic like it was his own.

"Maybe. I don't know," Elias replied honestly. "Ever since the warehouse, I keep second-guessing every instinct, every magical insight, every tactical decision. It's like I can't trust my own judgment anymore."

"So you started taking bigger risks to force situations where you'd have to rely on your abilities?"

"Something like that." Elias looked directly at Alex for the first time since the conversation had begun. "If I could prove my magic still worked under extreme pressure, maybe I could start trusting it again for normal operations."

Alex understood the psychological trap his partner had been caught in, the way self-doubt could drive someone toward increasingly dangerous behavior in desperate attempts to rebuild confidence. The warehouse incident had damaged more than their partnership. It had undermined Elias' faith in his own capabilities.

"And how did that work out?" Alex asked gently.

"It didn't. I just got more reckless and more convinced that my abilities couldn't be trusted when it mattered most." Elias said softly. "Lindsey was right to pull me from the assignment. I was going to compromise the case trying to prove something that can't be proven through reckless behavior."

As they approached Northwestern's campus, Alex processed what his partner had revealed about his recent state of mind and the dangerous patterns that had characterized his approach to undercover work. Alex glanced at Elias, but his partner kept his gaze fixed out the passenger window, jaw tight, saying nothing. The silence pressed heavier than the traffic noise, both of them skirting over the words that might have mattered most.

"For what it's worth," Alex said as they pulled into the Northwestern parking area, "your magical insights on the Torres and Cameron cases have been exactly as reliable as they were before the warehouse. The problem isn't your abilities, Elias. The problem is that you're not trusting them."

"Maybe," Elias replied, as he opened the car door. "I guess we'll find out."

Northwestern University Campus

Dr. Stephanie Panahi hurried across the parking lot behind the Materials Science building, her arms full of research files and her mind focused on the dinner plans she'd been forced to reschedule twice this week. The November wind cut through her wool coat as she fumbled for her car keys, eager to get home before the evening traffic made the drive to Evanston even more miserable.

She didn't notice the two men approaching from the shadow of a delivery truck until one of them called her name. "Dr. Panahi? We need to speak with you about your research."

Stephanie looked up to see strangers in dark coats, their expressions carrying the kind of intensity that made her think they were either federal agents or corporate security. Her grip tightened on her purse.

"I'm sorry, who are you?" she asked, noticing both men position themselves to block her path to her car.

"Dr. Panahi, you need to come with us," the taller man said, his hand moving toward something concealed beneath his coat. "Your research has attracted attention from people who value your expertise. People who can offer you opportunities your current position can't provide."

Stephanie didn't have magic abilities but she didn't need them to sense the hostile intent radiating from both strangers. These weren't federal agents or corporate recruiters. These were people who meant her harm, and she knew that this had to be related to her work on Avalon.

She opened her mouth to scream just as Alex and Elias exited a vehicle parked three cars away from her.

"FBI!" Alex's voice carried across the short distance as he and Elias hurried from their car preparing to draw their magic. "Step away from her!"

But one of the assailants was already a couple feet from her and raised his hand.

Alex moved instantly. He reached for her, magic already flaring. A defensive shield formed in front of him, glowing hot and sharp. It wouldn't reach her in time.

The air cracked with heat, heavy and blinding. A blast of elemental force struck Panahi in the back, lifting her off her feet. She hit the ground hard and didn't move. Smoke curled from her coat.

Alex and Elias moved in sync, using parked cars for cover while advancing toward the attackers. But more men emerged from concealed positions around the parking lot, turning the rescue into a firefight that sent students and faculty diving for cover behind vehicles and concrete barriers.

"Six hostiles," Alex shouted to Elias, his combat magic forming a protective barrier around them that deflected incoming rounds. "This is a coordinated operation."

The fight intensified as the attackers focused on eliminating the agents who'd interfered with their mission.

"They're running!" Elias said, noting the way several attackers were moving toward motorcycles parked at the edge of the lot.

Alex and Elias reached their car as engines roared to life around them. Three motorcycles accelerated toward the parking lot exit while their riders continued to fire back toward them.

The pursuit began on main streets where afternoon traffic provided cover for both hunters and hunted. Alex wove their SUV between cars and buses while Elias coordinated with FBI backup units by radio.

"Three motorcycles heading south on Sheridan," Elias reported. The riders went in different directions as they hit downtown Evanston. "They're trying to split up."

"Which one do we follow?" Alex asked, cutting across traffic near Church Street. His combat magic heightened his reflexes, but the tires still squealed through the turn.

"Left bike," Elias said, eyes unfocused for a moment as he reached out with his magic. "He's the leader."

Alex accelerated, tailing the rider as he veered west onto Dempster Street, dodging cars and blowing through intersections. The bike wove recklessly through traffic, clipping bumpers and brushing mirrors.

"He's heading for the highway," Alex said as the motorcycle cut west, then shot toward the I-94 on-ramp.

"He hits open speed, we lose him," Elias muttered.

Alex pressed harder on the accelerator, engine roaring as the expressway came into view.

But as they neared the highway entrance, the other two motorcycles reappeared from opposite sides, merging in from parallel streets. In seconds, the car was boxed in, surrounded by hostile riders who opened fire. Automatic bursts shredded the side mirror and turned the windshield into a spiderwebbed sheet of cracked safety glass.

"It's a coordinated assault," Elias said, ducking as bullets shattered their rear window. "They're not running anymore."

Alex's combat magic flared around them, protective barriers deflecting the worst of the gunfire while he searched for tactical advantages. But they were outgunned and outnumbered by attackers who'd clearly planned for vehicle pursuit.

"I need more than memory magic," Elias said.

"Alex, can you maintain protective barriers if I try something else?"

"What kind of something else?"

"Elemental magic. Wind pressure, thermal shifts. Make it harder for them to control the bikes."

"Alex looked at him skeptically. 'You sure about that?"

Elias didn't answer him but he saw Elias' focus shift, moving away from memory magic and into the secondary magical skills he rarely used. Subtle, elemental, and very unpredictable. It was never his preference to use it, but it didn't need to be perfect. It just needed to throw them off balance.

Alex reinforced his protective wards while Elias extended his magic toward the attacking motorcycles. He reached out and manipulated the air currents and thermal patterns around the moving vehicles. The effect was immediate and dramatic. The motorcycle to their left hit a pocket of superheated air that made its engine sputter and lose power. Its rider fought to maintain control as thermal distortions interfered with his vision and targeting.

"It's working," Alex said. The way attack was becoming less precise as Elias' elemental magic created unexpected obstacles. "Can you affect all three bikes?"

"I'm trying," Elias replied, as he attempted to influence multiple targets simultaneously. Wind patterns shifted around the motorcycles, creating crosswinds that forced riders to reduce speed and focus on maintaining control rather than accurate shooting.

The elemental magic required sustained concentration, but it was proving effective against the motorcyclists. Alex watched the pursuit dynamics shift as the attackers found themselves struggling with environmental hazards rather than maintaining offensive pressure.

But their tactical advantage was temporary. The motorcycle riders were adapting to Elias' elemental manipulation, adjusting their formation and attack patterns to minimize the effects of wind and thermal interference.

"We need to end this now," Alex said, channeling his combat magic into offensive capabilities he rarely used in urban environments. "Hold on."

Silver energy erupted from Alex's hands and back toward the lead motorcycle, a focused kinetic blast that sent the bike tumbling across three lanes of traffic in a shower of sparks and twisted metal. The rider hit the asphalt hard and didn't get up.

But the two remaining motorcycles immediately shifted tactics, accelerating ahead of their SUV before turning to face them in a coordinated assault that filled the highway with automatic weapons fire.

Alex swerved desperately to avoid the frontal attack, but their car was already damaged and losing power. The SUV's engine coughed and died as they stopped sideways partly on the shoulder of I-94 with two hostile motorcycles closing in for a final attack. Traffic behind them had long since come to a grinding halt as drivers saw the danger and came to a stop, distancing themselves from gunfight.

"Out of the car," Alex said as they rolled to a stop. "We fight on foot."

The battle that followed tested every aspect of their magical coordination. Alex's combat magic created shields and launched counterattacks while Elias used elemental manipulation to disrupt the motorcycles' mobility. But they were outnumbered by opponents who demonstrated professional training and sophisticated tactical coordination.

Fire magic erupted across the highway as one rider launched sustained attacks while the other maneuvered for flanking position. Alex deflected the worst of the assault while Elias created wind gusts that disrupted targeting, but their defensive position was becoming increasingly untenable.

"Elias, move!" Alex shouted, but Elias was focused on maintaining the wind and pressure fields that kept the motorcycles from closing in.

He didn't see the truck until the last second.

Alex's shield snapped into place on pure instinct, silver light flaring between Elias and the oncoming grille. The impact cracked the barrier like glass under a hammer, but it held long enough to throw the force sideways instead of through him. The ward shattered, and Elias hit the asphalt hard and rolled, tumbling across the highway median before coming to rest.

"Elias!" Alex sprinted toward him.

He wasn't moving. Blood was already pooling near his head. For one awful second Alex thought he was gone, until he saw it, the faint rise of his chest, shallow and fragile, like it could stop at any moment. The protective ward had held just long enough to keep the impact from killing him outright.

Alex turned back to the road as the pickup's doors flew open and new attackers advanced with weapons drawn.

Alex's combat magic erupted with power that exceeded anything he'd ever accessed previously. Silver energy blazed around him like controlled lightning as he channeled fury into force that made the remaining threats inconsequential.

The kinetic blasts that followed tore both motorcycles apart, sending their riders flying across multiple lanes of traffic. The pickup truck tried to escape, but Alex's magic reached it before it could gain distance, crushing the vehicle like an empty can.

Then his focus snapped back to Elias, lying unconscious on the ground, injuries demanding immediate medical attention.

"Officer down!" Alex shouted through his radio as he knelt beside his partner. "I need immediate medical evacuation on I-94 southbound, mile marker forty-seven. Agent injured, unconscious, possible internal injuries."

Northwestern Memorial Hospital

Morning light filtered through the hospital windows as Alex woke from an uncomfortable night in the room's reclining chair, his neck stiff and his clothes crumpled. He'd barely slept, too focused on monitoring Elias' breathing and the steady beep of medical equipment to trust that his partner was truly going to recover.

Elias blinked against the morning light, his gaze sliding from the monitors to the unfamiliar walls. He shifted, then sucked in a sharp breath as pain pulled across his ribs.

"Hey," Alex said softly, leaning forward as relief flooded through him. "How do you feel?"

"Like I got hit by a train," Elias replied, his voice hoarse from the breathing tube that had been used during the surgery. "Which, now that I think about it, is probably exactly what happened."

"Pickup truck, actually. T-boned our car on your side." Alex's expression grew more serious as memories of the previous evening returned. "You were unconscious for several hours. The doctors had to operate to repair internal bleeding."

Elias tried to sit up, wincing as the movement pulled at surgical incisions and aggravated cracked ribs. "Dr. Panahi?"

"Alex's expression answered the question before he could speak. "They killed her."

"Did we get any of them?"

"One dead in the highway crash, two others deceased from the fight. The pickup truck driver didn't survive either." Alex helped Elias adjust his position against the hospital pillows.

Before Elias could ask anything else, the door opened to admit Dr. Morris accompanied by a woman in her thirties wearing the distinctive light blue lab coat that marked her as a healing magic specialist.

"Agent Sinclair, I'm Dr. Sarah Washington," the healing specialist announced, consulting her tablet. "I've been asked to evaluate your injuries for accelerated magical healing. The surgical repairs were successful, but magical intervention could reduce your recovery time from weeks to days."

Elias stiffened, eyes narrowing as he drew back against the pillows, registering the implications of magical healing that would require psychic contact with a stranger. "I appreciate the offer, but I prefer conventional recovery."

"Agent Sinclair, the internal trauma you've sustained will take six to eight weeks to heal naturally." Dr. Washington's voice was calm, professional. "Magical healing could have you back to full function within forty-eight hours with no long term complications."

"No, thank you," Elias replied firmly. "I don't allow psychic contact with anyone."

Dr. Morris intervened with the diplomatic skills that came from years of managing patients who had strong opinions about their treatment. "Agent Sinclair, Dr. Washington is fully certified in medical magical applications. Her credentials include—"

"It's not about credentials," Elias interrupted, his pulse rate increasing and his expression growing more closed with each attempt at persuasion. "I don't do psychic contact with strangers. Period."

Alex didn't need the explanation. He knew the refusal had nothing to do with skill or effectiveness. Elias would never accept psychic contact from a stranger. It was about the intimate nature of psychic contact required for magical healing, the kind of mental connection that left a person vulnerable. It was too easy for an unscrupulous healer to attempt to read a person's most private thoughts. As a memory specialist, Elias knew all too well how easy that was.

After eighteen months of doubting his abilities and questioning every magical insight, Elias had built psychological barriers that protected him from potential manipulation or betrayal. Opening his mind to a stranger's magical influence would feel like surrendering control of the very abilities he was still learning to trust again.

"The accelerated healing really would be beneficial," Dr. Washington pressed, consulting assessment data that showed the scope of Elias' injuries. "Without magical intervention, you're looking at significant recovery time and potential complications from the internal trauma."

"He said no," Alex interrupted abruptly. "He's told you no three times. I think it's time for you to leave."

Elias stared at him in surprise. "He's right. It's time for you to leave. I've made my decision." The doctors exchanged a look and walked out of the room without further comment.

Alex walked to the door they'd just exited through and shut it. He returned to Elias' bed and sat down in the chair beside him.

"What if I do it?" he said cautiously.

Elias didn't answer immediately. Healing magic required the kind of psychic contact they hadn't attempted since before their partnership had ended. It was a personal magical connection that would require absolute trust from both participants.

"Alex, you don't need to—" Elias started, but Alex cut him off.

"I know I don't need to. I want to." Alex's voice was steady, certain.

"You'd heal faster, get back to work sooner, avoid weeks of pain and complications. And you still trust me, right?"

"Of course I do. I always have. And I know that you have healing magic that you've never told anyone else about," Elias replied.

"I'm not trained for complex medical procedures, but I have experience with trauma healing. We've done it before," Alex said quietly, his eyes meeting Elias'. "Remember Arizona?"

Elias did remember. A case that had taken them far from Chicago to desert landscapes where federal jurisdiction intersected with tribal law enforcement. A joint investigation that had somehow evolved into the closest thing to a vacation either of them had experienced in years.

"The Navajo Nation case," Elias said, with the first smile

Alex had seen from him since the hospital admission. "You said we should see the desert while we were there."

"And you insisted we go horseback riding like we were tourists instead of federal agents," Alex replied. "Even though neither of us had any business on horseback."

"You were so competitive about it," Elias continued. "Racing across open desert like we were the cavalry instead of FBI agents investigating magical artifact smuggling."

"You were the one who suggested we race," Alex protested, grinning at the memory of afternoon sunlight and desert wind while their horses thundered across the landscape. "I was just trying to keep up."

"And failing miserably until I got overconfident and took that ravine jump too fast," Elias finished, his expression growing more serious. "My horse balked at the landing. I went flying."

Elias was thrown from his horse and hit the rocky ground with enough force to snap his left leg cleanly in two places. Miles from the nearest medical facility, hours from conventional emergency services, in terrain that would have made rescue evacuation difficult even if communication had been possible.

"Compound fracture, complete break in two places," Alex said. "You were going into shock from blood loss and pain. I had to choose between waiting for evacuation or attempting field healing."

"And you chose to heal me," Elias said quietly, remembering the moment when Alex had knelt beside him in desert sand and offered magical assistance that would require deep psychic contact. "Even though we'd never attempted anything that complex before."

"I wasn't going to let you suffer waiting for a helicopter that might not even reach us for hours," Alex replied. "Besides, I knew that you trusted me."

The healing had required thirty minutes of sustained

magical contact, Alex's abilities working through Elias' body to repair bone and tissue while managing pain that could have overwhelmed him. An intimate connection that had left both agents feeling closer than any magic coordination they'd ever attempted.

"It worked," Elias said, flexing his left leg unconsciously as he remembered waking up with Alex sitting beside him on the ground, his broken bones completely healed and his pain reduced to manageable levels. "Better than conventional medical treatment would have managed."

"And we never told anyone afterward," Alex added. "Just wrote it up as field medical assistance in the official report."

"You didn't want anyone to know you had that ability. It was an easy secret to keep," Elias said casually.

"The trauma you've sustained is more complex than a simple fracture," Alex stated. "The healing will require more than an hour of sustained psychic contact. But I can handle it."

Elias held Alex's gaze for a long moment. The offer was more than medical assistance.

"You're sure you want to do this?" Elias asked. "It's not like Arizona. We have no privacy and this is more involved. If something goes wrong—"

"Nothing's going to go wrong," Alex replied. "No one will know what I did."

"If we ward the door so anyone who looks in just sees you sleeping, then we have privacy."

After watching Elias nearly die in a highway attack, Alex couldn't let him suffer through weeks of painful recovery.

"Okay," Elias said quietly. "Let's do it."

Alex positioned himself closer to Elias' hospital bed as Elias cast a warding spell that shielded them from intruders.

"Ready?" Alex asked, extending his hands toward Elias. Silver energy began to flow around his fingers.

"Ready," Elias replied, allowing his mental defenses to

lower as he prepared for psychic contact that would leave him completely vulnerable.

Alex's magic slid into Elias' mind, steady and deliberate as he knitted wounds. For the first time since the warehouse, their magic aligned again. Alex felt Elias' pain, sharp and immediate. Felt his exhaustion beneath it. Felt the edges of his thoughts, careful and guarded.

Elias felt Alex's presence in return, protective and certain. Neither pushed deeper. The link remained steady, present, just enough.

The healing would take time. An hour, maybe more. For the first time in eighteen months, Alex felt like the distance between them didn't matter, and maybe something had begun to mend.

7
The Secrets We Share

Shared secrets are the currency of trust
—Douglas Coupland (attributed)

Three Days Later

Through the windows, Chicago stretched toward Lake Michigan under a sky the color of old pewter. Holiday decorations had taken over the Loop, installed the moment Halloween ended. Garland wrapped around streetlights glowed with minor warming charms, window displays shimmered with perpetual motion spells, and a few early Christmas trees lit the lobbies of downtown offices, their lights powered by small magical generators that never burned out. In five days, families across the country would gather for Thanksgiving, sharing gratitude and turkey, unaware of the danger already taking shape around them.

Alex arrived at his desk to find Agent Cross and Agent Rivera waiting, both holding coffee cups and looking relieved to see him.

"How's Elias?" Cross asked immediately, extending one of the cups.

"He's better. Discharged this morning," Alex replied, accepting the coffee. Elias had spent two days in the hospital, mostly to keep the doctors from asking more questions. His recovery hadn't made sense, and he wasn't offering explanations. He'd kept Alex's secret, as he always did.

"Good," Rivera said, though her tone suggested she wanted more details. "Because what happened the other day was completely insane. Multiple assailants on motorcycles, a pickup truck attack, and a magical murder in broad daylight. He's lucky you were there to shield him from that truck."

Alex's jaw tightened. "It wasn't luck. That truck would have killed him if I hadn't stepped in." Elias frozen in the path of the oncoming truck. No time to react. For a heartbeat, Alex had thought he was too late. "He never saw it coming."

Cross gave a short nod. "Point is, he's still here. Because of you."

Alex settled into his chair, reviewing overnight reports. The highway attack had been coordinated, executed with precision and timing that pointed to a trained organization.

"Any intelligence on the attackers?" Alex asked.

"Four bodies. No IDs, no fingerprints in any database," Rivera said, scrolling through the forensic report.

"The serial numbers were filed off all the weapons. Motorcycles were stolen from a dealer in Wisconsin two weeks ago. The pickup truck was rented with fake documents."

Cross checked his notes. "They weren't improvising. The assault team was out front, but they had backup staged and ready. This was obviously coordinated."

Alex nodded, eyes still on the reports. "The same people who killed Torres and Cameron."

"Speaking of the investigation," Rivera said, glancing toward the elevator where Elias had just appeared, "how's he really doing? After yesterday?"

Alex looked over. Elias walked in like nothing had happened, posture steady, expression unreadable.

"He's fine," Alex said, though his eyes lingered on Elias as he approached.

Elias reached their desks, his expression focused and composed, but fatigue clung to him in subtle ways. In the set of his shoulders, the slight tension around his eyes.

"Morning," Elias said, settling into the chair beside Alex's desk.

"Elias," Cross said, leaning forward. "Dude, you all right? That scene was brutal."

"I'm fine, Marcus," Elias said with an easy shrug. "The doctors at the hospital patched me up."

Rivera studied him. "You look tired."

"You ever tried sleeping in a hospital?" A faint smile. "Let's get back to work. Any leads on our motorcycle friends?"

"Dead ends. Literally," Rivera replied wryly.

"Which reminds me," Rivera said, glancing toward ASAC Lindsey's office. "Lindsey wants to see both of you. Something about Baltimore."

They walked in silence, their steps unconsciously in sync as they made their way toward Lindsey's office. Alex didn't speak, but the memory of the healing still lingered. Not just the magic, but what it revealed. He'd felt Elias' loneliness, heavy and unresolved, and the strain of holding so much emotion without a place to put it. Elias wasn't the only one grieving. Alex just hid it better. Memory magic came with a cost. That much Alex understood. Emotions didn't just pass through Elias, they rooted. A man with his kind of power couldn't afford to be unmoored. And right now, Elias was more alone than he let on.

"Good morning. Have a seat."

Alex and Elias settled into the chairs across from her desk.

"Agent Sinclair, how are you feeling?"

Elias shifted slightly, the motion just stiff enough to hint at lingering soreness. "I'm fine, ma'am. No lasting effects."

"Glad to hear it. You made a miraculous recovery, I see." Lindsey gave Alex a long, sidelong look. Not accusatory, but not casual either. It lingered just long enough to make them both wonder how many close calls she'd catalogued over the years. Elias always walked away from the worst of it. And Alex was always there when he did.

Lindsey tapped her tablet once, locking the screen. "Follow me."

Alex and Elias exchanged a glance but said nothing as she led them out of her office and through the secure wing of the field office, past two security checkpoints and into a quiet hallway with restricted access. At the end of it, a door marked SCIF 3A waited, already unlocked. No one spoke until they stepped inside.

The Sensitive Compartmented Information Facility was a secure windowless conference room, its white walls interrupted only by a large screen on one side and a mounted camera above. Lindsey closed the door behind them with a solid click.

The monitor blinked to life. Across the top of the screen, bold red letters marked the classification of the briefing, followed by the seal of the Department of Magical Affairs, and the name of the person about to brief them.

TOP SECRET//SI-AVALON//DMA//APG

Deputy Director Catrin Rowan, Magical Operations Division

The woman who appeared was mid-forties, composed, and unmistakably sharp. Her dark auburn hair was loose around her shoulders, and steady green eyes that gave nothing away.

"Agents Sutton and Sinclair." Her voice was clear and deliberate. She paused, letting her gaze rest on Elias. There was no surprise in her expression, only recognition, as though she were remembering someone long forgotten. Then she continued, eyes still fixed on him.

"You are being read into Project Avalon."

Elias straightened slightly. Alex didn't move, but his posture sharpened. Lindsey remained behind them, silent and watching.

"Colonel Joseph Cameron wasn't targeted at random. Before retiring to teach, he oversaw access protocols for the DMA's secure vault at Aberdeen Proving Ground. That facility holds several recovered artifacts under joint jurisdiction. His clearance would have given him detailed knowledge of the vault's contents and their storage conditions. Whoever killed him likely wanted to silence him."

"The site itself is heavily warded and classified. Under normal circumstances, DMA would take full control of the investigation."

Rowan's tone shifted slightly.

"However, given your unique qualifications, we're treating this as a joint operation. Your combination of memory and combat magic, both at rare high proficiency, makes you uniquely capable of evaluating what you'll find there."

She finally looked away from Elias.

"You'll be given limited access to the Avalon vault and surrounding records. Learn what you can and report back."

Elias spoke, calm but direct. "What is the history of these artifacts?"

Rowan's eyes returned to him. She didn't reply at once. Then, with the barest tilt of her head, she said, "You've encountered their magic. Have you not?"

"Yes."

Her tone softened.

"Then you already know their power."

Elias didn't answer. He held her gaze for a second too long, and Alex caught something unreadable in his expression. Understanding, perhaps. Or suspicion.

Alex couldn't tell. But he knew that look. It meant Elias was filing something away. The way he did when a memory wasn't ready to be examined yet.

She held Elias' gaze a moment longer, then the video feed faded into the DMA seal.

A soft tone indicated the end of the briefing. Lindsey stepped forward to unlock the exit as she said, "You leave this afternoon. They'll be expecting you at 9 a.m. tomorrow."

They didn't speak until they separated from Lindsey.

"She's a Rowan," Alex said quietly.

Elias nodded once. "Yeah."

A pause. "That magical family is older than modern civilization,"Alex continued.

"Yes, they are," came the quick response from Elias.

"She couldn't take her eyes off you."

"I noticed."

"She seemed to think you know more about the ancient magic."

"Yeah. I've got a bad feeling about it."

"About her?"

"About all of it."

Alex didn't push further. Elias' answer had come a beat too fast, the kind of response he gave when he didn't want to lie but wasn't ready to say more. Alex had seen that tone before, usually when Elias' memories brushed up against something personal. There was more to that "yeah" than agreement. And Rowan had looked at him like she already knew what it was.

Back in the conference room that he and Elias had commandeered, Alex pulled out his phone to check the message that had arrived during Lindsey's briefing. It was from his mother, a cheerful text asking if he was still planning to join the family for Thanksgiving dinner at his parents' house in Annapolis.

The timing was almost surreal. Annapolis was less than an hour from Baltimore, close enough that he could easily attend the family gathering after completing the investigation. What should have been a convenient coincidence now felt like another layer of complexity in an already challenging assignment.

He stared at the text for a long moment, then called his mother's number.

"Alex." Colleen Sutton almost shouted with excitement.

"I was just thinking about you. Are you still planning to

come for Thanksgiving? Your father's already threatening to deep-fry another turkey despite what happened last year."

Despite everything, Alex found himself smiling. His family's Thanksgiving traditions were legendary for their combination of military precision and cheerful chaos. His father, a retired Air Force colonel, approached holiday meal preparation with the same systematic planning he'd once used for fighter jet missions. His mother coordinated the family gathering with the calm efficiency of a nurse who had spent thirty years managing emergencies.

"I'm still planning to be there," Alex said, then hesitated. "But I'm being assigned to a case in Baltimore. Should be finished by Thursday, unless something urgent comes up."

"Oh, honey." His mother's voice sounded concerned. "Is it dangerous?"

"Just basic investigative work." Alex hoped that description would prove accurate, though the DMA briefing confirmed that the case was more complex than investigating a murder. "But you know how these things can develop. If something critical comes up, I might have to work through the holiday."

"Well, if you do have to work, at least you'll be close by. Baltimore's practically next door." His mother's easy acceptance reflected years of adapting family plans to the demands of a law enforcement career.

"And if you get a break, even for a few hours, please try to come."

"Thanks, Mom. I'll call Thursday morning to let you know how things look."

"Be careful, sweetheart. And remember that whatever you're working on, it's important work. You're protecting people, even if they never know it."

As Alex was ending the call, Elias walked in holding a couple of soda cans and handed one to Alex.

Alex studied the photographs laid out before them as Elias sat at the head of the table nearest to him. Dr. Torres at her desk, peaceful in death. Colonel Cameron at his university office, reading glasses still perched on his nose. Dr. Panahi, dead before they could warn her.

"Walk me through it again," Alex said, his voice quiet in the empty conference room. "What you're sensing at these scenes. Not what you told Rivera or Lindsey. What you're actually picking up."

Elias looked up from the case files, his expression guarded. Around him, the air shimmered faintly with suppressed energy.

"I've told you what I found. Professional memory manipulation, an ancient and dangerous magic, magical traps to prevent detailed investigation," he replied sharply.

"That's the official assessment," Alex replied, leaning forward slightly. "Rowan made it sound like you know more than you've let on. I'm asking what else you sensed."

For a moment, Elias remained silent, his attention focused on straightening the crime scene photos.

"Alex, I don't know if I can trust what I'm sensing anymore," Elias said finally, his voice barely above a whisper.

"Ever since the warehouse, every magical insight feels unreliable. Like my abilities might be showing me things that aren't real."

"But you did sense something else."

"Yes." The admission came reluctantly. He'd been holding this back for days.

Elias glanced toward the conference room door, making sure they were alone before continuing. When he spoke again, his voice was even quieter, "Something I haven't mentioned to anyone because I wasn't sure it was real. But now, after that briefing I don't know what to believe."

"What did you see?"

Elias closed his eyes for a moment, reaching back through the impressions he'd pulled from the scene. They felt less like the usual memory traces and more like flashes of something older.

"I saw dirt. Cold, packed ground. A ring of tall stones worn down by time. They weren't just standing there. They were part of something. A ritual, maybe. I'm not sure. The sky was gray and heavy. The air felt thick, like rain was coming."

Alex watched his partner's face as Elias spoke, describing images that sounded nothing like their usual casework.

The magical energy around him had stilled, as if his abilities were focused entirely on recalling details that challenged rational understanding.

"There was a woman in the center of the circle," Elias continued, his voice taking on the distant quality that came with deep memory work. "Barefoot. Her arms out. Not in surrender. Something more deliberate. Her eyes were rolled back, but she wasn't unconscious. It was like she was offering herself. There were others standing just outside the stones. They weren't speaking, but I could feel them focusing on her. Like they were pushing something into her and anchoring it at the same time."

The conference room fell silent except for the distant sounds of the FBI building's daily operations. Alex found himself leaning forward, drawn into descriptions that painted a picture of magical practices unlike anything in contemporary training.

"The wind wasn't natural," Elias said, his jaw tightening as he relived whatever he'd experienced through his magical connection to the crime scenes.

"It moved with the rhythm of whatever was happening. Like it was responding to the ritual, not the weather. And there was this hum. Not sound exactly. More like a vibration under the skin. It made my teeth ache."

He opened his eyes, looking directly at Alex with concern. "I don't know what it was. But it wasn't symbolic. It was real, deliberate magic that felt very old."

Alex studied his partner's face, seeing the tension there. "Will you show me?"

Elias hesitated, "Alex, I don't know if—"

"I can shield the room so nobody sees," Alex said quietly, understanding his partner's concern.

Elias glanced toward the conference room's glass walls, then nodded. "Okay, make a shield that blocks the view into the conference room and make sure it doesn't allow anyone inside."

Alex stood and moved to the windows, silver energy flowing from his hands to create a barrier that would prevent anyone from seeing inside. The shield settled across the glass like a mirror, reflecting the hallway back to anyone who might look in while leaving their view outward unobstructed.

Elias extended his hand, palm down, across the table.

Alex grasped his partner's hand, feeling the immediate surge of magical connection beginning to form between them. Green and silver energies intertwined as their abilities synchronized, the familiar weaving of their magic they'd always shared clicking into place with startling ease.

The air around them began to shimmer as Elias' memory magic reached toward the ancient traces he'd detected at the crime scenes. Green energy swirled through the conference room, gathering substance and form as it reconstructed images from some distant past.

The modern FBI building faded around them, replaced by something far older and more primal. Cold earth materialized beneath their feet, packed hard and stained dark. The air grew heavy and damp with the smell of trees and dirt.

Standing stones rose around them in a perfect circle, each one taller than a man and worn smooth by countless years. Power hummed through the ancient rock, magical energy that felt alien and hungry, older than anything in contemporary practice.

"God," Alex whispered, feeling the power from the stones coming through the construct like a physical force.

The sky above was gray and oppressive, heavy with clouds that pulsed with their own energy. Wind moved through the circle with deliberate purpose, following patterns that had nothing to do with weather.

A woman stood at the center, barefoot on the cold earth, her arms spread wide. Her eyes had rolled back until only the whites showed, but she remained conscious, aware, participating in whatever was being done to her. Around her bare feet, symbols had been carved into the ground.

Other figures moved just outside the stone circle, their faces hidden by deep hoods but their intent unmistakably focused on the woman at the center. They weren't speaking, but Alex could feel the weight of their concentration, magical energy being drawn and shaped into something that made his combat instincts scream warnings.

"The hum," Elias said, his voice distant as he guided the construct deeper into the ancient memory. "Can you feel it?"

Alex could. It wasn't sound so much as vibration, something that resonated in his bones and made his teeth ache. The magical energy being manipulated here exceeded anything in his experience, raw power being refined into purposes he couldn't understand.

The woman's expression never changed, even as the hooded figures drew something from her into their working. She remained willing, offering herself completely to whatever they were creating.

The wind grew stronger, moving in spirals around the stone circle as the ritual reached some kind of climax. The woman's form began to waver, growing pale and translucent, until finally her body collapsed onto the cold earth.

The hooded figures remained for a moment longer, then melted away into the darkness beyond the stones, leaving only the circle itself and whatever terrible purpose it had served.

The construct began to fade, the ancient landscape dissolving back into the familiar conference room. But the feeling of what they'd witnessed remained, pressing down on both agents with the certainty that they'd seen something that should have been lost to history.

"That's what I've been seeing at every crime scene," Elias said, releasing Alex's hand as the magical connection ended. "Traces of that magic, like echoes."

Alex sat back in his chair, processing what they'd experienced together. The ancient magic, the deliberate cruelty, the sense of power being gathered for unknown purposes.

"Someone's using the same magic," Alex said finally.

"But I don't understand how," Elias replied. "Or why the traces are so strong at our crime scenes. It's like——" He struggled for words. "Like whatever happened in that circle is still happening now."

The magical energy in the conference room had grown heavier. Alex could see the strain in his partner's expression, the cost of sharing insights he'd been afraid to trust.

"Why didn't you tell me this before?" Alex asked gently.

"Because I wasn't sure it was real," Elias replied, his voice sounding resigned.

"Because every magical insight I've had since the warehouse feels questionable. Because I was afraid that if I shared these visions and they turned out to be fantasy, it would prove that my magic really had failed."

Alex understood the psychological trap his partner had been caught in. The warehouse incident had undermined Elias' faith in his abilities so completely that he'd been second guessing even his most reliable magical insights.

"Elias, these aren't fantasies," Alex said firmly.

"You're describing patterns that connect all three crime scenes to the artifact that Rowan mentioned. That's not unreliable magic. That's exactly the kind of insight that makes you the best magical investigator in the Bureau."

"But what if I'm wrong? What if these visions are just my imagination trying to make sense of magical signatures I don't understand?"

"Then we investigate and find out. But we don't ignore crucial intelligence because you're afraid your abilities might be unreliable."

"You really believe this is connected to the murders?" Elias asked.

"I think you're detecting patterns that no one else would be able to find," Alex replied. "And I think whoever's behind these murders has access to magic we don't understand."

"This is what Rowan meant when she said you'd seen their power," Alex stated with certainty. "Which tells me that the DMA knows more than they're telling us."

Elias glanced at the photographs, then back at Alex. "Aberdeen," he said quietly.

Alex nodded. "Aberdeen."

Alex leaned forward in his chair, letting out a slow breath. Their partnership was starting to feel almost normal again. The visions of the stone circle held details only Elias could have drawn from his powerful memory magic. Fragments that might help them understand a murderer whose power was beyond anything they'd encountered before.

By afternoon they were packed for Baltimore. What had begun as a case about infrastructure attacks and murder had shifted into something neither of them fully understood.

8
Something Wicked
This Way Comes

By the pricking of my thumbs,
Something wicked this way comes
—Macbeth, Act 4, Scene 1

Aberdeen Proving Ground, Maryland—November 25

The military archive facility at Aberdeen Proving Ground looked like standard government architecture from the outside, but its interior security measures reflected the sensitive nature of the materials stored within climate-controlled vaults. Magical preservation spells maintained optimal conditions for documents dating back decades, while security enchantments prevented unauthorized access or copying.

Privacy wards shimmered around the structure, preventing unauthorized surveillance while protective enchantments monitored every approach.

Defensive magic layered the facility, scanning every visitor for hostile intent while concealment charms prevented sensitive conversations from being overheard. Even the parking lot was warded against magical surveillance, creating a dead zone where foreign intelligence services couldn't penetrate.

The call had come at 6:30 a.m. while Alex and Elias were preparing to leave their Baltimore hotel. Dr. Robert Lane had been found dead in his office by security personnel conducting routine morning checks. The circumstances matched their Chicago murders exactly, but this time there was more. Seven Celtic artifacts from Project Avalon had been stolen from Aberdeen's secure vault overnight.

Dr. Jennifer Walsh, Aberdeen Proving Ground Deputy Director for Research, met them at the security checkpoint. She was a woman in her early fifties with blond hair and wire-rimmed glasses.

"Agents Sutton and Sinclair," she said, extending her hand. "This is a terrible situation. Dr. Lane's death, combined with the theft from the Avalon vault, represents exactly the security breach we've been fearing."

Alex shook her hand. Her grip was firm, strained. "Deputy Director Rowan briefed us on the artifacts yesterday. Seven of them were taken?"

"Dr. Lane discovered the theft around midnight," she replied, leading them through multiple security checkpoints toward the research wing. "Security logs show his keycard accessing the vault at 11:47 p.m., then returning to his office at 12:15 a.m. He was found dead this morning at 6:30."

Elias' expression darkened. "So someone with knowledge of both the artifacts and your security protocols killed the one person who discovered the theft."

"That's our assessment," Dr. Walsh confirmed. "The seven stolen artifacts are ancient gold disks no larger than a child's palm. Celtic knotwork covers their surfaces, intricate patterns that catch the light. They're dangerous. In the right hands, they can reach into someone's mind and rewrite memory itself."

The elevator carried them to the fourth floor, where wide

corridors led past laboratories and offices filled with the quiet intensity of people working on problems that couldn't be discussed outside secure facilities. Warning signs marked areas requiring special clearances, while display cases showed awards and commendations that represented breakthrough research in fields most people had never heard of.

Dr. Lane's office occupied a corner position with windows facing the research corridor, its interior arranged with the careful organization of someone who processed large volumes of classified information daily. Bookshelves lined the walls, packed with dense academic journals and thick technical manuals detailing some of the country's most sensitive magical protocols and equipment. Diagrams of ancient artifacts, energy calibration matrices, and field tested countermeasure procedures sat alongside worn binders stamped with security clearance levels.

The body sat behind the desk exactly as they'd seen in Chicago and Baltimore. Dr. Lane appeared to have simply fallen asleep while working, reading glasses perched on his nose, coffee cup positioned beside his computer keyboard. Peaceful except for the fact that he was dead, and the subtle magical signatures that lingered in the air like invisible fingerprints.

But unlike their previous crime scenes, this office buzzed with residual magical activity. Traces of foreign energy signatures clung to every surface. The security wards that normally protected the office flickered weakly, their defensive matrices disrupted by whatever had happened during the night.

Elias approached slowly, letting his abilities focus on the magical traces. "Same resonance as our other cases," he reported quietly. "He was murdered, and I'm sensing that he knew the attacker. It was a man but I can't see his face. Dr. Lane thought to call for help but the attacker was fast."

Alex studied Dr. Lane's computer screen. Research reports dating back twenty-five years, academic papers from multiple universities, and classified assessments. One name appeared repeatedly throughout the documents, highlighted by the computer's analytical magic in glowing text:

Project Avalon

"Dr. Lane was investigating unauthorized access to the Project Avalon files?" Alex asked.

"For weeks," Dr. Walsh confirmed. "He'd identified patterns in our system logs that suggested someone had been systematically studying our security protocols and artifact storage procedures."

"Someone preparing for this theft," Elias observed.

"He'd been tasked with assessing whether any of the older research projects might be relevant for current security threats. Experiment outcomes that could potentially be adapted for Defense Department purposes." Dr. Walsh consulted her notes. "Project Avalon represented some of the most advanced theoretical research ever conducted on ancient magical artifacts."

Alex said, "We'll need to review Dr. Lane's research notes."

"Those are kept in a different building. Colonel Jackson is expecting you."

Elias continued his investigation of the crime scene. The magical traces revealed more details about the killer's presence, someone with extensive knowledge of Aberdeen Proving Ground security procedures, able to access the building without triggering alarms or leaving electronic evidence.

But there was something else in the residual traces, something that made Elias concentrate harder. The impressions weren't clean. They felt distorted and fragmented. Some rang true, while others felt wrong, as if someone had planted false impressions to mislead whoever tried to read the scene.

Eighteen months of studying defensive techniques let him

push past the interference, separating fractured impressions from what remained authentic.

"Alex," he called softly. "There are distortions layered into the traces. But I can read through them to the real residue."

Alex approached cautiously. "What do the true traces show?"

Elias pushed deeper. Authentic images surfaced. Dr. Lane in his final hours, poring over classified files on ancient artifact research, drawing connections between old projects and present threats. Realization sparked into urgency. Then silence.

"Dr. Lane uncovered something," Elias said. "A link between Project Avalon and current security risks. He was killed to keep him from reporting it."

He opened his eyes, meeting Alex's gaze. "We need those files."

Colonel Jackson met them at the security checkpoint for the vault building, his uniform sharp, the rows of ribbons marking decades of military service. He was in his late forties, with close-cropped black hair.

"Agents Sutton and Sinclair," he said, reviewing their authorization documents with methodical precision. "Deputy Director Rowan said you'd been briefed on the Avalon arti-facts. This theft represents our worst case scenario. Seven of the most dangerous pieces in our vault are now in hostile hands."

"We need to understand exactly what was taken and who had access," Alex said.

"The seven stolen artifacts were part of the original collec-tion," Colonel Jackson replied, leading them through multiple security checkpoints toward the archive vaults. "Each disk is small, fits in your palm. Polished gold etched with Celtic patterns. But they're weapons. Memory magic makes them capable of stripping away identity, leaving only the thoughts the wielder allows to remain."

He guided them into a secure reading room where boxes of files had been arranged on a central table. The documents bore classification markings that indicated research deemed highly sensitive even by military standards.

"The project was officially terminated in 2005," Colonel Jackson explained. "But certain aspects of the research were continued under different oversight structures due to the strategic implications."

Elias opened the first box and froze. The principal investigator's name appeared on nearly every document. Dr. Edward Sinclair, University of Chicago, Department of Neuroscience.

Alex noticed his partner's reaction immediately. Elias' face went pale. "What is it?"

Elias stared at the documents. "That's my father's name. But this implies that he was lead scientist on a classified military project. That's impossible. He was just an academic researcher."

The words held implications neither of them wanted to consider. Elias had believed his entire life that his father was simply an academic researcher who'd died in a random terrorist attack. Learning that Edward Sinclair had been leading classified military research changed everything he thought he knew about his family.

"What kind of research?" Alex asked quietly.

Elias reviewed the documents, reading through documentation of artifacts he'd never imagined existed. "Understanding how the artifacts functioned as magical amplifiers."

He held up one file. "This one details methods for using the artifacts to create and implant memories through memory magic manipulation." He looked up at Alex. "I had no idea he was involved in anything like this."

Alex studied research notes that showed sophisticated

experiments in magical ability manipulation. The results appeared far more advanced than anything they'd encountered in their investigation. The work represented a breakthrough understanding of how the artifacts operated, with implications for both defensive and offensive applications.

"The artifacts themselves," Alex asked Colonel Jackson, "what do they look like?"

He held up his hand. "Ancient Celtic pieces, probably brought to America over centuries through immigration and collectors. Small enough to fit in your palm, made of gold with tessellation patterns. We believe they were used by druids, though we're not entirely sure for what purpose. Probably to fight enemies." Colonel Jackson consulted his briefing materials. "The government's been collecting them for decades. Ever since it was discovered they were dangerous."

"How do they work?" Elias asked.

"They're conduits for the darkest applications of memory magic," Colonel Jackson explained. "The wielder must hold the artifact while focusing on their target. The disks amplify their natural abilities far beyond ordinary limits, allowing them to slip past mental defenses. Once inside, they can plant false memories so vivid and detailed that the victim believes them more than their own past. Worse, they can seize control of the target's magical abilities, turning them into unwilling puppets who think they're acting of their own free will."

Elias reflected on that. "I've detected the artifact's magic at multiple crime scenes. But only two victims so far show signs of being forced to use their own abilities."

Colonel Jackson's expression hardened. "Like I said, it enhances whatever magic the wielder has and twists it into a weapon. But in the hands of a memory magic user, it becomes something worse. The amplification allows them to overwrite or even implant memories so vivid the victim can't tell they're false. That's what makes these artifacts so dangerous."

"Who else was involved in this research?" Alex asked Colonel Jackson.

"The original team included researchers from five universities and representatives from multiple agencies." Colonel Jackson consulted his briefing materials. "After official termination, access was restricted to personnel with specific authorization."

He provided a personnel list that included names from universities and intelligence agencies. Most of the original researchers were listed as deceased or retired, but several names had notes indicating that they may still be involved in other projects.

"Any of these researchers still active?" Elias asked.

"A few. Dr. Jonathan Pierce was a secondary researcher who returned to Cambridge University after the project ended. Our records show he left academic research around 2005 and remained overseas. No current address."

Alex thought to himself that someone with knowledge of classified ancient artifact research and international connections would be perfectly positioned to coordinate sophisticated terrorist operations across multiple countries.

"Dr. Pierce had access to the complete Project Avalon research?"

"He was involved in assessments of potential applications. He understood how the artifacts could be adapted for various purposes." Colonel Jackson's expression grew more serious. "If he's involved in your investigation, you're dealing with someone who understands both the theoretical foundations and practical applications of this research."

They spent two hours reviewing Project Avalon documentation, mapping connections between twenty-year-old research and current evidence. The pattern that emerged pointed to Dr. Pierce as someone with the knowledge and skills to use the artifacts effectively.

But more disturbing was the scope of the theft. Seven

Celtic artifacts in the hands of people who understood their capabilities represented a threat that exceeded anything in their previous experience.

"The stolen artifacts," Colonel Jackson said as they prepared to leave, "in the hands of someone who understands their true potential, represent a nightmare beyond conventional warfare. Seven golden disks that can turn ordinary citizens into unwitting operatives, their minds rewritten to serve purposes they'd never consciously agree to.

By five o'clock, they had enough evidence to confirm that their investigation involved people with access to classified research that most people had never heard of. Someone was using decades old military artifacts for purposes that could threaten national security at levels they were only beginning to understand.

Baltimore Hotel — November 25 7:30 PM

The hotel restaurant was quiet, half the tables cleared for the holiday. At a corner table, Alex and Elias leaned over their notes, the weight of Aberdeen heavy between them. Every discovery seemed to twist deeper into the case and into Elias' family history.

The artifacts were more complicated than either of them had expected. Ancient, dangerous, and disturbingly familiar. Elias kept circling back to that feeling he'd had during the Torres scene in Chicago, a thread of recognition he hadn't been able to place. Now, thinking about everything he'd learned, that sense of recognition no longer felt like a coincidence.

"My father's research provided the foundation for everything we've been chasing." Elias closed his eyes, exhaustion slipping through the discipline he'd held all day. "I never knew he was involved in classified work. I thought he was just a neuroscience professor."

Alex's phone rang. His mother's name lit the screen.

"Alex, honey!" Colleen Sutton's voice was warm. "I'm calling to confirm dinner for tomorrow. Your father's already working on his famous dry rub for the turkey, and I need to know about place settings. Is Elias coming with you?"

Alex glanced at Elias, who had turned back to his notepad with deliberate focus. The question caught him off guard, though it shouldn't have. Elias had been part of everything for the last six years. Holidays, weekends, family trips, always welcomed like one of their own. He wasn't just a friend. He'd been the brother Alex never had, and somewhere along the way, had lost.

"He didn't come last year," his mother added when Alex didn't respond right away. "I've been hoping to see him again. You know how much your father enjoys having him around, and I always make enough food to feed half the neighborhood anyway."

Alex studied Elias as he wrote, his partner's attention fixed a little too firmly on the page. The avoidance was obvious, and it tugged memories of past Thanksgivings when Elias had fit seamlessly into their family's celebrations.

Thanksgiving — Six years earlier

Their first year after the Academy, still learning to navigate life as federal agents. Elias had planned to spend the holiday alone in his Chicago apartment, but Alex's mother had insisted he join them. "Nonsense," she'd said when Alex mentioned his friend's situation. "Bring him home. Family is about more than blood."

Elias helping in the kitchen, listening to family stories with the fascination of someone who'd grown up without extended family traditions. Alex's father explaining military history while Elias asked thoughtful questions and contributed his own insights about federal law enforcement. The easy way Elias had fit into their family dynamic, like he'd always belonged there.

"You're welcome anytime," Alex's mother had told Elias as he prepared to leave with containers of leftovers. "This is your family now too."

And it had been, for years, until everything fell apart.

"Just me this time, Mom. Elias has other commitments." The lie came automatically, designed to avoid explanations about their complicated relationship.

"Oh." His mother's disappointment was audible through the phone's privacy enchantments. "Well, you know there's always a place for him if he changes his mind."

"I know Mom. I'll tell him you asked about him."

"Please do. And Alex? Drive carefully tomorrow. The weather forecast shows possible rain, and holiday traffic can be unpredictable."

After ending the call, Alex remained quiet for a moment, studying Elias' profile as his partner continued reviewing case notes. "Your mother?" Elias asked without looking up from his notepad.

"Thanksgiving plans. She asked about you."

"That's kind of her," Elias said politely, but Alex caught the slight tension around his eyes. "Your family always made me feel at home. I've never forgotten that."

"What about tomorrow?" Alex asked, noting the way Elias' expression grew more guarded. "Any plans?"

"I plan to review the reports that Nicole prepared." Elias' voice was matter-of-fact, but Alex could see something else in his expression. The quiet resignation that came from spending last Thanksgiving alone and preparing to do so again.

They finished dinner in silence. Around them, the restaurant's quiet magic maintained perfect comfort, a sharp contrast to the way the case had just turned personal.

By nine o'clock, they were back in their respective rooms. Alex tried to relax, but found himself thinking about Elias processing the discovery that his father's academic work had been connected to classified military research.

Around ten-thirty, Alex felt an instinctive unease that he couldn't immediately identify. Something was wrong, though he couldn't pinpoint what. The feeling grew stronger, and then he knew it was Elias.

Without conscious decision, Alex extended his magic toward Elias' room. The same subtle probe he'd used countless times during their partnership to keep an eye on him during difficult memory work.

This time, something was off. The spell extended, but instead of finding Elias, it found nothing. Just empty space where his presence should have been.

Alex was out of his room and down the corridor before he'd fully processed the implications. Elias' door was locked, but his partner was gone. No note. No sign of where he'd gone, or why he'd left the hotel at nearly eleven o'clock the night before Thanksgiving.

Alex pulled out his phone and called Elias' number, getting voicemail immediately. Either the phone was turned off or Elias wasn't in a position to answer. Neither option suggested anything good.

Moving on instinct, Alex put his coat on, grabbed his holstered weapon and left the hotel. The downtown Baltimore area was quiet for a holiday evening, most businesses closed and foot traffic minimal. Alex walked the perimeter of their hotel, extending his magical abilities to search for any trace of his partner's presence.

Two blocks away, in an alley behind a closed restaurant, Alex's abilities detected hostile magical energy signatures that made his combat instincts flare to full alert. Ancient and hostile, and aimed squarely at Elias, who was trying desperately to resist the magical assault.

Alex ran toward the alley, drawing his weapon as his combat magic rose to the surface. The scene that greeted him confirmed his worst fears. Elias backed against a brick wall, blood running from his nose, his expression dazed as he fought against whatever the magic was doing to him. A dark clad figure gripped a palm-sized golden artifact pulsing with magic. Sharp, hostile, and aimed directly at Elias.

Around the attacker, malevolent magical patterns crackled with ancient fury. One of the stolen Celtic disks blazed in his hands. Polished gold catching the alley's dim light, its intricate knotwork seeming to writhe and pulse as it channeled power older than civilization. The artifact's energy wrapped around Elias like invisible chains, overwhelming his magical defenses and leaving him helpless against the invasion of his mind.

"FBI! Step away from him!" Alex's shout cracked through the alley, silver light blazing around his hands as combat magic flared in answer.

The attacker turned toward Alex, revealing a face twisted with hatred and desperate fury. Instead of complying, he intensified the magical assault on Elias while reaching for a weapon with his free hand.

Alex didn't hesitate. Combat magic flowed through him, force shields deflecting the attacker's weapon while kinetic blasts sent him sprawling across the alley pavement. The disk went flying, its energy discharge cutting off abruptly as it struck the brick wall and shattered in a shower of sparks.

Alex reached Elias in three quick steps. Blood ran from his nose, his expression dazed. "Are you hurt? Can you hear me?"

Elias blinked slowly, his green eyes struggling to focus as his magical defenses slowly reasserted themselves. "Alex? How did you—"

"I felt something was wrong. Used our link to check on you." Alex kept one eye on the unconscious attacker while steadying Elias, silver energy flowing through him to anchor and heal. "What the hell were you thinking, meeting someone alone?"

"They said they had information about Dr. Pierce and

Project Avalon. About my father's research." Elias' voice was weak but growing stronger as the artifact's effects faded. "I thought I could handle it."

"You thought you could handle it? We're dealing with an ancient magical artifact and someone who's willing to kill." Alex's anger cracked through. "He was trying to kill you."

Elias didn't respond, which was answer enough. Alex studied him. No panic. No instinct where there should have been.

"Elias," Alex said quietly, silver energy continuing to flow around them both. "Are you trying to get yourself killed on purpose?"

The question hung between them. Elias looked away, his silence confirming Alex's growing suspicions about his partner's increasingly reckless behavior.

Alex pulled out his phone to call for backup and medical assistance, but his mind was already made up about tomorrow's plans. Whatever was driving Elias toward self-destruction, he wasn't going to face it alone.

The Baltimore police and FBI backup team arrived to secure the scene and took the attacker into custody. Alex provided statements and coordinated evidence collection while keeping Elias under close observation. His partner seemed surprised to find himself still alive rather than grateful.

By 1 a.m., they were back at the hotel with medical clearance and a terrorism suspect in federal custody. Alex walked Elias to his room but didn't leave, settling into the chair by the window while his partner sat on the edge of the bed, staring at his hands.

"You should get some sleep," Elias said quietly.

"I'm fine here." Alex's tone made it clear he wasn't going anywhere. The silence stretched between them for several minutes before Alex spoke again. "You're coming home with me," Alex said. "My parents' house. No arguments, no excuses."

Elias looked up, surprised. "Alex, you don't need to—"

Elias started to protest, but Alex cut him off with a look that ended the conversation. "This isn't a discussion. We'll leave around noon." Alex used the authority he'd used in the alley.

"Your mother isn't expecting me."

"Of course she is. She's been asking about you for the last year and a half." Alex studied his partner's expression. Gratitude warred with stubborn independence. "I'm not leaving you alone anymore, Elias. Whatever's driving this self-destructive behavior, you're not dealing with it alone."

Eighteen months of staying out of each other's way had nearly gotten his partner killed. That ended here.

9
Homecomings

One of the most beautiful qualities of true friendship is to under-
stand and to be understood
     — Lucius Annaeus Seneca

Interstate 95 South
Thanksgiving Day 11:45 AM

The drive from Baltimore to Annapolis stretched through
Maryland countryside painted in November browns and
grays, bare trees reaching toward overcast skies that promised
rain before evening. Alex kept his eyes on the road while Elias
stared out the passenger window, both of them wrapped in
silence that felt heavy with unspoken thoughts about the
previous night's attack.

They'd been driving for an hour without conversation, the
radio providing background noise that neither paid attention
to. Alex glanced at his partner every few minutes. Elias held
himself carefully, his expression distant.

"Thank you," Elias said suddenly, his voice quiet but clear. "For last night. For coming after me."

"You don't have to thank me for that. I'll always have your back." Alex paused, then decided they needed to address what had happened. "But I need to understand something. Who called you?"

Elias was quiet for a moment. "Someone claiming to have information about Dr. Pierce. About my father's research."

"Someone you didn't recognize?"

"No. They said they'd been monitoring the investigation, that they had intelligence about the connection between Project Avalon and the recent attacks."

Elias kept his voice level, gaze on the window. "They wanted to meet privately."

Alex felt a chill that had nothing to do with the November weather. "And you didn't think to question why an anonymous caller would have classified intelligence? Or why they'd want to meet you alone in the middle of the night?"

"I thought about it."

"But you went anyway."

"I thought I could handle it." Elias turned to look out the window again. "I thought maybe if I could gather intelligence on my own, prove that my abilities were still reliable…"

"By walking into an obvious trap?" Alex's voice was frustrated, concerned. "Elias, that wasn't investigative work. That was… that was almost like you wanted something bad to happen."

The accusation hung in the air between them. Elias didn't deny it, which was more troubling than any protest would have been.

"The attacker," Alex continued more gently. "Did you recognize him? Did he say anything about why he was targeting you specifically?"

"He kept saying that magical freaks like me were ruining everything. That federal agents with abilities were making it impossible for normal people to fight back against magical threats." Elias' voice grew quieter. "He seemed to know exactly who I was, what my magic was, how to counter it."

"Someone's been tracking our investigation closely enough to know where we're staying, what we're working on, how to get to you personally." Alex gripped the steering wheel tighter. "This wasn't random, Elias. Someone wanted you specifically."

"Maybe they wanted to eliminate the psychic investigator before we got too close to the truth," Alex said glancing at his partner and noticing the way Elias seemed almost disconnected from the conversation. "Either way, going alone was—"

"Stupid, yeah, I know." Elias' voice was flat, accepting. "I've been making a lot of stupid decisions lately."

"That's not what I meant."

"Isn't it?" Elias looked at him directly for the first time since they'd started driving. "Alex, I got seven people killed eighteen months ago. Last night I nearly got myself killed for no good reason. Maybe the common denominator isn't bad luck."

The words made Alex realize how close to the edge his partner had been drifting. This wasn't just about confidence or guilt over the warehouse incident. This was about someone who'd stopped believing his life had value.

"Elias…"

"I'm not saying I want to die. I'm just saying that maybe I don't care as much as I should about staying alive." Elias returned his attention to the window. "And maybe that makes me dangerous to work with."

Alex wanted to pull over and have this conversation properly, but they were expected at his parents' house and this revelation required more time and privacy than the roadside could provide. Instead, he reached across the console and grabbed Elias' shoulder, his grip firm and grounding.

"We're going to figure this out," he said quietly. "Whatever's been eating at you, whatever guilt you're carrying, we're going to work through it together."

"Together?"

"Yes, together. But no more anonymous meetings, no more taking unnecessary risks, and no more pretending that your life doesn't matter to people who care about you."

The remaining hour of their drive passed with less tension, but Alex found himself watching his partner with growing concern. The reckless behavior wasn't just about proving himself professionally. It was about someone who'd lost his sense of purpose and was drifting toward a darkness that could destroy him if left unchecked.

Annapolis, Maryland

The Sutton family home sat on three acres of wooded property outside Annapolis, a colonial-style house that had housed three generations of military families with the kind of solid comfort that came from decades of careful maintenance and genuine affection. Alex pulled into the circular driveway behind his father's pickup truck as Elias straightened in his seat as they approached.

Before they could knock, the door swung open to reveal Colleen Sutton, she pulled him into a hug before he could speak. She was a woman in her late fifties with light brown hair and the kind of warm energy that had made her the center of every family gathering for thirty years.

"Elias!" she exclaimed. "Oh, sweetheart, I've missed you so much. Look at you, you're too thin. Are you eating properly?"

Alex laughed as his mother let him go and went straight for Elias. Elias hugged her back and his shoulders eased. Elias had been a regular presence at family gatherings for years, but he'd also joined them for long weekends, holidays, any excuse Alex could find to bring him home when he knew his partner would be spending too much time alone.

"Hello Colleen," Elias said, his voice warm despite his exhaustion. "Thank you for having me."

"Nonsense. This is your home too, and don't you forget it." She kept one arm around his shoulders while reaching for Alex with the other. "Both of my boys, home for Thanksgiving. Alex, your father's in the kitchen pretending he knows what he's doing with the turkey."

Colonel James Sutton emerged from the kitchen wearing an apron that read "World's Greatest Dad" and carrying a meat thermometer like a weapon of warfare. He was a man in his late fifties with salt and pepper hair and the kind of bearing that came from thirty years of military service, but his face softened when he saw Elias.

"Good to see you, son," he said, extending his hand for a firm handshake that turned into a brief but meaningful embrace. "Been too long."

"Yes, sir. Good to see you too, James."

"That's better. None of that formal stuff." James clapped Elias on the shoulder with the easy affection he'd shown since their first meeting years earlier. "Come on, let me show you what I'm doing with this turkey. Got a new dry rub recipe I want to try."

Alex watched his father guide Elias toward the kitchen, noting the way his partner's posture relaxed slightly when James threw his arm over his shoulder. James Sutton had always treated Elias with the same pride and concern he showed his own son, recognizing something in the young man that needed the stability of family support.

Colleen kept her arm linked through Alex's as they followed the men into the kitchen, where the familiar chaos of Thanksgiving preparation was in full swing. The dining room table was set with good china and autumn decorations, while the kitchen counters overflowed with ingredients for side dishes and desserts that had been family traditions for decades.

"I made your favorite stuffing," Colleen told Elias, gesturing toward a casserole dish that smelled of sage and celery. "And that sweet potato casserole you always request seconds of."

"You didn't have to go to any trouble."

"It's no trouble when it's for family." She squeezed his arm with maternal possessiveness. "Now, you boys go wash up while your father and I finish the last preparations. Dinner will be ready in thirty minutes."

Alex led Elias upstairs to the guest bathroom. Elias flicked the bathroom light without looking and turned right toward the guest room when he was done, moving like someone who'd walked this hall a hundred times. Family photos lined the hallway, including several that featured Elias at various gatherings over the years, evidence of how naturally he'd been incorporated into their family traditions.

"Your parents seem happy to see me," Elias said quietly.

"They love you. They always have." Alex paused at the top of the stairs. "You're family here, Elias. Missing last year doesn't change that."

"I wasn't sure you'd want me to come back."

"I wasn't sure either, until last night. But seeing you in that alley, realizing how close I came to losing you..." Alex met his friend's eyes directly.

"I'm done pretending that keeping our distance is more important than making sure you're okay."

They rejoined Alex's parents in the dining room, where Thanksgiving dinner proceeded with the kind of comfortable tradition that had characterized Sutton family gatherings for years. James carved the turkey with military precision while Colleen orchestrated the flow of side dishes with the organizational skills that had made her a successful nurse. Conversation flowed easily around topics that avoided work stress. Family updates, neighborhood news, plans for the Christmas holidays.

After dinner, while Colleen and Alex handled cleanup duties, James invited Elias to join him on the back deck for coffee and what he called "proper Thanksgiving conversation." The two men settled into deck chairs overlooking the wooded property, their discussion initially focused on the mild weather and James' plans for winter property maintenance.

"You know," James said after a few minutes of comfortable silence, "I lost my wingman in my third deployment. Jake Morrison, good pilot, better friend. We'd been flying together for two years when his plane went down over hostile territory."

Elias looked up from his coffee, recognizing the tone of someone sharing difficult memories.

"For months afterward, I questioned every decision I'd made that day. Every tactical choice, every communication, every moment leading up to his crash." James stared out at the trees, his voice heavy with old grief.

"I kept thinking maybe if I'd done something different, if I'd been faster or smarter or just paid better attention…"

"Did the questioning ever stop?"

"Eventually. But it took time, and it took accepting help from people who cared about me." James turned to face Elias directly. "Something's eating at you, son. Has been for a while now, from what Alex tells me."

Elias was quiet for a moment, considering how much to reveal. "Lost some people on the job. Made some bad calls."

"Your job does that. Puts you in situations where there are no good choices, only necessary ones." James lowered his voice, elbows on knees. "But carrying guilt for circumstances beyond our control doesn't honor the people we've lost. It just makes their sacrifice meaningless."

"I'm not sure how to stop second-guessing myself."

"Start by trusting the people who've never given you reason to doubt their loyalty. That boy in there has been worried sick about you for months. Whatever happened between you two, whatever wall you've built, it's not protecting anyone."

"I know. I just... I don't know how to get back to where we were."

"One conversation at a time. One honest moment at a time." James finished his coffee and stood up. "But you can't do it alone, son. Healing never works that way."

Inside the house, Colleen had cornered Alex in the kitchen for her own version of the same conversation. She dried the dishes as she fixed Alex with a look that said he couldn't talk his way around this.

"There's something wrong with Elias," she said without preamble. "He's lost weight, he's too quiet, and he looks like he hasn't been sleeping properly."

"Work has been stressful lately."

"Don't give me that. I know what stress looks like, and this is something deeper." Colleen set down her dish towel and fixed Alex with the look that had made him confess childhood mischief for almost thirty years.

"He's hurting, Alex. Really hurting. And you're both too stubborn to talk about whatever happened between you."

"It's complicated, Mom."

"Love always is. But that boy has been part of this family for years, and you've always looked at him like the little brother you never had. He's sitting out there looking like he's forgotten what home feels like."

Colleen's voice softened. "Whatever complicated means in your world, it doesn't change the fact that he needs his friend right now."

"I know. I'm trying to help him."

"Then stop trying and start doing. He trusts you more

than anyone else in the world, even if you've both forgotten that." Colleen resumed her dish drying with purposeful energy. "Friendship like yours doesn't come along often. Don't let pride destroy something that important."

As evening approached, Alex suggested they take a walk around the property while the weather was still mild. Elias agreed readily, both of them recognizing the need for a private conversation.

The wooded trails behind the house stretched for acres through Maryland forest that had been preserved by local conservation efforts. Alex and Elias walked in comfortable silence for the first few minutes, their path lit by late afternoon sun through bare branches.

"Your father talked to me about post-traumatic stress," Elias said finally.

"He's good at recognizing it. Losing his wingman nearly broke him when he was younger." Alex kicked at the fallen leaves as they crunched under his boots. "My mother thinks you've forgotten what home feels like."

"Maybe I have," Elias stopped walking and faced Alex. "I've been so focused on proving I could still do my job that I forgot why it mattered in the first place."

"The job matters because we protect people. But that doesn't mean we have to destroy ourselves doing it."

They walked deeper into the woods, their conversation circling back to the things they had avoided for eighteen months. The warehouse incident came first, then the guilt they had both carried, and finally the misunderstandings that had pushed them apart when they should have been leaning on each other.

"Alex," Elias said as they reached a small clearing ringed with tall oaks. He hesitated, searching for the right words. "There's something I need to tell you about last night. About what that attacker was trying to do to me."

"What do you mean?"

"He wasn't just trying to kill me. He was trying to implant something. False memories, I think. Something about it felt familiar, but I couldn't place why until now."

Alex's attention sharpened "Familiar how?"

"It felt like the warehouse. The way I was so certain about what I'd read that day, how clear and detailed everything seemed. But underneath, something felt distorted." Elias sat down on a fallen log, his expression troubled.

"Alex, what if I didn't mess up that day? What if someone fed me false information that felt more real than authentic traces?"

The implication hit Alex hard. If one of the artifacts had been used during the warehouse incident, then Elias' abilities hadn't failed. He'd been attacked.

"You think the warehouse was connected to our current case?" Alex asked, already knowing the answer.

"I think someone used the same magic on me eighteen months ago that they tried to use last night. Only last night wasn't subtle. But I can't be sure."

Elias looked up at Alex, determined but apprehensive. "I need to go back through the memory of using my magic at the warehouse. Try to distinguish between authentic traces and whatever artificial information was planted there."

"That's dangerous. That was a traumatic event, and if false memories were involved—Elias, they could overwhelm the real ones before you realized it was happening."

"I know. That's why I can't do it alone." Elias met his eyes directly. "I need someone I trust to help anchor me during the recall. Someone who can provide psychic support if the false memories try to take over."

Alex understood immediately what his partner was asking. Psychic support during memory recall required the kind of mental connection they hadn't attempted since the healing he'd performed at the hospital a few days earlier. This would be deeper still, more intimate, and far more dangerous if it went wrong. It demanded absolute trust and careful coordination.

"Are you sure you want to do this? I know how strongly you feel about that level of psychic connection."

"I need to know what really happened. We both do." Elias' voice was steady.

"I'm asking you to connect with me psychically, to help ground me if the artificial memories or the emotions become overwhelming. That's not something I would trust anyone else with."

Alex sat beside him on the fallen log. "Tell me what you need."

"Just keep me grounded."

Alex placed his hand on Elias' forearm and squeezed gently, feeling the psychic connection form between them. The connection locked, as if it had always existed, dormant and waiting. Their magic aligned with a precision that neither of them controlled, like something old coming back to life.

It felt like tuning two instruments that had once played in perfect harmony but had drifted slightly out of sync. The adjustment came easier than it should have. More instinct than effort. A faint shimmer of silver light, characteristic of Alex's combat magic, began to wrap around Elias' arm like a protective grounding current.

"Okay," Alex said quietly, his voice resolute. "I'm here. Take it slow."

Elias closed his eyes and began the careful process of accessing memories he'd spent eighteen months trying to suppress. Alex focused his magic to provide stability and support, feeling his partner's consciousness reaching back toward the warehouse incident.

Elias' brow furrowed in concentration, as he began the careful process. Alex focused his magic even tighter. A precise energy that could redirect mental pathways and pull Elias out if he had to.

"The warehouse," Elias said slowly, his voice strained as he went deeper. "I remember approaching it, letting my magic open to read the psychic traces, the echoes of emotions and intentions left behind."

"What did you sense initially?" Alex asked, his focus unwavering, his magic acting as a filter, allowing Elias to access only what he needed, while subtly guarding against overwhelming feedback.

"Fear, desperation, tactical planning. The emotional residue felt authentic, like genuine traces from the terrorists' preparation." Elias' breathing remained steady, but Alex could feel tension building in the psychic connection.

"But there was something else. A quality to the memories that feels different. Like maybe they were enhanced."

"Enhanced how?"

"More detailed than usual. More vivid. The emotional resonances were stronger than typical traces."

Elias paused, his concentration deepening. "At the time, I thought it meant the terrorists had been under extreme stress. But now…"

Alex tightened his grip on his partner's forearm, the silver light around his hand intensifying, a physical manifestation of their psychic anchor. Through their connection, he could sense Elias encountering layers of memory that felt artificially amplified, like a meticulously constructed illusion woven into the fabric of the past.

"There." Elias gasped, then said, "The tactical planning traces. They felt incredibly specific, showing me exactly where the terrorists would position themselves, what weapons they'd use, how they'd coordinate their attack."

"Too specific?" Alex asked.

"Real magical traces are usually less sharp, emotional rather than tactical. But these showed me detailed plans, precise timing, coordinated movements." Elias' breathing began to quicken. "I was so confident. I told you it was safe to proceed, that we had complete intelligence on their positions."

Alex could feel tension building through their magical connection, Elias' consciousness pulling deeper into the traumatic memory. Around them, the Maryland forest began to shimmer as Alex's magic responded to his partner's distress, reality bending to accommodate the power of their joined consciousness.

"Then the explosion," Elias continued, his voice growing strained.

"Will you show me?" Alex asked quietly.

Elias' magic flowed with bright green energy, drawing the construct together. Silver light blazed as Alex's power wove into it, their abilities meshing with a precision neither fully controlled. His combat magic, normally defensive, became something far more dangerous when fused with memory work. It extended into places it was never meant to go, into thoughts, emotions, the fragile structure of consciousness itself.

He could anchor Elias. He could also shatter him.

That was why Alex never attempted this with anyone else. The risk of causing permanent damage was enormous. But Elias trusted him completely, opening his defenses without hesitation. And because Elias allowed him access, his magic settled. It knew Elias. It remembered.

Suddenly the woods around them transformed. Alex's magic swirled through the air like silver mist, and the past came alive before them.

The warehouse materialized around their seated forms. Concrete walls, industrial equipment, the acrid smell of explosives. Alex could see it all through Elias' memory, could feel every emotion his partner had experienced.

The building erupted in a ball of fire and debris. Alex watched himself turn and run toward Elias extending a protective shield to his partner, then being thrown, his body slamming into a support beam before crumpling to the floor. Blood pooled beneath his motionless form while seven other agents lay scattered throughout the wreckage.

Through the magical connection, Alex experienced Elias' absolute terror as his partner crawled across the debris-strewn concrete, his own injuries forgotten. Seeing Alex's eyes barely focused on him and then shutting. The desperate search for a pulse, the horror of finding none at first, the frantic attempts at CPR until paramedics arrived.

"Alex, you were on the ground, not moving," Elias whispered, lost in the memory. "Blood everywhere. Your back was bleeding from the shrapnel."

The magical construct around them intensified. Alex could see himself through Elias' eyes, as he lay injured, dying, his life hanging by the thinnest of threads.

He watched his partner's vigil in the hospital. Three days of sleeping in an uncomfortable chair, refusing to leave, talking to his unconscious body in hopes that familiar voices might call him back.

Alex felt Elias' consciousness spiraling deeper into the trauma, the memory consuming him. The magical construct began to darken, Elias' guilt and despair threatening to trap them both in an endless loop of regret and self-recrimination.

"Elias, come back to the present." Alex let his combat magic flow through their connection with focused intent, wrapping protective energy around Elias' mind like a shield against the consuming memories.

Alex's magic found the pathways where trauma had carved deep channels in his partner's mind and gently redirected the flow of memory away from the most destructive patterns. The warehouse vision began to fade, replaced by the reality of the Maryland forest.

"I'm here," Alex said firmly, his magic anchoring Elias in the present moment. "I'm alive. You're safe. Come back to me."

The green mist swirled once more, then settled, leaving them sitting on the fallen log surrounded by bare trees and autumn silence. Elias opened his eyes, tears falling down his face, but his consciousness was his own again.

"Seven people died because I couldn't tell the difference between real magical traces and whatever artificial information was planted there. I failed them, Alex. That's on me."

"That's not what happened." Alex stood up, pulling Elias with him, silver and green magic still sparking faintly between them.

"They weaponized your gift. You didn't fail them. Your magic was attacked."

Elias staggered to his feet, his voice rough. "But people still died because of my assessment. And you were nearly killed."

Alex pulled him into a fierce embrace, holding on tight enough to anchor them both against the emotional storm they'd just weathered. For a moment Elias remained rigid. Then his defenses crumbled, and he returned the embrace with the desperate gratitude of someone who'd been drowning and suddenly found solid ground.

"Your magic was sabotaged by a kind of power that you'd never encountered before," Alex said quietly. "But even knowing that, it's going to take time to rebuild confidence in yourself."

"I don't know if I can."

"Then we'll figure it out together. Step by step, case by case, until you remember why you're one of the best magical investigators the Bureau has ever seen." Alex's grip tightened, conveying through physical contact what words couldn't fully express.

"I missed having my partner. My best friend. My brother. I'm not letting you disappear again, Elias. Whatever happens with this case or any other, we face it together."

"Together," Elias whispered, his voice carrying the first note of hope Alex had heard from him in months.

"I'm sorry I walked away. I made a choice for both of us that wasn't mine alone to make."

Alex could feel his own tears falling as he replied, "I forgive you, Elias. Just promise you'll never do that again."

"I promise," Elias said quietly. "I missed having someone who understood my magic, who knew when I was struggling even when I couldn't admit it myself."

They released each other and sat in the Maryland woods as afternoon faded toward evening, both of them processing revelations that changed everything about their understanding of the past eighteen months. They weren't fully back to normal.

Elias still struggled with trusting his abilities, and Alex still fought protective instincts that sometimes felt overwhelming. But the wall that had stood between them for eighteen months had fallen. What remained was a renewed determination to support each other through whatever challenges their investigation might bring.

As they walked back toward the house, rain began to fall through the bare branches, creating the kind of November evening that drew people inside to warmth and quiet conversation. Colleen had prepared hot chocolate and leftover pie, while James built a fire in the living room fireplace that would provide warmth and comfort through the evening hours.

The weekend settled into an easy rhythm. Long walks through the wooded property where the air smelled like pine, shared meals and late-night conversations by the fireplace.

Alex watched the tension slowly drain from Elias' shoulders, the lines around his eyes softening as he allowed himself to exist within the Sutton family's unconditional embrace. And Alex, in turn, remembered how much he had missed having his friend there.

The weekend passed in a blur of family stories, laughter, and quiet moments that helped them both heal. Elias seemed steadier, anchored by the simple act of being wanted. Alex knew with certainty that whatever lay ahead, they were back on the same path.

Sunday Morning — November 30 8:15 AM

The call came while they were having breakfast with Alex's parents. ASAC Lindsey's tone was all business and indicated they needed to return to work. Alex stepped into the living room for privacy while Elias helped Colleen clear the breakfast dishes.

"How are you both doing?" Lindsey asked without preamble. "Ready to get back to the investigation?"

Alex glanced toward the kitchen, where Elias was accepting another helping of scrambled eggs, his appetite better than it had been in months. The weekend had been good for both of them, providing time to process their revelations about the warehouse incident and begin rebuilding the trust that had been damaged by eighteen months of misunderstanding.

"We're ready," Alex said. "What's the latest on the case?"

"Several developments while you were away. I need you both back in Chicago tomorrow morning for briefings. The investigation is expanding in directions we didn't anticipate."

After ending the call, Alex rejoined his family in the kitchen. Elias looked up immediately, noticing his change in expression.

"Work?" Elias asked.

"Lindsey wants us back tomorrow morning. New developments in the case." Alex accepted his mother's offer of more coffee while considering their travel arrangements. "We need to head back to Chicago this afternoon."

They spent another hour with Colleen and James before packing their bags and preparing for the drive back to Baltimore-Washington International Airport. The weekend had provided exactly what both agents needed, time away from the investigation's intensity.

James walked them to their rental car. "Take care of each other out there," he said, gripping both their shoulders with paternal affection. "Whatever this investigation brings, you're stronger together than apart."

Colleen emerged from the house with turkey sandwiches for their lunch. "Drive carefully, call when you can, and remember that there's always a place for both of you here."

She hugged Elias with particular warmth, holding on just long enough to convey the message that he would always be welcome in their family.

"Don't be a stranger, sweetheart. You know we worry about you."

"Thank you," Elias said quietly, his voice carrying gratitude for more than just the weekend's hospitality. "For everything. I needed this more than I realized."

"That's what family is for," Colleen replied, stepping back to include Alex in her maternal gaze. "Both of you remember that you're not alone in this work. You have people who care about you. And make sure you ask for time off at Christmas. Both of you."

The drive to BWI took forty minutes through Maryland countryside that looked different in daylight than it had during their emergency trip three days earlier. Alex and Elias drove in comfortable silence, both processing the weekend's emotional breakthroughs while mentally preparing for whatever new developments awaited them.

"Thank you," Elias said as they approached the airport. "For bringing me home with you. For not letting me spend the weekend alone."

"Thank you for coming," Alex replied. "It felt right, having you there again. Like things were getting back to normal."

"Not normal," Elias corrected. "But better."

BWI Airport

The airport buzzed with post-holiday travel, families returning from Thanksgiving celebrations while business travelers resumed their routines. Alex and Elias moved through security with their FBI credentials and carry-ons, bound for Chicago.

Their flight would take two and a half hours, arriving in time for them to rest before reporting back to work the next morning. The investigation that had taken them to Baltimore, and revealed a family connection neither had anticipated, was still unfolding. In the air, they discussed the implications of what they'd learned about Project Avalon and Dr. Pierce's potential involvement. The weekend at Alex's parents' house had provided emotional healing, but it had also cemented their commitment to stopping whoever was orchestrating the attacks.

"Whatever Lindsey has discovered," Alex said as the Chicago skyline came into view, "at least we're facing it together."

Elias nodded, his voice carrying the confidence and humor that had been absent for eighteen months.

"Guess you're stuck with me again."

The plane touched down at O'Hare in late-afternoon light, bringing them back to the city where their investigation began—and where the next phase waited. They had only begun to glimpse how far the conspiracy reached, and every answer uncovered two more questions. The danger was only beginning.

10

Fractured Foundations

We shall know the truth and the truth shall make us mad
—Aldous Huxley

The Monday after Thanksgiving felt different as Alex and Elias walked through the FBI building together after meeting for breakfast at their favorite coffeehouse. They had both avoided it for the last eighteen months. The baristas, who had always known their orders by heart, still remembered that Elias asked for a second shot of espresso. Alex wondered aloud, "What kind of magic could keep their recall that sharp?"

Elias rolled his eyes and looked at him like he was insane. "They're baristas, it's literally their job to remember what regulars like. It's not magic, Alex."

And just like that, eighteen months of separation evaporated. Alex smiled and thought to himself, all is right with the world again.

Agent Rivera met them at the elevator. "Lindsey wants to see you both. Full debrief on Aberdeen."

ASAC Lindsey's office was warmer than usual when they entered, sunlight streaming through windows that looked out over downtown Chicago. She gestured toward the chairs across from her desk, noting how they seemed less tense, more at ease.

"Morning, gentlemen. Don't forget to turn your timesheets in when we're done here if you want to get paid. Accounting's on my ass again."

"Yes, ma'am," Alex and Elias said in unison.

"Now, tell me about Maryland," Lindsey asked, her tone curious.

"We spent the weekend at my parents' house," Alex replied, settling into his chair while Elias pulled out their files.

Lindsey glanced at Elias and back at Alex. With a wide smile she said, "I hope your parents are well."

Alex smiled back. "They are. We all are."

Elias looked up at Alex with an embarrassed grin and directed his words at Lindsey. "Aberdeen gave us answers we didn't expect."

Lindsey leaned forward. "What kind of answers?"

"Seven Celtic artifacts were stolen from Aberdeen's secure vault," Alex said, opening the technical documentation they had gathered. "Ancient gold disks that can amplify memory magic to control other people's consciousness."

Elias spread the Aberdeen files across the desk. "The research shows they can implant false memories, override magical abilities, even force a user to weaponize their own magic."

"The worst part," Alex added, "is the training manuals. Step-by-step instructions on how to deploy the artifacts, program victims, control them."

Lindsey frowned. "Control how?"

"By making the false memories feel real," Elias said. "The victim doesn't just believe the lie. They act on it. The artifact pushes a magic user beyond their limits until they are fighting with someone else's intent."

"How long does the control last?"

"It isn't clear," Elias admitted. "The artifacts were supposed to be locked away permanently. But the files suggest there was more testing than anyone admitted. And it requires someone with memory magic to make it work."

Alex slid over a personnel list. "Several researchers from Avalon are still alive. One name stands out—Dr. Jonathan Pierce. He had complete access to the project. If he's involved, he could be coordinating a network of operatives right now."

"Do you know what they're planning?" Lindsey asked.

"Not yet," Elias said. "But with seven artifacts in circulation, whatever it is, we won't see it coming."

"Dr. Lane was killed with the same ancient magic that took Torres and Cameron," Alex added. "We believe he uncovered who was behind it, and they silenced him. The work was rushed, sloppier than the others. We missed the assailant by only a few hours."

"They know we're closing in," Elias finished. "They're moving faster."

"We need authorization from DMA to bring in the rest of the unit," Alex said. "Full SCIF briefing, full counterterrorism team."

Lindsey reached for her phone. "I'll call Washington. If someone has trained operatives and seven artifacts—"

Her phone rang before she could dial. At the same time, emergency alerts shrilled across the building.

She answered, listened, and looked up at them. "Multiple incidents across the city. Magic users losing control in populated areas. We need to move."

◇✧◇

Union Station — 11:45 AM

The grand hall of Union Station looked like a war zone. Classical architecture twisted into impossible shapes. Marble columns cracked and bent. Steel beams spiraled into abstract sculptures. Emergency responders worked to evacuate the building while treating casualties whose injuries ranged from minor cuts to serious trauma.

"Four maintenance workers," Detective Brianna Lee reported when Alex and Elias arrived. "All registered magic users with perfect safety records. Witnesses say they went crazy around ten-thirty and started destroying everything they could reach."

Alex studied the damage pattern while Elias approached one of the witnesses. A businessman in a torn suit sat on a bench, his hands shaking as he gave his statement to a uniformed officer.

"They were working on the electrical systems," the man told Elias. "Normal maintenance. Then something changed. Their eyes went blank and they started tearing the building apart with their bare hands. Like they were possessed."

Elias extended his memory magic toward the scene, letting the echoes settle across his senses. The resonance was twisted —authentic memories overlaid with distortions that didn't belong. Fragments bent into patterns designed to control rather than record, the unmistakable signature of artifact interference.

"Artifact magic," Elias said quietly to Alex. The distortion was obvious now that he knew what to look for.

"Multiple artifacts activated simultaneously. Someone was controlling all four workers at the same time."

"How long did it last?" Alex asked Detective Lee.

"Twenty minutes of destruction. Then they all collapsed. All four are dead."

Through the station's damaged windows, they could see news crews setting up outside. Early reports were already describing "magic users going berserk" and calling for immediate government action to protect non-magical citizens.

"There," Alex said, spotting movement in the debris. "Someone's trapped under that beam."

They moved toward the collapsed section where a child's cries could be heard beneath twisted metal. The steel beam was too heavy for conventional rescue and too unstable for normal cutting equipment.

One wrong move and the entire wreckage could collapse.

Alex dropped to one knee beside it, his palm against the scorched concrete. "She's wedged under a support strut. Maybe a twelve-inch gap."

"There's fire on the west side," Elias said, eyes narrowed as he scanned the creeping flame near the gas-line rupture. "We've got less than two minutes before this whole pocket lights up."

"Normal shielding won't hold," Alex said.

Elias didn't look away from the smoke. "No. But an elemental weave might."

Alex's eyebrows rose. "We haven't done that in a couple of years."

"She's terrified, Alex," Elias said, his voice tight as he brushed the girl's psychic trace. "If we don't move now, she doesn't think she's getting out."

Elias gave a tight nod. "Then let's remember fast."

They didn't speak again.

Elias raised both hands, green magic forming an arc of pressure against the fractured ground. Moisture in the air condensed instantly, sweeping in with a sharp chill. Frost spread across the steel beam's edge, cooling the structure just enough to slow the warping.

Alex moved beside him, silver light igniting around his

arms. His magic settled into the metal—not lifting, not forcing —just easing the strain along the weakened seams, working with the cold Elias had drawn into the steel.

Their magic laced together without planning or speaking, just years of trust.

Steam hissed. The steel groaned.

"Now," Elias said.

Alex held the beam steady with raw force while Elias reached into the narrow gap. His arm disappeared up to the shoulder. A moment later, he pulled back, cradling a soot-covered child against his chest.

Alex released the magic all at once, letting the beam settle as gently as the wreckage allowed. The air around them snapped as the last threads of their weave dissipated.

"Nice work," Detective Lee said as paramedics carried the child to safety. "I've never seen magic users coordinate quite like that."

Alex and Elias exchanged glances, both recognizing that their magic had woven together more completely than either had expected. But before they could discuss what had happened, Detective Lee's radio crackled with reports of another incident.

"Northwestern Memorial Hospital," she said. "Similar situation. More people are dead."

Northwestern Memorial Hospital

The medical facility felt wrong the moment they entered. The emergency department buzzed with controlled chaos as staff struggled to manage both the aftermath of Union Station and a crisis within their own building. Dr. Cindy Hale met them at the main desk.

"Dr. Christina Sanchez and Nurse Patricia Booker," she said without preamble. "Thirty years of experience between them. Perfect healing records and completely reliable. This morning they were providing magical enhancement for critical patients. Then something happened."

She led them through the corridors. "Dr. Sanchez was performing cardiac surgery on a six-year-old when suddenly, instead of healing, she began causing damage. The child died before we could get her away from the table."

Alex studied the hospital's security footage while Elias approached the treatment room where Dr. Sanchez had been working. The magical traces here were similar to Union Station but more disturbing. Someone had turned healing magic into a weapon.

"Nurse Booker was worse," Dr. Hale continued. "She was in pediatric intensive care with five children under her watch. She attacked them with magic that should have been keeping them alive."

"Where are they now?" Elias asked.

"Dr. Sanchez is sedated in psychiatric observation. Nurse Booker is dead. Looks like a massive stroke." Dr. Hale swallowed. "She died while killing her own patients. It's horrific."

Elias extended his memory magic toward the body of Nurse Booker, seeking any traces that might explain what had happened to her. But when his abilities made contact with her remains, he staggered backward as chaotic magical static flooded his consciousness.

"What is it?" Alex asked, moving to steady his partner.

"Her memories are chaos. They aren't memories at all," Elias said, steadying himself on the wall. "They've been shredded into just fragments of pain and commands," he said, pulling back from the body. "Whatever happened to her, I can't make sense of it. "

"The artifacts?" Alex asked.

"Yeah, same signature I think." Elias placed a hand on the wall to steady himself as he lowered his head.

"You good? Do you need me to help?"

Elias looked at him and shook his head. "No, I'm okay. Thanks. Just needed a minute. That was disorienting."

Through the hospital windows, they could see protests beginning to form. Signs demanding immediate action against magic users mixed with news crews interviewing families whose children had been attacked by hospital staff they had trusted with their lives.

"This is what they wanted," Alex said, watching the coverage develop. "Maximum emotional impact. Turn healers into killers. Turn protectors into threats."

By three o'clock, Chicago felt like a city under siege. Two major incidents involving trusted magic users attacking the people they were supposed to protect had created exactly the crisis someone wanted. News coverage was uniformly negative, social media exploded with calls for immediate detention of all magic users. Politicians were already scheduling emergency sessions to address the "magical threat."

FBI Chicago Division — 4:45 PM

The emergency command center hummed with urgency as federal and local agencies scrambled to manage the aftermath. Alex and Elias moved between workstations where analysts processed evidence from both incident sites, searching facial-recognition patterns that might reveal who was behind the coordinated assault.

"Two incidents. Six magic users hijacked. Seven civilians dead." Agent Rivera reported. "All the magic users are dead. Medical scans show no evidence of drugs or conventional coercion."

Lindsey studied the attack timeline, noting how each incident built upon the previous one's psychological impact. "Surgical precision designed for maximum emotional trauma. Someone understands exactly how to turn public opinion against magical integration."

Alex reviewed the technical evidence while Elias processed witness statements from both scenes. The magical signatures were consistent with the Avalon artifacts, but deployed with a sophistication that suggested experience and training.

"The coordination required multiple operators," Alex said, reviewing the technical analysis. "Someone has trained teams working throughout the city."

"And they aren't finished," Elias added, studying patterns that suggested systematic preparation rather than random strikes. "This feels like a trial run. They're testing their capabilities before something bigger."

Their analysis was interrupted by the arrival of two officials in dark coats. The lead figure approached Lindsey. "ASAC Lindsey? I'm Agent Eleanor Hartford, Department of Magical Affairs. We're here to coordinate the response to these incidents."

Lindsey straightened when she heard the name. "Agent Hartford. I wasn't expecting DMA to send anyone."

"Today's attacks involved registered magic users turning on the general population." Hartford replied. "This falls in our jurisdiction. We're here to provide specialized support."

Behind Hartford, another figure emerged with military bearing. "Agent Austin Ryan, DMA tactical coordination. We'll be standing up a temporary operations post here."

Alex studied the DMA personnel with interest, noting the way they moved with confidence and authority. These weren't typical federal agents. This was the highest magical authority in the country and no one questioned their presence.

"We'll brief your team tomorrow morning," Agent Hartford told Lindsey. "But first, we need to speak with Agent Sinclair privately."

Elias looked up from the evidence files, surprised to be singled out. "Me?"

Alex's eyes flicked to his partner, sharp with concern. Elias masked it well, but Alex saw the tension in his shoulders, the hesitation in his breath. The DMA carried weight wherever they went. They were the authority on magical regulation, their word enough to override Bureau procedure. Their presence alone was power, and Elias felt it.

"Some aspects of this investigation concern you directly," Ryan said, his tone measured. "We'd prefer to discuss them away from the office. Would your apartment be suitable?"

Elias' Apartment — 7:30 PM

Elias' apartment occupied the top floor of a fifteen-story building in the West Loop, its floor-to-ceiling windows providing panoramic views of Chicago's downtown skyline. The space reflected his background, elegant but lived in, with clean architecture softened by warm lighting and natural textures.

Books lined dark wood shelves in quiet, thoughtful arrangements. Magical theory, neuroscience, literature, and a few worn novels clearly read more than once. The kitchen was spacious and well used, with high-end appliances, cast iron pans hung neatly above the stove. A half-finished crossword sat on the counter beside a mug. His apartment wasn't a show-piece. It was a home. A place where Elias could cook, read, think, and be alone with the silence that he trusted more than most people

Alex had been here many times during their partnership years ago, but this was his first visit since they'd started working together again. The apartment looked exactly the same, down to the photograph on the mantelpiece showing him and Elias at the summit of Mount Washington, taken shortly after graduating from the FBI Academy. Both grinning at the camera in hiking gear, arms around each other's shoulders, looking like they could conquer the world together.

"I never moved that," Elias said quietly, noticing Alex's attention on the photograph.

Alex studied the image, remembering the week they flew to New Hampshire to celebrate finishing their Academy training. "We looked so young."

"We were young. And stupid. And convinced we were going to save everyone." Elias moved to the kitchen, pulling out beer and wine. "Beer or wine? I've got both."

"Beer's fine."

Alex settled onto the couch. Here, Alex didn't have to pretend to be fine. And Elias didn't have to explain why he kept the lights dim in the evening or played the same old Miles Davis record while he cooked.

They'd opened their drinks and were beginning to relax when the building's security buzzer sounded. Agent Hartford's voice came through the intercom.

"Agent Sinclair? It's us."

Elias buzzed them up, exchanging glances with Alex. "This feels ominous."

Agent Hartford and Agent Ryan entered the apartment and Hartford accepted Elias' offer of coffee while Agent Ryan positioned himself where he could observe both men, posture relaxed but watchful.

"Thank you for agreeing to meet here," Hartford said, settling into the chair across from the couch where Alex and Elias sat. "What we need to discuss is sensitive, and we felt you should hear it privately rather than in front of your colleagues."

Elias felt tension building despite the polite tone. "What kind of sensitive?"

Hartford opened a classified file, revealing documents that made Alex sit forward sharply. Academic papers, research reports, and photographs that looked decades old but yet were well preserved.

"Agent Sinclair, what we're about to tell you will be difficult to process," Hartford lowered her voice and set the file down gently. "We've been investigating illegal magical activities for several years. The Celtic artifact research you read about at Aberdeen Proving Ground, the coordinated attacks today—all of it traces back to someone who was supposed to have died almost twenty years ago."

She placed a photograph on the coffee table between them. The image showed a man in his thirties with dark hair and green eyes, wearing academic robes at what looked like a university ceremony. Elias stared at the photograph, his face going pale.

"Dr. Edward Sinclair," Hartford said quietly. "Your father. He didn't die in the London bombing."

The words hit Elias like physical blows. His father's photograph lay on the coffee table like an accusation, proof that everything he'd believed was wrong.

"That's impossible," Elias said, his voice barely above a whisper. "My father died in London. I was there. I have the death certificate."

"It was all falsified," Agent Ryan replied. "The bombing was real, but your father used it as cover to fake his death. He's been operating under false identities for twenty years, building networks throughout North America."

Hartford provided additional documentation that included financial records, operational planning, and intelligence reports that painted Edward Sinclair as the mastermind behind sophisticated magical terrorism. "The attacks today were his work. Testing capabilities he's been developing since shortly after his supposed death."

Alex watched his partner process revelations that challenged every foundation of his understanding about his family. "How long have you known?"

"We've suspected for years, but couldn't confirm until recently," Hartford replied, but it all matches his academic work from before the London incident."

"He's been planning this operation for decades," Agent Ryan added. "Building a network, training operatives, positioning assets throughout major American cities."

Elias stared at his father's photograph. "He's been alive for twenty years while I thought he was dead."

"And based on today's attacks, his network is approaching operational readiness for something much larger than what we've seen," Hartford replied.

The apartment fell silent except for the distant sounds of Chicago traffic and the subtle hum of the building's heating system. Elias continued staring at the photograph, his hands beginning to shake as the full implications hit him.

"We'll brief the full details tomorrow morning," Hartford said, beginning to gather her files. "But we felt you deserved to know privately rather than learning in front of your colleagues."

Professional courtesy," Agent Ryan added. "One law enforcement officer to another."

After they left, Elias remained on the couch, staring at the space where his father's photograph had been. Alex moved closer, providing a physical presence without trying to force conversation.

"Eighteen years," Elias said finally. "I spent eighteen years thinking he was dead. Mourning him. Building my entire life around the fact that he was gone."

"Elias—"

"He's been alive the whole time. A terrorist! Training

people to use magic as weapons against innocent civilians." Elias' voice grew stronger, green sparks snapped between his fingers, the window frame buzzing with residual charge. "I thought he was dead and instead, he was building networks to attack the system I dedicated my life to protecting."

Alex had never seen his partner this angry. Green energy began crackling around Elias' hands as his magical abilities responded to emotional stress, power sparking through the apartment's air in patterns that made the windows vibrate.

"He let me think he was dead," Elias stood suddenly, his magic sparking stronger. "Let me grow up alone. Watched me become a federal agent investigating the exact kind of crimes he was planning to commit."

"Hey," Alex said, moving closer and placing a hand on Elias' shoulder. The contact grounded some of the chaotic energy, but didn't eliminate the raw fury building in his partner. "I'm here."

Elias looked at him. "Are you? Because anyone else would be running for the door right now."

"Elias. I'm not going anywhere," Alex said, voice steady.

Elias was quiet for a moment. "I don't know how to handle this."

"You don't have to handle it alone." Alex sat beside him on the couch, close enough to provide stability if Elias' magic became unstable again.

"Whatever happens tomorrow, whatever we learn about his plans, we face it together. I'm staying tonight." Alex stated.

"Is my favorite pillow still in the guest room?"

Only Alex would say something that normal after a day like this. Not to distract, but to remind him he wasn't alone. Elias didn't answer right away. His throat was tight, his chest still hollow from everything he'd learned. But somehow that simple question cracked through the numbness. Absurd, familiar, so very *Alex*.

He huffed a laugh that caught halfway to breaking. "Of course it is."

The evening continued with Alex making sandwiches in the kitchen and insisting that Elias eat. Outside the apartment windows, Chicago's lights sparkled in the darkness. They ate in silence, Elias wondering why his father had chosen this path, and what waited when they met again. Tomorrow would likely bring more questions than answers. At least he didn't have to face it alone.

11

Room 101

There are things that have to be forgotten if you want to go on living
  —*Jim Thompson, The Killer Inside Me*

FBI Chicago Division—December 2

The DMA briefing room had been established overnight in the FBI building's most secure conference space, equipment and personnel transforming the familiar environment into something that felt like mission control. Alex and Elias arrived to find Lindsey, Cross, Rivera, and the rest of their team already assembled, coffee cups and notepads suggesting they'd been there for a while.

Agent Eleanor Hartford stood at the front of the room beside displays showing Edward Sinclair's network in comprehensive detail. Agent Austin Ryan sat near her with the laptop controlling the presentation.

"Thank you all for coming," Hartford began. "What we're

about to discuss will fundamentally change your understanding of the investigation you've been conducting."

She advanced to the first slide showing the connections between the murders and several other unknown individuals suspected of being operatives. "The resonance amplifier technology, the training protocols you discovered at Aberdeen, and the coordinated attacks that started in this city two weeks ago, all trace back to a network that's been operational for almost eighteen years."

Rivera looked up from her notepad. "Eighteen years?"

"Since 2007," Agent Ryan confirmed, consulting files on his laptop. "We've been tracking illegal magical activities throughout the Midwest and Eastern seaboard. Financial networks, training facilities, personnel recruitment. The scope exceeds anything we've encountered in domestic magical enforcement."

Lindsey studied the information on the screen. "You're talking about a major operation. How many people?"

"Conservative estimate? Maybe eight to ten trained operatives who know how to use the Celtic artifacts and coordinate operations. Easily another twenty-five or more magic users throughout the city who are true believers and providing logistics and safe houses," Hartford replied. "All of them potentially following protocols developed through years of systematic research and field testing."

Alex asked, "Is it just the seven artifacts that were stolen from Aberdeen?"

"We aren't sure of the total number in Edward's possession," Agent Ryan said. "We don't even know how many exist in total, only what has been recovered to date. But we believe Edward has maintained possession of at least one artifact for years." He looked at Alex and Elias as he continued. "He used one in the warehouse explosion that nearly killed you both."

Elias went very still and then spoke, anger evident in his voice. "Are you saying you knew?"

"Your magic didn't fail that day, Agent Sinclair," Ryan replied evenly. "Edward used his artifact to manipulate the minds of the terrorists you were tracking. He convinced them they weren't in possession of explosives."

Hartford didn't look away from Elias. "We believe Edward was testing the artifact's capabilities with you."

"You're telling me," Elias said slowly, his voice dangerously quiet, "that my father used me to test weapons that got seven agents killed?"

"That's exactly what I'm telling you," Hartford answered.

Alex felt rage building in his chest. "How long have you known this?"

"We suspected after the recent attacks," Ryan said. "I requested a reexamination of the warehouse evidence with new artifact resonance detection methods. The confirmation came just before we started this briefing."

Elias' voice cut in, sharp, his eyes locking on Alex. "In Maryland, I said the traces felt too precise. He was already manipulating what I read."

Ryan gave a single, grave nod. "That would fit. Our reexamination showed resonance consistent with artifact interference. If Edward had one of the disks then, he could have altered the psychic residue before you ever touched it."

Elias' jaw tightened. "So I wasn't just wrong. I was being used."

Hartford leaned forward, steady. "You were deliberately deceived, Agent Sinclair. Those deaths weren't your fault. They were caused by ancient magic designed to distort perception itself."

Elias stood abruptly and crossed to the window. His reflection in the glass looked pale and drawn, his voice rough when it came. "He's been using me. Testing me. Letting me take the blame while he sat back and watched."

Hartford spoke up, saying, "Edward manipulated the terrorists' perception of events, and the evidence team had no way to know they were dealing with ancient magic. They dismissed any anomalous readings as chaos from the explosion."

The others in the room exchanged confused looks until Rivera spoke up. "What do you mean your father? What are you all talking about?"

"Which brings us to the most difficult part of this briefing," Hartford said, her voice more careful now. She activated a new display showing academic records and photographs from decades past. "The network we're tracking has connections to Project Avalon research from nearly twenty years ago. Officially terminated, but elements clearly continued operating."

"The artifacts represent the most sophisticated magical warfare research ever conducted. They can amplify abilities or, when wielded by a memory specialist, override human consciousness, create false magical traces, and turn magic users into weapons against their will."

Hartford paused, then advanced the display. A dark-haired man in his thirties, standing before a university backdrop, his gaze steady and unreadable

"Dr. Edward Sinclair," Hartford said quietly, watching the room's reaction. "The original lead researcher on Project Avalon. Officially declared dead in the London bombing eighteen years ago."

Rivera frowned. "What do you mean officially?"

Lindsey's mouth set and her pen stopped mid-note.

"Agent Sinclair was there. He survived the bombing. How did this happen?"

"The bombing was real," Hartford confirmed. "But Edward Sinclair used it as cover to fake his death while continuing his research into classified and illegal magical applications. He's been coordinating extremist activities throughout the United States ever since."

Rivera's eyes went wide as she stared at Elias. Cross opened his mouth to speak but then stopped.

"How long have you known?" Lindsey asked.

"We've suspected for years, but couldn't confirm until recently," Hartford said. "A field operative here in Chicago made visual contact. That's how we know he's alive."

Rivera glanced at Elias with obvious concern. "He's been planning this for eighteen years?"

"Building a network, training operatives, positioning assets throughout the city," Agent Ryan confirmed. "The attacks yesterday were his work. He's progressed from testing infrastructure weaknesses to executing a sophisticated plan."

Alex watched his partner struggle to process the information. The rest of the team seemed to grasp what it meant for him personally.

Cross spoke from the back of the room. "What's his endgame?"

"Based on operational analysis, systematic destabilization of magical integration policies across the country," Agent Ryan replied. "Create enough chaos to prove democratic systems can't handle magic."

"Force governmental overreach that radicalizes moderate magical communities," Hartford added. "Push both sides toward extremism while positioning his network as the reasonable alternative to chaos. Clearly, he's decided to start in Chicago."

Hartford took a deep breath before continuing. "There's something else. Based on operational needs, we believe this network may try to recruit high level memory magic specialists. Memory specialists are extremely rare, maybe only a few dozen in the entire country with the abilities needed to operate these artifacts effectively."

She looked at Elias. "Someone with your capabilities would be invaluable to his operations. His psych profile indicates that Edward may try to recruit you. It's possible he orchestrated the incident eighteen months ago with one goal. To drive a wedge between you and your partner."

She looked at Alex as she continued. "By manipulating events so you'd stop working together, isolating Elias from the person he trusted most. He may have been setting the stage for his return all along."

Alex looked at Elias and saw him staring down at the table. He didn't think his partner could handle any more surprises.

The briefing continued for another hour, with technical analysis and coordination plans. But throughout the discussion, Alex remained focused on Elias, noting the way his partner withdrew more with each new revelation.

"We'll coordinate tactical response with your team," Hartford concluded.

The briefing ended and personnel began dispersing toward their assignments. Elias didn't move when the room emptied.

Lindsey approached carefully. "Elias, take whatever time you need to process this. But I want you to know this team supports you completely."

"Whatever he planned, whatever manipulation he attempted, you became someone who dedicated his life to protecting people," Rivera added. "That's what matters."

Elias looked up at her. "Thanks, Nicole."

Alex didn't move from his seat, and waited until the room had cleared before speaking to his partner. "How are you handling this?"

"I don't know," Elias admitted. "Everything about my life, my career, our partnership... what if none of it was real? What if I'm just a weapon he spent eighteen years creating?"

"Whatever your father planned, he doesn't get to decide who you are."

But Alex could see the doubt in his partner's expression,

the way the revelations had planted questions about everything Elias thought he knew about himself.

The report came from Agent Sarah Patterson, who was
coordinating with neighboring medical facilities. Alex listened
while keeping one eye on Elias, who hadn't looked away from
the photograph of his father.

"We've got a situation you might want to see in person,"
Patterson said. "Possible use of advanced memory manipulation, but something went wrong. The subject is aware and
experiencing severe psychological trauma."

Alex's attention sharpened. "What sort of awareness are
we talking about?"

"Janine McCarthy, thirty-two, elementary school teacher
in Milwaukee with minor magical ability," Patterson replied.
"Yesterday she was found in her classroom screaming. The
symptoms match artifact activation. But instead of pushing
her to act, the process fragmented her consciousness."

Elias moved closer, his expression tightening. "Fragmented
how?"

"She knows who she is," Patterson explained, "but she's
carrying artificial memories that feel real. She remembers
planning terrorist operations that never happened, participating in attacks she never saw, receiving training she never
had."

Alex and Elias exchanged a glance. A partially aware
victim of the artifact's magic who could provide intelligence
about Edward's network they couldn't obtain anywhere else.
But accessing her fractured consciousness would require
magical techniques that held enormous risk.

"Where is she?" Alex asked, already calculating the drive
time to Milwaukee.

"She's being treated at the Milwaukee medical facility. Her

condition is deteriorating fast. Whatever they did to her, she's not stable." Patterson hesitated. "Dr. Kincaid estimates forty-eight hours before the artificial memories completely over-write her original personality."

Milwaukee, Wisconsin

The Milwaukee Federal Medical Facility occupied several floors of a downtown building, its reinforced construction designed for patients whose conditions exceeded normal human medical capabilities. Alex and Elias arrived to find security protocols that suggested they were dealing with some-thing far beyond a standard medical emergency.

"Elementary school teacher. Minor illusion magic for class-room work. No criminal background, no extremist ties," Elias said, studying the profile. The woman's only notable trait was a magical ability that made her useful for Edward's purposes.

"She was selected because her magic could be weaponized, not because of any ideological alignment," Elias added.

"Which means her artificial memories will feel completely foreign to her real personality," Alex observed, recognizing how that fracture would make memory extraction especially complex.

"She'll be fighting against the false memories, but that resistance might also be destroying her sanity."

"If I can access her consciousness carefully enough, I might be able to separate the originals from the artificial ones," Elias said, though his voice sounded uncertain. "But the level of psychic contact required would be deeper than anything I've attempted before."

He looked at Alex. "Except with you, of course."

Alex's concern sharpened. The kind of contact Elias was describing would leave him exposed to whatever distortions had been planted in Janine's mind.

"We'll need to be careful," Alex said. "If this magic can fragment consciousness, it might pull you into it too."

Dr. Rebecca Kincaid met them at the checkpoint. A woman in her forties with years of experience treating magical trauma.

"Ms. McCarthy's condition has been deteriorating since admission," Dr. Kincaid reported, leading them through corridors lined with reinforced observation windows designed for patients in magical crisis. "The artificial memories are becoming more vivid and detailed while her original personality fragments under the pressure."

"What kind of artificial memories?" Elias asked, his senses already detecting the familiar resonance of ancient magic woven into her consciousness.

"Terrorist training, operational planning, participation in attacks that caused civilian casualties. All of it feels completely real to her, despite having no basis in her actual life." Dr. Kincaid consulted her chart, the notes documenting a systematic violation of identity.

"She believes she's a terrorist operative while simultaneously knowing she's an elementary school teacher. The contradiction is destroying her sanity."

They approached a reinforced observation room where Janine McCarthy sat in restraints designed to prevent magical discharge during episodes. Through the one-way mirror, Alex saw an ordinary woman who looked like she should have been grading homework or reading to her students. Instead, a troubled look settled in her eyes.

"I remember killing people," Janine said to the staffer monitoring her. "I remember planning attacks, coordinating with other operatives, choosing civilian targets. But I also remember reading stories to third graders yesterday morning."

"Both sets of memories feel equally real to her," Dr. Kincaid explained. "The amplifier didn't just implant them. It fused them into her identity so thoroughly that she can't tell where reality ends and the false memories begin."

Elias focused his magic, reading the distorted residue. The false impressions were tangled with fragments of her true self, an overlay of conflicting lives.

"I need to access her consciousness directly," Elias said. His voice was steady, but Alex caught the weight beneath it.

"If I can separate what's false from what belongs to her, we might understand how the artifact's magic twists identity, and how to stop it."

"That's extremely dangerous," Dr. Kincaid warned. "Those artificial memories might try to anchor themselves in your mind as well. We don't yet understand the limits of this magic."

Alex's concern sharpened, but the intelligence value was undeniable. They needed answers before Edward's network could inflict this on anyone else.

"I'll monitor the contact," Alex said, his abilities already reaching toward Elias in preparation to anchor him.

"If the artificial memories try to transfer, I can sever the connection and pull you back," Alex said firmly.

"The level of psychic contact required will be extensive," Dr. Kincaid warned again, her tone edged with unease. This wasn't a medical procedure. It was stepping into dangerous territory that normal healing protocols were never meant to reach.

Elias studied Janine through the observation window. Her fractured mind was tearing itself apart, the false memories consuming her sense of self.

"I need to try," he said quietly.

Dr. Kincaid prepared the secure treatment suite, setting

protective wards and placing safeguards meant to stabilize a patient in psychic crisis. Alex positioned himself beside the bed where Janine would be brought, every line of his body ready to anchor Elias if the magic turned against him.

"Remember," Alex said as he rested a hand on Elias' shoulder, "don't let the false memories convince you they're real. I'll hold the connection and pull you back if anything goes wrong."

Janine was led in under restraint, her face pale, eyes wide with confusion and terror. The moment she saw Elias, magic curling faintly at his fingertips, her expression broke into desperate relief.

"Can you help me?" she asked, her voice trembling, raw with weeks of strain. "I don't know which memories are mine anymore. I don't know who I am."

"I'm going to try," Elias said, extending his hands. Green light flared softly around his fingers, steady and deliberate. "But I need you to trust me. Let me in, and I'll help you separate what's real from what was forced into you."

Alex tightened his grip on Elias' shoulders, silver energy flowing through the contact and weaving into the green current. The familiar harmony of their magic settled around them, anchoring Elias for what was about to happen.

"Ready?" Elias asked, his voice calm despite the weight of what he was attempting. His magic reached toward Janine's consciousness, preparing to cross the fragile boundary between healer and patient, memory and illusion.

"Ready," Alex replied, his magic forming protective barriers around both their minds.

Elias' abilities flowed into Janine's mind like water seeping into a cracked vessel, his consciousness immediately colliding with artificial patterns that felt wrong. The false memories were sophisticated beyond anything he had ever encountered, woven so deeply into her mind that separating truth from fabrication demanded impossible precision.

Through his link with Alex, Elias felt the steady pull of silver energy anchoring him while he navigated Janine's fractured landscape. The artificial memories felt real because they had been engineered to simulate authentic experience, each threaded with emotional detail. Precision unlike anything he had faced before.

Beneath it all, though, Elias could still sense fragments of her true self. Authentic memories of a woman who had dedicated her life to helping children learn and grow. The false memories layered over them weren't just fabrications. They had been designed to break her.

Then he saw the real horror.

These weren't random visions, they were precise, targeted psychological weapons. Memories of Janine murdering children who looked like her students, engineered to make her believe she had done it. To make her feel it, again and again.

"Dear God," Elias whispered, reeling from the cruelty etched into the artifact's magic. "He's not just controlling them. He's torturing them while they do his work."

Through their bond, Alex felt the wave of revulsion hit him. Edward hadn't built a weapon. He'd created psychological warfare, memory by memory, customized to each victim.

"I can see the pattern," Elias said. "Each memory set creates a false personality. One that fits the role he needs while destroying the person beneath."

"Can you remove them?" Alex asked, his magic maintaining protective barriers while his attention stayed locked on Elias' mental state.

"Maybe. But the integration is so complete that tearing out the false memories might also rip apart her authentic self."

Elias pressed deeper into Janine's mind. The artificial memories reacted like a defense system, disguising themselves as real, cloaking each scene in emotional detail, and trying to overwrite his perception. Then they turned on him directly.

They showed him his parents' deaths. Vivid, brutal memories that had never happened. In one, his father tortured his mother Sinclair before killing her. Every detail was precise, every emotion sharpened until it felt true.

Through their link, Alex felt the pressure building inside Elias' mind. The artificial memories pressed against his thoughts like an infection trying to take hold. Alex responded immediately, silver magic flaring in strong, controlled pulses as he strengthened the barrier between them. He didn't sever the connection. He held it steady, ready to pull Elias back the moment it tipped too far.

"They're fighting back," Elias said, his voice strained as the false memories tried to convince him that terrorist operations were authentic experiences he had personally witnessed.

"The memories have a defensive protocol. They activate when magic tries to analyze them."

"Can you maintain the connection?" Alex asked, feeling the rising pressure as the artificial memories tried to override Elias' consciousness through manipulation that should not have been possible.

"For now. Edward's design is more sophisticated than I realized."

The assault intensified. Through their connection, Alex could feel Elias' defenses buckling under pressure that exceeded anything their training had prepared them for.

The psychological attack turned vicious. Elias saw false visions of Alex dying slowly in the warehouse explosion, bleeding out as he called his name.

This wasn't psychic bleed. They were targeting him.

"Elias, you need to pull back," Alex said, his energy reinforcing the barriers while preparing to sever the link if the false memories broke through.

"He planted these for you! They're designed to attack you! This is an ambush!"

"Almost finished," Elias forced out, pushing deeper into Janine's consciousness. "I can see the damage. If I can understand how the memories were implanted, I might be able to stop it."

But as he pressed further into Janine's subconscious, the false memories launched a coordinated assault too strong for his defenses. They tried to convince him his entire life was a lie. That his career as an FBI agent was fabricated, that his loyalty had been engineered by those in power, and that he had personally caused the warehouse explosion that nearly killed Alex.

Through the bond, Alex felt the artificial memories probing toward his own mind, seeking to transfer through the connection. His magic blazed, sealing barriers that kept him untouched. He prepared to pull Elias free before the infection could take root.

But Elias was too deep. Alex could feel his partner's defenses beginning to collapse under the weight of the attack.

"That's enough," Alex said. "I'm pulling you out."

Silver light blazed as his magic severed Elias' connection to Janine's mind. The disconnection was not clean. It tore through layers of artificial memory that clung to Elias, ripping him free with force that left his mind reeling.

The recoil hit like a physical blow. Elias collapsed against Alex with a sharp gasp, body trembling. His abilities guttered out, spent from battling the false constructs, and his mind reeled from the violence of being wrenched out of Janine's mind without warning.

"I'm sorry," Alex said immediately, arms steadying him while his own heart hammered with guilt. "I had to pull you back before they corrupted your consciousness."

Elias clutched Alex's sleeve, grounding himself in the here and now. "Don't apologize. I trust you. I was lost in there, Alex. I needed you to drag me out even if it hurt."

His voice was raw, exhaustion threaded with relief. He had always accused Alex of being too protective, but in this moment those instincts had saved him.

"I could feel myself losing track of what was real," Elias admitted. "If you hadn't yanked me out, I don't think I would've found my way back." His voice was hoarse, but the gratitude was unmistakable.

Alex's concern lingered, unspoken but obvious.

Elias caught it and gave him a steady look. "Alex, listen to me. I don't let anyone connect that deeply for a reason. But with you—it's different. You have my permission. If I ever get lost again, you bring me back. No matter what it takes. I trust you."

The tension in Alex's shoulders eased just enough. "All right," he said. "I'll hold you to that."

"What did you discover?" Dr. Kincaid asked, monitoring both agents for signs of neurological damage.

"The magic is more sophisticated than we realized," Elias said. He explained the details of what he had found, his voice heavy with fatigue.

"The level of sophistication suggests decades of research and refinement. Can the artificial memories be removed?" Dr. Kincaid asked.

"Not without risking permanent damage to her personality," Elias replied. "The false memories are engineered to be irreversible. They create lasting psychological harm, not just temporary illusions."

The medical suite fell silent as everyone processed the implications of a type of magic capable of permanently altering human consciousness through artificial memories.

"What's her prognosis?" Alex asked.

"Permanent psychological damage," Dr. Kincaid said. "If the artificial memories are too integrated to remove, the contradiction with her authentic personality will eventually destroy her sanity until one framework overwhelms the other. Worse, the design ensures psychological torment no matter which identity survives."

"Meaning she'll either live convinced she's a terrorist who

murdered children, or break completely trying to cling to her original identity," Elias said.

When Elias tried to stand, the room tilted. A wave of weakness hit hard, the kind that left his muscles shaking and his thoughts slow to catch up. The psychic contact had stripped him bare, his magic drained, leaving him moving like a man half-asleep and struggling just to stay upright.

Alex saw it instantly. The way Elias' balance faltered, the hollow look in his eyes, the raw cost of what he'd just endured. Concern spiked, and before his partner could go down, Alex caught him in a firm grip.

"Easy. That was intense work. You need time to recover."

"I'm fine," Elias said automatically.

"No, you're not," Alex countered, holding him firm as they walked toward the exit. "What you just did was extraordinary. Anyone would be wrecked after that."

Dr. Kincaid regarded them with concern. "Agent Sinclair, your partner is right. The depth of psychic contact you reached would be exhausting under the best conditions. You could suffer lasting effects. You should stay overnight for observation and let our healing specialists examine you."

"No, thank you," Elias said sharply, turning away before she could press further.

As they made their way to the parking area, Alex stayed close, watching his partner carefully.

He drove the two-hour trip back to Chicago, glancing at Elias often. His partner's magic still seemed drained, weighed down by the false memories and the horror he had faced inside Janine's mind.

"Thank you," Elias said quietly at last. "I couldn't have done that analysis without you anchoring me."

"Thank you for trusting me enough to let me," Alex replied.

Elias stared out the window, voice low. "It showed me memories of you dying in the warehouse explosion. You calling my name. They felt completely real. More real than my actual memories of that day. I finally understand how victims lose themselves in the false imprints."

Anger simmered in Alex as he absorbed the cruelty Edward had engineered. Beside him, Elias had already fallen asleep, his magic drained and his body sagging against the passenger door. Alex kept his eyes on the road, knowing Edward Sinclair had already turned memory into a weapon and that they were running out of time to stop him.

12

The Maelstrom

Nearly all men can stand adversity, but if you want to test a man's character, give him power
— *Abraham Lincoln*

Elias woke to the smell of coffee and the quiet sounds of someone in his kitchen. For a brief, disorienting moment he was alone again, as he had been for eighteen months. Then the memories returned. The sterile white of the hospital, Janine's shattered mind, and Alex's desperate pull, dragging him out of the psychic wreckage before Edward's trap could claim him too.

He found Alex at the stove, still in yesterday's clothes, cooking eggs with an easy, practiced familiarity that made the kitchen feel less like a solitary refuge and more like home. Two coffee mugs sat on the counter, steam curling from their rims.

"Morning," Alex said without turning from the pan. "You were dead to the world when we got back. Figured you needed the sleep more than you needed to argue about me staying."

Elias accepted the mug, struck by how Alex remembered

exactly how he liked it. He took a sip, the warmth steadied him. Sweetened just the way he liked it. He glanced around the room. "I don't remember getting upstairs."

"You were half asleep," Alex replied, plating the eggs. "You barely made it into bed before you crashed." He handed Elias a plate. "How's your head?"

"Better. Still feels like someone used my skull for target practice, but the worst is gone." Elias sat at the kitchen table, his eyes on the coffee rather than Alex. "Alex, I don't think I can handle this."

He hadn't told Alex everything about Janine. The feeling of being inside her mind, the labyrinthine wreckage where reality had been overwritten so many times it had blurred into a void. The terrifying part wasn't what he saw, but the moment he'd almost given in to the impulse to fix it. To smooth the chaos, impose his own order, and shape something that made sense. It would have been his version of the truth, not hers. It was a line he hadn't crossed, not yet.

Elias gripped the mug tighter. "It's not just my father. It's what I could become if I stop being careful."

Alex's fork paused midair. The easy morning atmosphere vanished. "Handle what?"

"All of it. My father being alive. The manipulation. Him targeting me specifically." Elias' voice was quiet, but edged with panic. "All these years of thinking he was dead, building my entire life around believing I had no family alive. And now I find out he's been pulling the strings the whole time?"

Alex set his fork down and leaned in closer. "Elias—"

"He's been watching me, studying me, probably laughing at how easily I fell into every trap he set." Elias finally met his eyes, and Alex saw not just exhaustion but a profound concern. "The Academy, our partnership, my career with the Bureau. What if none of it was my choice? What if I'm just some experiment he's been running?"

"That's not true."

"How do you know?" Elias stood abruptly and paced toward the window, agitation in his every step. "How do we know anything about our lives is real if he's been manipulating everything from the beginning?"

Alex recognized the signs. The careful control was fracturing. Elias had spent years building walls around his vulnerabilities, but the revelation about Edward had ripped through them.

"Because I know you," Alex said simply. "Whatever Edward planned or manipulated, he couldn't create who you are. He couldn't manufacture your sense of justice, your loyalty, your ability to see the good in people even when they can't see it themselves."

"You don't understand." Elias pressed his palms against the window glass. "I was barely holding it together before this started. After losing our team at the warehouse, almost losing you, I was... God, Alex, some nights I didn't see the point in waking up the next morning."

The admission hit Alex like a blow. He'd known Elias was struggling, but he hadn't realized how close his friend had come to giving up entirely.

"But you did wake up," Alex said, moving to stand behind him. "Every morning, you got up and you kept fighting. That wasn't Edward's manipulation, that was you choosing to survive."

"And now he wants to take even that away." Elias' reflection in the window showed only defeat. "Turn me into another Janine, another broken mind he can use as a weapon."

Alex set his hands on Elias' shoulders, feeling the tension wound tight under his grip. "He can try. But he's not accounting for one thing."

"What?"

"You're stronger than he knows," Alex said, steady and unwavering.

"What if I'm not strong enough? What if next time I can't resist the artifacts?"

"Then I'll pull you out, same as I did at the hospital." Alex's hands tightened on his shoulders. "That's what friends do, Elias. We anchor each other when the world gets too chaotic to handle alone."

They stood like that for several minutes, Alex a steady presence while Elias struggled through the fears he'd carried alone. Finally Elias straightened and turned.

"I'm sorry. I know you've got your own life. You shouldn't have to babysit me because I can't handle my family drama."

"I'm your partner. Keeping you out of trouble is part of the job. And stopping Edward's network is our priority," Alex replied. "Everything else can wait."

Their conversation was interrupted by Alex's phone buzzing with a text. He checked the display, and the warmth in his expression hardened into professional focus.

"Nicole. We've got another incident, and this one's different."

Alex studied the surveillance photos spread across their desk while Elias reviewed the encrypted communications they'd intercepted the night before. The intelligence had come through DMA channels. Chatter about a meeting scheduled for this morning at an abandoned steel mill on Chicago's South Side.

"Three vehicles spotted at the location yesterday," Alex said, pointing to timestamps on the photos. "Black SUVs, tinted windows, no plates visible."

"Communication intercepts mention 'the specialists' and 'final preparations,'" Elias added, consulting the transcripts. "Could be Pierce or Edward coordinating with cells."

Agent Rivera approached their desks with fresh coffee and

the impatient energy she brought to promising leads. "Lindsey wants you two to check it out. Hartford and Ryan are coordinating from tactical command, but they're twenty minutes out if you need backup."

Alex gathered his tactical gear while Elias reviewed building schematics downloaded from city planning records. The steel mill had been abandoned for five years, its massive structures creating perfect cover for clandestine meetings while offering multiple escape routes through the industrial maze.

"Standard approach?" Alex asked as they headed for their vehicle.

"Reconnaissance first, then assessment," Elias replied. "If it's just a meeting, we observe and gather intelligence. If they're planning something immediate, we call for backup."

The drive to the South Side took twenty minutes through Chicago's morning traffic, giving them time to coordinate their approach and review what they knew about the area.

South Side Steel Mill

The rusted frames and shattered windows made the place look dead under the gray December sky. Alex parked their SUV behind a concrete barrier that provided cover while maintaining sight lines to the main building.

"Two vehicles in the loading area," Elias observed, extending his abilities toward the complex. "Six people inside the main structure. They're not doing anything, they're just waiting on something."

Alex studied the building through binoculars, noting the way the occupants weren't moving but rather just casually positioned around the room.

Elias said, his concentration deepening as he probed the building's interior. "But something feels wrong. Too obvious."

They approached the complex through the maze of abandoned machinery and storage containers that littered the industrial site. The December air felt bitterly cold as broken glass crunched underfoot despite their careful movement.

"Loading dock," Alex said quietly, pointing to an entrance that offered the best approach angle. "We can get close enough to see what they're doing."

The steel mill's interior cavernous space echoed with the weight of its own ruin, its high ceilings supported by massive beams while broken windows let in shafts of pale sunlight. Edward's people had positioned themselves in the central area, but instead of working, they were waiting.

"It's a trap," Elias whispered, his magic picking up on their thoughts that suggested an ambush rather than a real operation. "They're set up to capture, not plan another attack."

Alex counted six operatives, all armed and their attention focused on the entrances rather than conversation.

"They want us specifically," Elias said, his focus narrowing on the residue of intent that clung to the room. It wasn't memories, not yet, but impressions and flashes of anticipation and directed purpose. The operatives weren't here to kill indiscriminately. Their attention was fixed on him. The sensation had an undercurrent he recognized from Janine's mind, a controlled push meant to see how far he could be driven.

"This whole thing is bait to lure us in."

The moment they tried to retreat, alarms began blaring throughout the complex. Motion sensors activated, flooding the area with harsh light while the six operatives moved with coordinated precision to block all escape routes.

Alex's combat magic erupted before the first gunshot sounded. Silver energy blazed through the industrial space, kinetic blasts hitting three of the operatives before they could fully raise their weapons. The remaining three scrambled for cover, their carefully planned ambush disrupted by Alex's aggressive counterattack.

"Move!" Alex shouted, launching another wave of silver force that shattered concrete pillars and sent debris flying.

But one of the operatives pulled out a small golden disk. A Celtic artifact that pulsed with power and energy.

He concentrated and directed the ancient magic toward Elias, attempting to override his consciousness. The artifact's power struck Elias' mind just as his own memory magic put up defenses to counter it and strike back. Green energy and ancient magic collided in a violent discharge that sent both men staggering.

Elias felt the artifact's magic slide into his thoughts with surgical precision, stitching false memories together as if they had always been his. The pressure was probing with cruel precision, testing how long before he broke and turned on Alex. But he had been able to fight back, disrupting the artifact's influence.

"Elias!" Alex shouted, seeing his partner locked in magical combat with the artifact wielder.

Gunfire erupted from the remaining operatives, forcing Alex into cover while he sent silver force to deflect bullets and keep Elias from being overrun. But the artifact's assault pressed harder, and Elias could feel his resistance slipping. For one terrifying instant, he saw himself standing over Alex's fallen body, weapon raised under someone else's command.

No. Not Alex.

Something inside him snapped. Elias' elemental magic surged outward with a fury he couldn't restrain. Winds howled through the mill, tearing steel beams from their mounts. Heat shimmered as the air itself ignited, rupturing gas lines and turning the structure into a furnace. The operatives broke formation, survival overriding their orders as the collapsing steel frame buckled around them.

But Elias wasn't stopping with defensive measures. His magic reached beyond the immediate building, drawing power from atmospheric pressure across the entire district. Natural gas lines ruptured and ignited, creating columns of flame. Wind patterns shifted throughout the South Side as Elias manipulated weather systems on a massive scale.

The steel mill began to collapse as wind and fire exceeded its structural limits. Metal beams twisted under pressure while the building's framework buckled. Edward's operatives fled as the situation became pure survival.

The operative using the artifact against Elias was caught in the elemental assault, his concentration broken as superheated air made it impossible to maintain the complex magical working. The artifact's power faltered, releasing Elias from its influence just as a section of roof collapsed around the man's position and sent him scrambling away.

The operatives who had surrounded Alex were gone. But Elias' magic was still escalating, driven by fury that burned through his control. Fire spread to adjacent buildings while wind threatened to carry the destruction throughout the district.

"Elias, stop!" Alex ran toward his partner, recognizing forces that were becoming too large to contain.

He saw Elias standing in the loading dock, surrounded by a maelstrom of fire and wind that warped the air into a living storm around him. His eyes showed no recognition, only elemental fury directed at anyone who had threatened Alex.

"Look at me," Alex said, placing his hands on Elias' shoulders despite the dangerous energies. "Look at me, not them."

Green eyes focused on Alex's face, and the elemental assault faltered as conscious thought returned.

"I can't stop it," Elias said, his voice barely audible over rushing wind and crackling flames. "It's too strong."

"Yes, you can," Alex maintained contact while his own magic provided stability. "Guide it, redirect it, give it somewhere safe to go."

The process of controlling forces that had been unleashed without planning took nearly fifteen minutes. Together, they redirected wind patterns to prevent fire from spreading, while carefully venting superheated air to prevent explosive pressure buildup.

When it was over, the steel mill lay in ruins, a collapsed shell of twisted metal that still smoldered. The surrounding area looked like a war zone, with scorched concrete and shattered windows marking the extent of Elias' fury.

Edward's operatives had retreated, escaping the powerful display of violent elemental magic that none of them had likely ever witnessed.

Agent Eleanor Hartford and Agent Austin Ryan arrived at the edge of the destruction with a tactical team that had been racing toward the steel mill when the elemental assault began. They stared at the devastation with shock.

"Holy shit," Hartford said, stepping out of her SUV. "What the hell happened here?"

Ryan consulted his tablet, scrolling through readings from monitoring equipment that had detected the magical disturbance across the city. "Atmospheric pressure changes, thermal spikes, wind patterns that triggered weather alerts throughout the South Side. This wasn't normal magic."

Alex and Elias emerged from the wreckage, both covered in dust but unharmed. Hartford approached them, trying to understand the impossible scene.

"Are you injured?" she asked, noting how exhausted Elias looked while Alex stayed close.

"We're fine," Alex replied. "Edward's people set up an ambush. We defended ourselves."

"By creating what looks like a tornado?" Ryan studied readings that suggested magical output far beyond normal capabilities.

"What exactly did you two do here?"

Elias straightened despite his fatigue. "I used elemental magic to neutralize the threat."

Ryan studied the readings, his voice low. "These pressure

spikes and fire signatures don't come from secondary ability. This is specialist-level elemental control."

Alex stepped between Hartford and Elias. "Agent Sinclair used what was necessary to protect us. The situation required a proportional response."

"Proportional response is an understatement," Hartford said, studying Elias with obvious admiration.

Hartford exchanged glances with Ryan. "Agent Sinclair, this degree of elemental magic isn't listed in your personnel file. According to Bureau records, you're a memory magic specialist."

"I have some elemental abilities," Elias replied carefully. "I don't use them often."

"Why not?" Ryan asked. "Abilities like that would put you in the top tier of elemental specialists."

"No," Elias said. "I've always had the ability, but I don't usually access it. It's dangerous. When I was younger, I couldn't control it well. I learned to rely on memory magic instead."

Hartford glanced at the scorched ruins, then back at him. "But you controlled it today. You channeled enough force to bring down the mill without taking out the surrounding blocks."

"And a few buildings," Ryan muttered.

"Because Alex was there," Elias said simply. "His magic helps stabilize mine when things get intense."

Hartford and Ryan exchanged a confused look. They'd just witnessed a magical display they didn't see often, and it wasn't in either of the personnel files.

"We'll need detailed reports about this incident," Hartford said finally. "And Agent Sinclair, you'll need to undergo evaluation of your elemental capabilities. Power like this requires proper assessment."

"Fine," Elias replied.

As they coordinated with emergency services, Hartford

found herself reassessing both agents. They'd just demonstrated capabilities that exceeded their official classifications by considerable margins. She wondered just how far their abilities could go.

After the DMA agents left, Alex and Elias stood in the ruins of the steel mill. Smoke rose from the devastated area as fire crews worked to contain the remaining blazes.

"I may have gotten a little carried away," Elias said quietly.

"Yeah, you think?" Alex surveyed the destruction. "I appreciate you protecting me, but you always avoid using your elemental magic unless you really have to. I have to admit, this is a new level of power, even for you."

Elias met his eyes, exhaustion roughening his voice. "I could have killed you along with everyone else."

"But you didn't. When it mattered, you controlled it and redirected it safely." Alex placed a hand on his shoulder.

The drive back to FBI headquarters took place in relative silence, both agents processing what had occurred. The trap had been precise. Meant to catch them, and to measure what the artifact could do. But Elias' elemental power had turned the ambush into a failure.

"Good job back there," Alex said as they approached downtown Chicago. "You definitely sent them running."

"That artifact was starting to get to me. Another few seconds and I might have been shooting at you instead of them. I couldn't let that happen."

As they pulled into the FBI building's parking structure, Alex suddenly gave a quiet chuckle that grew into full laughter. The sound was unexpected after the tension of the morning, causing Elias to look at him with confusion.

"What's so funny?" Elias asked.

"I just remembered something," Alex said, still chuckling. "Do you remember that hostage scenario exercise at the academy? When you tried to use your elemental magic?"

Elias groaned. "Oh God. Please don't."

"You were supposed to create a minor distraction. Maybe a small wind to knock some papers around," Alex continued, grinning. "Instead, you generated a full thunderstorm complete with torrential rain and gale force winds."

"It got out of hand," Elias said defensively, but he was starting to smile despite himself.

"Out of hand? You soaked the entire training area and all the cadets. The exercise had to be canceled because nobody could see through the rain." Alex laughed harder. "And you were standing there in the middle of it, completely drenched, yelling at me 'I can fix this!' while making it worse."

"I did eventually stop it," Elias pointed out.

"After an hour, and only because I grabbed you and helped you focus," Alex replied. "That's when you swore off elemental magic, wasn't it?"

"That's when I realized I should stick to memory magic for anything that required precision," Elias admitted. "Nobody ever figured out it was me who caused the 'freak weather event.'"

"Lucky for you the instructors were baffled," Alex said. "They spent weeks trying to figure out how a thunderstorm could form and dissipate that quickly in a clear sky."

"And you never told anyone it was me."

"Of course not. Your secret was safe. But it's great to know you've got better control now," Alex said, his laughter fading into something more serious. "You saved both our lives back there."

"Just don't get used to it," Elias said. "I still prefer memory and basic defensive magic in most situations."

"Noted. But it's good to know you've got that in reserve if we need it."

Elias let the corner of his mouth twitch, the laughter gone almost as soon as it came. His thoughts drifted past the chaos of the day, past the weight of the case, to the first day at Quantico six years ago, and the moment he met Alexander Sutton. The slightly older trainee who would change everything.

13

Origins

FBI Academy, Quantico—Six Years Ago

The dorm room at Quantico was comfortable but sparse. Two beds sat against opposite walls, each with a desk and a closet. A single window looked out over the training grounds. Elias set his bag down at the foot of one bed and surveyed the space.

The door opened. A man stepped in, pulling a rolling suitcase and carrying a garment bag. He looked to be about six feet tall, just slightly taller than Elias, with a broader build. Where Elias was lean and athletic, this man had more muscle. He gave the room a quick once-over, then looked at Elias.

"Looks like we're roommates," he said.

"Elias Sinclair," Elias replied.

"I'm Alexander Sutton." He gave a quick nod. "Fair

warning, I talk in my sleep sometimes. If it bothers you, just throw something."

Elias let out a quiet breath that might have been a laugh. "I'll keep that in mind."

Alex started unpacking.

Elias opened his bag and began hanging clothes in the closet. The silence held for a minute, not strained, just practical. The rustle of fabric and the scrape of drawers filled the space.

When most of their things were in place, Alex leaned against his desk. "You're the youngest here by a mile, aren't you?"

Elias glanced over. "By several years. Most of them already worked field jobs or came out of law school."

Alex's mouth pulled into a quick grin. "Yet here you are."

"They wanted me for my memory magic," Elias said. "I can follow what people leave behind—echoes, residue, emotional traces. They pulled me in straight out of college."

Alex gave a small nod. "Not surprised. If they brought you in that young, you must be good at it."

Elias didn't answer.

"My speciality is combat magic," Alex went on. "Shields and kinetic strikes. I spent three years in the Army after college because of the Service Requirement. The Department of Defense gets first claim on combat-rated specialists."

"I obviously got tracked for law enforcement, which fortunately was the career I wanted anyway." For specialist magic users, careers were assigned by the government, not chosen by individuals.

Their eyes met across the room. Neither said anything more, but the recognition was clear enough. Alex straightened and pulled the last drawer shut. "I think we'll manage," he said.

Elias nodded once. "I think so too."

A knock sounded down the hall, followed by a voice

calling for the new trainees to assemble. Alex grabbed his jacket, stepped into the doorway, then glanced back. "You coming?"

Elias fell into step beside him. It was the first day at the Academy, and already he felt a little less alone.

Two days later their class met at the scenario training building. The instructors explained the exercise as if it were routine. One trainee would act as a subject moving through the mock offices. Two others would intercept before he reached the exit.

Pairs were called in turn. When Elias heard their names together, he wasn't surprised. They were roommates. The instructors probably thought it would be efficient to keep them that way.

"East entrance," the instructor said. "You have ten minutes."

Elias and Alex stepped inside. The fluorescent lights buzzed overhead, throwing pale light across the narrow hall. Desks and file cabinets lined the walls to make the space feel lived in.

The whistle blew.

Elias let his focus drop into the faint residue clinging to the corridor. The subject had passed minutes ago, but the trace of his movement still hung like a disturbed current in the air. Elias followed it left at the first junction.

Alex stayed with him, his presence steady at Elias' shoulder. When two "civilians" stepped from a doorway to block them, Alex lifted a hand. A ward shimmered into place, not flashy, just solid. It slid into Elias' awareness without pressing against it.

Elias felt the odd pull of it then. His tracing and Alex's defense didn't compete. They settled together as if they had been shaped for the same space. He had never felt that before.

The trail led them to the stairwell. The subject was halfway down when they caught him. Alex cut off his path with another ward, firm and unshaken. Elias followed the trace to its end and signaled the takedown.

"Four minutes," the instructor said, noting the time. "Clean."

They stepped aside for the next pair. Elias kept his eyes forward, but his thoughts stayed on the strange fit of their work. It had been seamless, as if each already knew where the other would move.

Back in the hall Alex gave him a sidelong look. "Not bad for our first run."

Elias nodded. "We didn't get in each other's way."

"That's a start," Alex said, his mouth lifting in a quick grin.

Elias didn't return the smile, but inside he felt a flicker of recognition. Something about their magic wanted to move together. He wasn't sure if that was chance or something rarer.

That night the dorm room was dark. Elias lay on his back staring at the ceiling, every muscle tense. Sleep would not come.

"My parents died in that bombing," he said into the quiet. His voice sounded strange, even to him. "I was ten. We were in the wrong place at the wrong time. I don't know how I survived. I woke up in the hospital, alone."

The room was still for a moment. Then Alex shifted on his bed. "That's rough man, I'm sorry."

Elias swallowed. "I don't normally share that with people."

"Thanks for telling me," Alex said. His voice was steady,

no trace of pity. "And I'll keep it to myself. If you ever want to talk about it, I'm here."

Elias turned his head toward him. He could make out the shape of Alex's face in the faint light from the window. Alex wasn't looking away.

"Thanks." Elias was quiet for a moment. "You ever wonder why you're here?" Elias asked.

"Sometimes," Alex admitted. "We're here because we can do things others can't. The Bureau couldn't pass that up."

Elias exhaled slowly. The tightness in his chest eased a fraction. "That's one way to look at it."

"Just because we're younger doesn't mean we don't deserve to be here," Alex said.

The room went quiet again. Elias closed his eyes, surprised to find sleep came easier than before.

Halfway through the Academy training, the scenarios had grown more complex. This one was staged in the outdoor yard, a hostage situation with trainees role-playing both suspects and civilians. The goal was to resolve it quickly and without harm.

Elias had intended to create only a small distraction. A shift of air, just enough to scatter the papers on a desk and pull attention away from the doorway. The control slipped before he realized it.

Wind rose sharp and sudden. Clouds pressed low, darker than they had any right to be. Then the rain came, sheets of it, blinding and relentless. Within seconds every trainee was soaked, the ground turning slick under their boots.

Instructors shouted for order, but the storm only built. Lightning cracked across the yard. Gale-force winds bent the training props until one toppled with a crash.

Elias stood in the center, rain streaming down his face,

fighting to rein it back. The harder he tried, the worse it became.

A hand clamped on his shoulder. Alex's voice cut through the roar. "Focus on me!"

Elias tried, but his grip kept slipping. Alex moved in front of him, eyes locked on his. "Stay with me. You can stop it."

Elias latched onto the steadiness in his voice, the unwavering presence in front of him. Slowly, painfully, the storm broke apart. The downpour eased to a drizzle. The wind dropped. After nearly an hour of chaos, the clouds finally scattered, leaving behind drenched trainees and waterlogged instructors.

The whistles blew at last, calling the scenario over. The yard looked like a floodplain.

Alex leaned against the wall under the overhang, water streaming from his hair. He let out a low laugh. "That was supposed to be a breeze, wasn't it?"

Elias forced a breath. "It got out of hand."

"You think?" Alex shook his head, still grinning. "You gave Quantico its own monsoon. You didn't mention you had elemental gifts that strong."

Elias winced. "I try not to use it. I'm not registered as an elementalist. I've always been scared of losing control, and that's exactly what happened. If they find out, they may hold me back until I've had training. The DMA is strict with unregistered magic."

Alex's grin faded. He lowered his voice. "Then don't let it happen again. And no one needs to know what you were trying to do. I'm not telling."

Elias searched his expression for judgment and found none. Only steady certainty.

"Why?" Elias asked.

"Because we all have secrets we'd rather keep hidden," Alex said simply. "Yours is safe with me."

◇✧◇

The cafeteria was crowded at midday, trays clattering, voices echoing against tile. Most trainees clustered at tables with their study groups, trading notes and complaints.

Elias set his tray down across from Alex. They had fallen into the habit of eating together without needing to say it.

A pair of women passed their table, both balancing trays. One wore her dark hair in a long braid, the other had it pulled back in a neat ponytail. They found seats a few tables away, laughter carrying with them.

Alex leaned forward slightly, voice pitched low. "Ponytail or braid?"

Elias followed his glance. He didn't usually comment, but the question drew an honest answer before he thought better of it. "Both."

Alex grinned. "Ambitious."

Elias felt heat rise in his face and shook his head. "I meant they're both attractive. That's all."

"Sure," Alex said, still grinning. He speared a piece of chicken with his fork. "So who's going to try first?"

Elias gave him a dry look. "You."

"What makes you think she'd even be interested in me?"

The question was delivered with mock seriousness that pulled a laugh out of Elias despite himself. Elias ignored the glances from the next table and focused on his food.

Alex smirked. "Fine. But if she laughs in my face, you're next."

That drew another short laugh from Elias. The ease between them settled deeper after that. They didn't talk constantly, but the rhythm was steady, built on small jokes and quick comments that helped get them through the long hours of training. Elias noticed it most when they were in scenarios. Alex knew where he would move before he made the choice, and Elias found himself adjusting instinctively to Alex's shifts.

It wasn't practiced. It was something else, something that fit too naturally to explain.

Graduation day came faster than Elias expected. The months had blurred into long lectures, drills, and late nights, the routine demanding enough that he hadn't noticed how quickly the end approached.

The ceremony itself was formal. Families filled the seats along the back wall, instructors lined the front. Trainees filed across the stage to collect their badges and shake hands. Elias felt the weight of the moment but little else. He had never cared for ceremony. What mattered was what came after.

The instructor pressed the badge wallet into Elias' left hand and shook his right. Then he handed him a sealed envelope. "You and Agent Sutton are posted to the Chicago Field Office. You will serve a probationary year under senior agents. If you perform as we expect, you'll be partnered permanently afterward."

Elias and Alex had both requested Chicago, and they had gotten it.

"Yes, sir," Elias said, smiling.

The instructor dismissed him, and as he stepped off the stage he glanced at Alex, who was behind him about to receive the same assignment.

In the reception hall after the ceremony, other trainees were surrounded by parents, spouses, and siblings. Voices rose with congratulations, laughter carried across the room. Elias stood apart, the envelope tucked under his arm, uncertain where to put himself.

"Elias." Alex's voice pulled him around. He was walking toward him with two people at his side. A tall man with the same brown hair and build. A woman with blue eyes and a smile.

"These are my parents," Alex said. "James and Colleen Sutton."

James offered a firm handshake. "Good to meet you. Alex has mentioned you several times."

Colleen stepped closer without hesitation. "So you're Elias. It's so nice to meet you."

Elias managed a small nod. "It's a pleasure to meet you, too."

"You don't have any family here do you?" she asked gently.

"No." The single word was easier than the truth.

Colleen's smile didn't falter. "Then you'll have to let us stand in for them. We're proud of both of you." She touched Alex's arm, then looked back at Elias. "You boys get a few days off before you're expected in Chicago. I insist you come home with Alex and spend a couple days with us in Annapolis."

Elias felt the answer catch in his throat. He settled for a quiet "Thank you."

Colleen gave his hand a squeeze before stepping back.

Alex glanced at him with a look that said nothing and everything. Elias returned it with the smallest nod. For the first time since he had arrived at the Academy, he felt the faint pull of belonging. He'd never had many friends, and now he had a new one—and a partner.

Present Day

Elias blinked, the memory slipping away, and Alex was still there beside him, no longer a trainee, but the same steady presence he had trusted from the beginning. That first bond had carried them further than he ever imagined. It was what Edward would try to twist next.

14
Edward's Choice

The hand that rocks the cradle is the hand that rules the world.
   —William Ross Wallace, "What Rules the World"
(1865)

Eighteen Years Ago

Edward Sinclair stood at the window of the cramped Whitechapel flat, watching rain streak down dirty glass. The television murmured in the background, BBC coverage of the "tragic terrorist attack" that had claimed dozens of lives including, according to official reports, Dr. Edward Sinclair and his wife Margaret. The dental X-rays had been convincing. Pierce's work was flawless.

On the scarred wooden table behind him lay a manila folder containing photographs and documentation that would never appear in any official investigation. Margaret's final moments, captured through surveillance that only Edward's network possessed. Her face, twisted with betrayal and horror, as she realized what her husband had become. What he had always been beneath the veneer of academic respectability.

Beside the folder rested a small case lined in black cloth. Inside, on a bed of padding worn from years of careful concealment, lay a gold disk covered in intricate Celtic knot-work. Its surface caught the weak daylight, sending muted glints of amber across the flat. Edward had acquired it years earlier through a private exchange with an archaeological contact who never fully understood what he had sold. The artifact had a faint hum at the edge of perception, an almost imperceptible weight in the air around it.

He felt its presence the way one senses a storm before it breaks. The artifact never spoke, yet it seemed to sharpen his thoughts and strip away hesitation. It reminded him of the clarity he had felt during his earliest academic breakthroughs.

He laughed softly. "They bind you with the Service Requirement and call it duty. Trained under their command, held in reserve like weapons on a shelf. That isn't equality—it's fear. They know we're superior and they cage us because of it. Rights and laws are constructs of the weak. Lions don't ask sheep for permission; they take their place."

"You're a monster," Margaret had said in that hotel room, moments before he ended her life. "Our son will be better off believing you're dead."

Edward felt nothing as he recalled her voice. No grief, no regret, no sense of loss. Margaret had been useful once, for research and for bearing his child, but her clinging to outdated moral frameworks had made her a liability. Killing her had been necessary for operational security.

The real question was what to do about Elias.

Edward consulted the file Pierce had compiled about his son's current status. Ten years old, survivor of a "terrorist attack," traumatized and confused, currently in the care of British social services while arrangements were made for repatriation to the United States. The boy would be sent to live with his maternal grandmother in Chicago, a woman whose declining health made her unsuitable for long term guardianship.

Edward opened a second folder containing assessments of Elias' developing magical abilities. The boy's memory magic already showed remarkable sophistication for his age. Early aptitude tests indicated he could grow into one of the most powerful specialists of his generation, perhaps even surpassing Edward himself. Useful. Potentially very useful.

He let his hand rest on the edge of the case containing the disk. The artifact's faint vibration was there as always, the same steady pulse that stripped emotion from his calculations.

But Elias was also ten years old, emotionally needy, and required the kind of daily care that would interfere with operational planning. Edward had twenty years of revolutionary development ahead of him. He could not waste time on child-rearing when civilization needed to be reordered under the dominion of magic users.

Edward pulled out a third folder, this one containing long term strategic projections. Eighteen years will secure the foundation. The artifact must be mastered, its power made obedient. Loyal operatives must be trained and placed where they cannot be removed. When the time comes, democracy will fracture under its own weakness, and magic will claim its rightful authority.

Nowhere in these timelines was there space for managing a traumatized child's emotional development.

But Elias' abilities represented a significant strategic asset. Memory magic at his level could be invaluable for intelligence gathering, psychological warfare, and eventual recruitment of other magic users. The boy's ancestry suggested he might develop even more sophisticated capabilities as he matured.

Edward considered the options with clinical detachment.

- Option one was to eliminate Elias and remove the potential liability while ensuring no future complications from family connections.

- Option two was to maintain minimal surveillance and allow others to raise the boy while monitoring his development remotely, recruiting him when his abilities reached operational usefulness.

- Option three was personal involvement, raising Elias directly, shaping his development to serve revolutionary purposes while managing the complications of active childrearing.

Edward dismissed option three immediately. He had neither the patience nor the interest in managing a child's daily needs. Emotional attachment would compromise operational effectiveness while providing no strategic advantages.

option one had merit. Elias represented a potential security risk if he ever developed suspicions about his father's death or began investigating the circumstances of the London bombing. But premature elimination would waste significant genetic potential.

option two offered the optimal balance between utility and convenience. Others would handle the emotional complications while Edward maintained strategic oversight of Elias' development. The boy could be recruited when his abilities reached maturity, providing maximum benefit with minimal personal investment.

Edward made his decision with the same clinical precision he brought to all strategic planning. The artifact's weight in the room steadied the choice.

He opened his laptop and drafted surveillance protocols for long-term monitoring of Subject E-7. Funds were allocated for periodic assessments of magical growth, academic progress, and psychological stability. Contact protocols would guarantee intelligence collection without risking Edward's operational security. The trust fund, masked as inheritance from his parents' deaths, ensured the boy would live in comfort, never questioning how carefully his life had been arranged.

When Elias reached sufficient maturity and capability, recruitment approaches could be implemented through carefully orchestrated circumstances that would seem natural rather than manipulative. The boy's career guidance, educational opportunities, and professional assignments could be influenced subtly to position him exactly where Edward needed him when his operations began.

Twenty minutes of typing completed the surveillance framework that would govern Elias' next eighteen years. Edward closed the laptop and glanced at the artifact before slipping it into a specially shielded pouch inside his coat.

By the time Edward's plane lifted off from Heathrow that night, Dr. Edward Sinclair would be officially dead while his operational planning entered its most critical phase.

Nearly twenty years of work lay ahead. When it was complete, magic users would govern humanity according to magical rule, rather than democratic chaos. Elias would play his assigned role in that transformation, whether he chose to cooperate or required more direct persuasion.

For now, let others raise his son. Let the boy develop his abilities through whatever educational opportunities mundane systems could provide. Let him form emotional attachments to inferior governmental structures and misguided moral frameworks.

All of it would serve Edward's purposes when the time came for recruitment.

Edward left the safe house without a backward glance, abandoning his son as easily as he had eliminated his wife. The artifact rested in the inner pocket of his coat, its steady pulse reinforcing the cold certainty of his choice. Sentiment was a weakness that superior minds could not afford. Revolutionary work required the kind of clarity that came from eliminating unnecessary emotional complications.

The revolution would succeed because Edward had the discipline to make necessary sacrifices. Even when those sacrifices involved walking away from his own child without experiencing so much as a moment's hesitation.

After all, civilization could only be remade under magical order. And those chosen to rule did not shackle themselves with attachments when history demanded sacrifice.

University of Chicago — Five Years Later

Edward reviewed the surveillance report with clinical satisfaction, the artifact resting on the table beside the papers like an unblinking observer. Subject E-7 was exceeding developmental projections in several key areas.

Edward made notes in the margin with precise handwriting.

Surveillance Report: Subject E-7

Developmental Overview: Subject continues to exceed projections in multiple domains. Memory magic ability measures at approximately twice peer baseline. Demonstrates natural aptitude for reading emotional residue and reconstructing events from minimal traces.

Below my own level, but still useful.

Emotional Vulnerabilities: Abandonment remains the

primary psychological lever. Subject shows minimal peer bonding and maintains distance from authority figures. Pattern indicates an unresolved need for belonging that remains unmet.

Subject demonstrates difficulty forming bonds, but once established, attachments are expected to be unusually intense. This dependency represents a predictable and exploitable condition.

Recommendation: Monitor carefully for the first instance of sustained attachment; such a relationship will likely become a critical leverage point.

Elemental Affinity: Appears to be strong, however, the subject demonstrates instinctive avoidance of wind, fire, and water manipulation despite measurable natural capacity. Assessment indicates psychological suppression rather than inability.

Irrelevant. Repressed power can always be forced out.

Recommendation: May require direct intervention to activate if deemed operationally necessary.

FBI Academy Quantico — Graduation Day

Subject E-7 graduation assessment:

Exceptional performance in magical applications, superior investigative methodology. Partnered with Alexander Sutton (combat magic specialist) for optimal capability complement. Recommend continued monitoring of partnership dynamics; first instance of sustained peer attachment observed.

Edward studied photographs from the FBI Academy graduation ceremony, watching his son receive awards for academic excellence and magical proficiency. Twenty-three years old, exactly where Edward needed him to be.

The partnership with Sutton was especially intriguing. For years Elias had kept his distance, avoiding lasting ties with either peers or mentors. Yet surveillance confirmed that Sutton was beginning to break through that barrier. From Academy roommates to potential partners, their trust was deepening rapidly. Sutton, an only child, had taken to Elias with the protectiveness of an older brother, while Elias responded with the loyalty of someone who had finally begun to find family.

Useful, but also problematic.

Edward's narcissistic nature appreciated having a son whose magical abilities reflected well on his genetic superiority. Elias was his creation, proof of his evolutionary advancement, a living extension of his legacy. But Sutton's influence was corrupting that natural hierarchy, giving Elias alternative sources of validation and belonging.

Still, the partnership served Edward's purposes for now. Sutton kept Elias functional and professionally effective, ensuring his continued development without requiring Edward's direct involvement. When recruitment time came, eliminating Sutton would be simple enough. The artifact's cool, steady presence assured him that such choices would never weigh on him.

Chicago FBI Division — Eighteen Months Ago

Edward examined the artifact within arm's reach on the desk, its quiet pull as familiar as his own breath. Years of careful preparation had created the perfect testing opportunity.

Operational objective: Test the artifact's magic amplification against Subject E-7's memory magic capabilities.

Secondary objective: Introduce controlled failure to existing partnership dynamic. Acceptable casualty threshold: Seven federal personnel.

The warehouse operation would serve multiple purposes. Edward needed to verify that the artifact's amplification magic could compromise Elias' abilities without permanent damage. More importantly, he wanted to fracture the partnership with Sutton, creating emotional vulnerability that would facilitate eventual recruitment.

Seven federal agents died during the warehouse incident. Acceptable losses for gathering crucial intelligence about his son's psychological resilience and magical limitations.

Edward noted with clinical interest how completely Elias blamed himself for the operational failure. The guilt and self-doubt were exactly what Edward had hoped to achieve. His son's magic had not actually failed. Edward's artifact had created a subtle memory interference that made accurate readings impossible. But Elias would never know that.

The partnership with Sutton survived the incident, unfortunately. Edward had hoped the catastrophic failure would destroy Sutton's trust in Elias' abilities. Instead, both agents had withdrawn from each other, creating distance but not genuine separation.

No matter. Edward was patient. The artifact's presence

reminded him that history favored those willing to wait. Other opportunities would arise.

Aurora Industrial Complex — Present Day

Edward stood over a spread of intelligence reports, maps, and magical resonance readouts, studying FBI response times, tactics, and vulnerabilities. Phase Two was accelerating beyond his original timeline, driven by opportunities that demanded immediate exploitation.

His son's recent partnership reconciliation with Sutton represented both a tactical challenge and a strategic opportunity. Their combined magic was stronger than Edward's projections had anticipated, requiring more sophisticated countermeasures. But their renewed emotional bond also created exploitable weaknesses.

"Dr. Pierce," Edward said without turning from his displays. "Initiate direct approach to FBI Chicago Division."

"Target specification?" Pierce asked, consulting tactical assessments on his tablet.

"Someone my son works with. An agent in the counterterrorism unit." Edward's voice was detached and uncaring. "I want to demonstrate to my son that his precious FBI can be compromised at will."

Pierce nodded, understanding the psychological warfare implications. "Artifact deployment?"

"Close proximity and extended duration. Let Elias watch someone he trusts lose control completely and turn on him. Let him understand that nowhere is safe from our capabilities."

Edward finally turned from his displays. "His faith in the Bureau needs to be shattered before recruitment can proceed."

Most importantly, it would demonstrate to his son that

emotional attachments were vulnerabilities that superior minds exploited without hesitation. The lesson would be painful but necessary.

Edward had spent eighteen years positioning Elias exactly where he needed him. Now it was time to begin active recruitment, starting with proof that everything his son believed in could be corrupted or destroyed at Edward's discretion.

After all, magical leadership required rational followers. And Elias would learn to be rational, whether he chose cooperation or required more direct persuasion.

The order went out within the hour. By tomorrow, someone in the FBI Chicago Division would become Edward's weapon.

Edward felt no concern for whoever would be selected for conversion. They were tools in service of his purpose, nothing more.

Just like everyone else in Elias' life.

15

The Night Is Falling Fast

The night is falling fast; within, the evening firelight fades
— A.E. Housman

December 7—FBI Chicago Division

The bullpen was winding down, but a few of the agents were still at their desks, papers stacked high and screens glowing in the fluorescent light. Marcus Cross looked up from his own half finished report, stretching the tension out of his shoulders. Across the aisle, Rivera was still working, her hair falling forward as she flipped through surveillance notes.

He smirked. She never quits.

"Careful," he called over, leaning back in his chair. "If you keep at it this late, Lindsey's gonna start charging rent for your desk."

Rivera didn't look up right away. When she did, it was with that sharp smile she used when she knew she had him. "That's rich, coming from you. You've been here just as long."

"Difference is," Marcus said, standing and wandering over

with his coffee mug in hand, "I was waiting for you to finish. Thought maybe I'd walk you out."

Her eyebrows lifted slightly. "Walk me out, huh? That supposed to be chivalry, or just an excuse to get me to your car first?"

"Little of both," Marcus said easily, leaning against the edge of her desk. "Besides, we've been eating Bureau cafeteria food for three weeks straight. I was thinking maybe something edible. Friday night? There's a place by the river. Good pasta, better wine. Less paperwork."

Rivera's lips curved, slow and amused. "You're asking me out while I'm still typing incident notes."

"Best time to catch you," he said. "When you're too focused to shoot me down."

She chuckled, shaking her head. "All right, Marcus. Friday. But if the pasta's bad, I'm telling everyone in the unit it was your idea."

"I'll take that risk." His grin was hard to hide, so he didn't bother.

Across the bullpen, Alex Sutton dropped a folder onto Elias Sinclair's desk a little louder than necessary. "Cross, you working your Bureau romance angle again?"

Marcus turned and caught both Alex and Elias watching. Alex had that half-grin of his, the one that made everything he said sound like a dare. Elias only arched an eyebrow, expression unreadable.

"Not an angle," Marcus said, lifting his chin. "Just good timing."

"Timing," Alex repeated, clearly amused. "Bold move."

Elias didn't comment, but Marcus thought he saw the faintest flicker of a smile before the memory specialist bent back over his file.

"Relax," Marcus said, waving a hand. "Some of us are allowed to have lives. Not all of us thrive on brooding in dark corners."

Alex snorted, but there was no heat in it. "Fair enough." He slid back into his chair, and Elias' eyes followed him, quiet but steady.

Marcus caught that look. The easy way they moved around each other now, the unconscious synchronization that had returned after eighteen months of careful distance. Rivera was still typing, pretending not to listen, but he saw her smile.

"Besides," Marcus added, grinning at Rivera, "some of us know how to ask someone out without making it a federal case."

"Subtle," Rivera said without looking up.

Alex laughed. "He's got a point. Remember when you spent three weeks analyzing optimal conversation timing before asking that prosecutor for coffee?"

Elias finally looked up from his file. "That was research. And it worked."

"After you'd mapped out her schedule, identified her preferred coffee shops, and practiced the conversation with your reflection," Alex said, clearly enjoying himself.

"Thorough preparation is not overthinking," Elias replied with dignity, but Marcus caught the way his mouth twitched.

"Right," Marcus said. "And I'm sure Rivera here appreciates the direct approach."

Rivera finally stopped typing, giving him that sharp look again. "I appreciate honesty. And decent pasta."

"Both of which I can provide," Marcus said.

The way Alex seemed more grounded when Elias was close by, the way Elias seemed more relaxed when Alex was within arm's reach. Whatever had gone down between them during their eighteen-month split (and Marcus had heard enough whispers to know it had been bad), they'd sorted it out. The whole unit felt more stable for it.

Alex had been different those months when they weren't working together. More solitary, keeping to himself between cases, working with methodical precision but without the easy confidence that made him such an effective agent. Marcus had partnered with him briefly during that time, and while Alex was always professional, always reliable, there had been something isolated about it. Like he was doing the work because it needed doing, not because he belonged there.

Now, watching them settle back into that natural rhythm, Marcus could see what the unit had lost when they'd split up. These two weren't just partners. They were the kind of team that made everyone around them better. They anticipated each other's moves, covered each other's weaknesses without thinking about it.

Truth was, Marcus admired them both. He'd seen Alex in the field during joint operations, that combat magic channeled with deadly precision when it mattered. And Elias. The man could walk into fractured memories and come back with answers that broke cases wide open. Together, they weren't just effective. They were the kind of partners who made you believe the impossible cases might actually be solvable.

Marcus was glad they'd found their way back to each other. The Bureau needed partnerships like theirs. Hell, the Chicago Division needed them, especially with Edward Sinclair's network still out there somewhere.

And selfishly, Marcus liked seeing his colleagues happy. Alex seemed lighter these days, more like the guy who'd graduated from the Academy with a reputation for both brilliance and reckless confidence. Elias had stopped looking like he was carrying the weight of the world alone.

It made the work feel more survivable somehow, seeing that even in this job, with its impossible hours and darker cases, some things could be repaired.

Later, as the bullpen emptied out, Marcus settled back at his own desk. He glanced at Rivera, still typing a final note with that sharp focus that had drawn him in from the start. He thought about Friday night and allowed himself a small smile.

He also glanced once more at Alex and Elias' corner, now empty but neat, chairs pushed in, side by side. It felt right seeing them back together. Solid.

Marcus picked up his pen, signed off the last page of his report, and closed the file. For the first time in weeks, he felt like maybe, just maybe, they would get through this chaos.

And he would be there with them.

16
Echoes of Control

The mind is its own place, and in itself can make a heaven of hell, a hell of heaven
— *John Milton, "Paradise Lost"*

They arrived without warning. Alex looked up to see Agent Hartford followed by Agent Ryan and a woman he immediately recognized as DMA Deputy Director Catrin Rowan.

Rowan was tall with auburn hair and sharp green eyes. Every step made it clear she was in charge, commanding the room. Her coat was dark and austere, as if chosen less for fashion than for the way it underscored her authority. Two DMA agents followed behind, one carrying a small metal case.

Alex's magic reacted the moment the case entered the room. Silver energy stirred around his hands, his combat magic responding to a threat that he couldn't define. Across the room, Elias straightened at his desk, green eyes locking on the case in recognition.

"Agents Sutton and Sinclair," Hartford said as they

reached them. "Director Rowan would like to speak with you immediately."

The case gave off a muted hum of suppressed energy, the lead lining enough to dull its resonance but not conceal it completely. Alex exchanged a glance with Elias, both recognizing the signature of ancient magic.

"SCIF briefing," Hartford added, gesturing toward the secure wing. "ASAC Lindsey is expecting us."

Rivera and Cross joined them in the corridor, both noting how the metal case drew the attention of every magic user they passed. Conversations stopped mid-sentence, the normal rhythm of the FBI division disrupted as if the air itself had shifted. Agents leaned back from doorways. Others closed their files and moved aside without being asked. Even non-magical personnel, people with no reason to notice subtle resonance, shifted uneasily as the case went by, instincts saying something was very wrong.

Lindsey waited in SCIF 3A, the secure conference room already prepared with layered privacy wards that shimmered faintly against the walls. Those protections were strong enough to block electronic surveillance and magical observation alike. As the group filed inside, Lindsey raised her hand and activated additional seals, each one locking into place with an audible click. The wards wrapped around the room like iron, cutting them off from the rest of the building.

Director Catrin Rowan stepped forward and set the case on the conference table with deliberate care, as though its weight was more than physical. Hartford and Ryan positioned themselves at opposite ends of the room, silent sentries with eyes on everyone present. Cross and Rivera took seats along the wall, both tense, their expressions showing the unease of agents who could feel history pressing into the room.

"I decided to bring this to you rather than continue theoretical discussions about what we're facing," Rowan said evenly. "You need to understand the scope of what Edward Sinclair can do."

She gestured toward the metal case. "What you're about to see is not one of the seven artifacts stolen from Aberdeen. This is an artifact the Department of Magical Affairs has safeguarded in a classified vault for over a century. Very few people even know it exists. It was recovered in Wales during an archaeological dig, part of a site that predates Roman occupation, and it has been kept under maximum security since the day it was unearthed."

Elias leaned forward slightly, attention fixed on the case. Alex saw green light begin to move around his partner, energy responding to whatever was hidden within the lead-lined container.

"The artifact is over two thousand years old," Rowan continued. "Celtic in origin, crafted by Druidic practitioners to turn individual magic users into weapons during their wars against Roman invaders. We believe they were capable of amplifying a person's natural abilities to devastating effect."

Pressure built in Alex's chest, his combat magic tightening. Silver light edged his fingers, not flaring outright but coiling close, restless in the presence of whatever lay inside the case. Across the table, Elias was already locked on the case, green light gathering at the edges of his vision.

"I didn't bring it here to rehash research," Rowan said. "I brought it so you would feel what Edward has in his possession and understand why he's so dangerous."

The locking mechanism released with a soft click. Inside, nestled in protective foam, lay a gold disc covered in intricate Celtic knotwork. The moment it was exposed to air, the energy in the room shifted, heavy and invasive. Even Cross, who had no magic of his own, pushed his chair back as if distance alone could mute the pressure.

Elias remained motionless, eyes fixed on the disc with fascination rather than revulsion. Green energy flowed around him, his magic answered the artifact's call. His magic reached for the ancient disc, drawn to secrets too terrible to resist.

He looked up at Alex without speaking. Alex moved to stand beside him, placing a hand on his shoulder and letting his own magic rise in a quiet, grounding presence between Elias and the artifact.

"Agent Sinclair?" Rowan said quietly, noting his reaction with a quick glance at Hartford before turning back. But Elias' memory magic was already weaving through the air around the disc, seeking connections to the visions that had haunted him since the crime scenes.

The conference room faded as ancient memories awakened. Stone circles materialized in misty landscapes, massive blocks aligned with precision, radiating a purpose darker than ceremony. Druids moved between the stones with robes that swept the ground, faces hidden, intent fixed on the figures positioned at the circle's center. Men and women stood with blank expressions. Their consciousness had been overridden by power channeled through artifacts identical to the one before him. They were not willing participants. They were weapons, their abilities amplified and directed against enemies who had no defense against assault by their own people.

The vision deepened, showing battles where Celtic warriors wielded impossible power, Roman legions falling not to conventional weapons but to magic that turned their own auxiliary forces against them. The artifacts did not just amplify power. They corrupted it, twisting natural abilities into weapons of fear and control.

"Agent Sinclair," Rowan's voice sounded like it came from far away. "What do you see?"

Elias looked up from the artifact, green eyes bright with memory magic. For a moment, he remained silent, unsure of what to say.

Alex's hand stayed on his shoulder. "Elias, show us what you're seeing."

The request broke the trance. Elias blinked, then nodded, shifting from receiving visions to projecting them.

Green energy surged through the conference room as he wove a construct more vivid than anything he had ever created.

The SCIF walls disappeared, replaced by ancient landscapes that felt more real than the building around them. Stone circles rose from misty ground, their blocks arranged with precise intent. Druids moved between the stones, faces hidden by deep hoods, attention fixed on the people at the circle's center.

Rivera gasped. Cross gripped his chair. Hartford and Ryan stared at the scene materializing around them. Even Lindsey, who had seen decades of magical investigation, sat transfixed by the construct's detail.

Alex's breath caught as the construct showed warfare on a scale beyond anything they'd seen. Celtic warriors wielded power that defied natural law, their abilities amplified by artifacts that twisted individuals into weapons, devastating entire armies. The cost was visible in the blank expressions of those pressed into service, their consciousness overridden by magic that left them aware but powerless.

The vision lasted only a couple of minutes before Elias pulled it back, the landscape dissolving into the conference room. But the weight of what they had witnessed remained.

"Holy shit," Rivera whispered.

"I have never seen anything like that," Cross said, his voice shaking.

Rowan studied Elias. "Agent Sinclair, we didn't realize you had this level of ability."

Her tone stayed level, but Alex saw calculation flicker in her eyes.

"What else can you tell us about the artifact?"

Elias looked down at the disc, then back at her. "The

Druids didn't only use it on enemies. They used it on their own people to control them."

"Their own people?" Hartford asked.

Elias nodded. "This artifact is more powerful than you realize."

"How much more powerful?" Lindsey asked.

Elias met her eyes. "You have no idea what my father has awakened."

The room went still. Unease tightened across every face. The sensation of contained energy had everyone entranced.

Rowan closed the case, the weight of what they had witnessed settling over the secure room. She cleared her throat. "We'll continue this discussion later."

The meeting broke up, people filing out past layers of security. Alex stayed close to Elias as they walked the corridor toward a smaller conference room reserved for interagency briefings. The space was still on a secure floor but lacked heavy SCIF restrictions, making it easier to coordinate with DMA field teams cycling in and out.

Inside, Cross had already set up on one side of the table with Hartford and Ryan. Laptops and field reports covered the surface. The shift in atmosphere was immediate, from Rowan's guarded presentation to the practical, detail-driven rhythm of operational planning.

Cross tapped a folder. "We've got patterns showing coordinated movements in at least four cities. Supplies, personnel, and magical equipment are being shifted to unknown staging points."

DMA surveillance data scrolled across the screen behind him. "They've gone dark in every city we've been monitoring. No chatter, no movement. It's as if they've shut down every visible operation at once."

Elias scanned the reports. "Because they did. He knows we're closing in. The question is whether we can get to him before whatever he's planning launches."

A knock sounded at the door. A man in a building services uniform stepped inside, an ID badge clipped to his chest and a tablet in hand. Average build, neutral expression—the kind of person who could pass unnoticed in a government building.

"Excuse me," the man said. "I'm from IT support. We need to update the network hardware in this room. It should only take a few minutes."

Cross frowned. "I didn't hear about any network work orders in this wing."

"Emergency security patch," the technician replied, tilting the tablet to show a digital work order with federal seals. "Came down from D.C. this morning. It applies to all classified facilities."

Alex studied the credentials. They looked real. The seals were correct. The name matched the badge.

"Go ahead," Cross said finally. "We can probably move to Lindsey's office for now."

They began gathering their files, moving toward the door. That was when Elias felt it—a trace of hostile magic in the air, subtle but familiar.

"Cross, wait," he said sharply. "Something's wrong."

Confusion flickered across Marcus's face, his mouth starting to form a question. Then his expression went blank. His eyes lost focus, as if something had been pulled away. When he looked back up, his voice was flat, not his own.

"Alex, you're working with them. I know what you've been doing—the contacts, the classified information you've been passing. I can't let you hurt anyone else."

His hand moved toward his weapon.

"Marcus?" Alex said carefully.

Cross drew, aiming at Alex's chest with smooth precision born from years of training.

"Put the gun down," Alex said, hands raised but silver light already building around his fingers. "You're being controlled. This isn't you."

"You're lying to me, Alex," Cross replied, finger twitching on the trigger. "I've seen the evidence. The meetings, the money transfers. You're selling us out."

Elias stepped between them, his memory magic reaching for the distorted traces laced through Cross's mind. "I can feel the artifact's influence," he said evenly. "His perceptions are being rewritten."

You're trying to get in my head. I won't let you.' Cross' finger tightened on the trigger. The first shot came without warning.

Alex's magic flared, deflecting the bullet into the wall. His barrier enclosed both himself and Elias as Cross adjusted position.

"The IT technician!" Elias shouted. "We have to find him."

Cross's eyes stayed on Alex. "That's exactly what a terrorist would say. Use magic to confuse federal agents."

The second shot shattered the conference room glass. Shouts came from the main office as agents moved in response to gunfire.

DMA Agent Ryan appeared in the doorway, weapon drawn. "Agent Cross, drop your weapon immediately."

"Federal agents compromised," Cross said, turning toward Ryan. "Request immediate backup. We've got terrorists in the building."

Elias scanned for the IT tech, but he was gone, his equipment still connected to the network panel.

"Ryan, don't shoot," Elias called. "He's being controlled. If I can trace the artifact's resonance, I can break the connection."

"He fired on you," Ryan replied.

"Give me thirty seconds," Elias said, still working to trace the signal.

Cross turned back toward Elias. "I can see what you are," he said, voice cold. "The evidence is right there."

He fired again. Alex's magic deflected the round, but Cross was already shifting for a clear angle.

A gunshot cracked through the room. Cross jerked as Ryan's round hit center mass, dropping instantly, his weapon clattering across the floor.

Silence followed. Alex stood frozen, staring at his fallen colleague. Elias' hand hovered where he'd been reaching for Cross's mind. Ryan kept his weapon up, scanning for threats.

"The IT guy," Alex said finally. "Where did he go?"

Ryan moved to the network panel. "He left everything running."

"Three weeks inside the building," someone said from the hall. "Same credentials, same work orders."

"He's been gathering intel on all of us," Alex said.

Through the shattered glass, people were already gathering on the street. Sirens wailed.

"North stairwell," Ryan reported. "Thirty seconds ago. On foot, heading toward the river."

Alex looked at Elias. "We have to go. Now."

They ran.

The north stairwell was empty when they reached it, emergency lighting throwing harsh shadows across bare concrete. Alex took the stairs three at a time, Elias close behind, both running on adrenaline after watching Cross die.

"Which way?" Elias asked as they burst through the exit.

Alex scanned the sidewalk. Office workers streamed past, coffee in hand, oblivious to the fact that a terrorist had just slipped out of the federal building.

"There," Elias said, pointing. A man in a building services uniform walked calmly toward Wacker Drive. Not running. Not panicked. Every step deliberate, the kind of movement that comes with a planned extraction.

They trailed him through the crowd, weaving between pedestrians. The man checked his phone once, then kept moving without hurry.

"He's heading for the river," Alex said.

They quickened their pace, cutting through the morning foot traffic.

The man turned down a dock where two figures waited beside high-performance motorcycles.

"Damn motorcycles," Alex muttered.

Instead of leaving, the newcomers reached into their jackets and drew pistols.

"They're not running," Elias said. "They're covering his escape."

Gunfire cracked across the dock. Bullets sparked off steel rails and shattered windows, sending civilians screaming for cover.

Alex's magic surged. Silver barriers flared, catching the first burst as he returned fire with concussive blasts that shook the dock. The operatives had come prepared, their counter-wards slamming into his defenses and forcing both sides into cover.

"Get people clear!" Elias called, pushing civilians back as gunfire stitched across the waterfront.

The motorcycle team moved with precision, laying down fire while their target sprinted to the end of the dock.

Alex blasted one rider off balance, but the second vaulted onto his bike and opened fire again, muzzle flash lighting the morning haze.

"Boat!" Elias shouted. A speedboat nosed up to the dock. The target leapt aboard as the last rider covered him with suppressive fire.

Alex hurled another blast, but the boat peeled away fast, engines screaming as it tore downriver. A moment later, the remaining motorcycles shot into traffic and were gone.

Silence followed, broken only by sirens and the cries of civilians crouched behind overturned benches.

"Casualties?" Alex asked, pulling Elias up from behind a shattered barricade.

"Three CPD officers were hit, multiple civilians shaken, but no fatalities." Elias scanned the wreckage. "Property damage is heavy."

The dock looked like a war zone. Shattered glass, bullet holes, and emergency crews rushing in made the message clear. Edward's network could infiltrate, kill, and still walk away.

On their way to Lindsey's office, Alex and Elias passed the conference room where Marcus had been shot. The blinds weren't drawn, and a dark stain marked the carpet. Neither of them spoke. A moment later they stepped into Lindsey's office, where she and DMA Agent Ryan were waiting for the debrief.

"The contractor had been working here three weeks," Lindsey said. "Perfect credentials. Real work orders, every protocol followed."

Ryan stood near the windows. "The credentials were forged, but the work orders were real. Someone inside the system is feeding them assignments."

"Which means clearances and schedules could be compromised," Lindsey said.

Elias stared at the reports. Cross's death pressed heavy on his chest. The man deserved better than to be twisted into a weapon.

"Someone with memory magic was channeling through the artifact," Elias said. "That's how they controlled him. They made him believe Alex was a terrorist."

"Could you have saved him?" Lindsey asked.

"Maybe—if I'd had time to trace the connection."

"He fired on you," Ryan said quietly. "Standard procedure is to stop the shooter."

"He was being controlled," Elias snapped. "Killing him is exactly what Edward wanted. One less agent, and more damage to morale."

"Ryan made the right call," Alex said. "Cross was about to kill you. If Ryan hadn't fired, I would have."

Elias looked at him. "You would have shot him?"

"To save your life? Yes. And you'd do the same for me."

Lindsey studied them both. "Edward's escalating. He's moving from manipulation to open assaults."

"Which means we're close to his real objective," Alex said.

"I can pull you from the case," Lindsey offered.

"No," Elias said instantly. "This is personal. He killed Cross. I'm not walking away."

Alex met Elias' eyes. "We're not stepping back. Not now."

Elias' Apartment — 8:30 PM

The apartment was quiet when they got back. Elias set two beers on the table and slid one across to Alex.

"To Marcus," he said.

Alex raised his bottle. "To Marcus." They drank in silence.

For a while neither of them spoke. The city noise outside was faint and muffled through the glass.

"He was a good agent," Elias said at last. "Didn't deserve to go out like that."

"No," Alex agreed. "He didn't."

They sat with the fact that a man they'd worked with wasn't coming back.

After a while, Elias leaned forward. "Tomorrow we go after my father."

Alex nodded. "Then let's finish this."

They sat a little longer, the beer going warm in their hands, the silence saying more than either of them could.

17

Fault Lines

A great civilization is not conquered from without until it has destroyed itself from within.
—Will Durant, "The Story of Civilization, Vol. III: Caesar and Christ"

December 9

The call came through while Alex was reviewing overnight intelligence reports. Director Rowan's voice left no room for argument.

"Agent Sutton, Agent Sinclair. SCIF 3A. One hour."

The line went dead.

Alex looked across the bullpen where Elias sat at his desk, working through witness statements from the warehouse attack. His partner looked up at the same moment, recognition passing between them.

"Both of us?" Elias asked.

"Both of us." Alex gathered his files. "Hartford and Ryan will be there too."

Rivera approached their desks, coffee in hand. "Everything okay? You both look worried."

"DMA wants another briefing," Alex said. "Probably about the artifact analysis."

"Or about yesterday's elemental display," Elias added quietly. "Hard to keep that kind of thing quiet."

The hour passed slowly. At 8:25, they walked toward the secure wing in silence.

SCIF 3A

Director Rowan waited inside with Agents Hartford and Ryan. Her expression was serious, edged with concern. The secure room felt smaller with all five of them present.

"Agents Sutton, Sinclair. Please, sit."

Alex and Elias took chairs across from the DMA officials, both noting the way Hartford consulted her tablet with unusual intensity while Ryan positioned himself near the door.

"This meeting is classified beyond your current clearance levels," Rowan began. "What we discuss here cannot be shared with your local colleagues or supervisors."

She activated privacy wards that made the air shimmer briefly around them. "Agent Sinclair, your recent magical displays have raised significant concerns."

Elias straightened slightly. "Ma'am?"

"The memory construct you created during the artifact demonstration exceeded anything in Bureau records. Witnesses described experiencing shared hallucinations so vivid they doubted their own perception of reality." Rowan's tone remained professional. "That level of cognitive manipulation requires capabilities we didn't know you possessed."

"It was a standard memory projection," Elias replied carefully.

"Standard projections don't allow non-magical personnel to experience sensory detail to that degree," Agent Ryan said. "What you created affected everyone in that room, regardless of their magical abilities."

Hartford tapped her tablet, displays showing technical readings. "And yesterday's elemental work, Agent Sinclair, you redirected weather patterns across a significant area. That requires magic at a level exceeding anything in your personnel file, by a considerable margin. The registration system exists for reason, Agent Sinclair. To track abilities before they become a liability."

Alex watched the exchange, recognizing genuine concern in the DMA officials' voices.

"The warehouse destruction shows sustained elemental manipulation that lasted fifteen minutes," Hartford continued. "Wind pressure, thermal shifts, atmospheric disturbances. These aren't secondary abilities, Agent Sinclair. This is specialist-level elemental magic."

"We need to understand the full extent of your capabilities," Rowan said. "More importantly, we need to understand your connection to the artifacts we're investigating."

"What kind of connection?" Elias asked.

"The kind that allows you to access ancient magical signatures with remarkable precision," Hartford replied. "The kind that suggests either exceptional natural ability or previous exposure to similar magical systems."

The room fell silent for a moment. Alex felt tension building as he processed the implications of what the DMA officials were suggesting.

Rowan leaned forward. "We need to discuss the operational implications of Agent Sinclair's capabilities and his connection to these artifacts."

The privacy wards intensified around them.

◇✦◇

Three hours later, Alex and Elias emerged from the secure wing together, both looking subdued as they returned to the bullpen. Rivera glanced up from her desk, noting the strain written across their faces.

"How'd it go?" she asked.

Elias dropped into his chair, staring at his computer screen as if it might give him answers. "They want me reclassified."

"Reclassified how?"

"Elemental specialist was added to my registration file," Elias said, his voice low.

"Quarterly psych evals. They're recommending restricted access to certain evidence. They think my connection to the artifacts makes me unstable."

Rivera blinked. "Unstable? That's ridiculous. You're the reason we even understand half of what we're dealing with."

"They see it differently," Elias said, finally glancing up. "When I come near the artifact, I connect with it. They assume it means that it's influencing me. Instead of thinking that it's just my level of skill."

Alex's crossed his arms. "That's bullshit. Your abilities are the reason we're even this far ahead of Edward."

Before Elias could reply, Lindsey appeared at their desks, sharp eyes flicking between the three of them. "My office. Now."

They followed her across the room, Alex noting the way other agents looked up from their work, curiosity mixed with unease. Extended DMA meetings never ended quietly.

Inside, Lindsey shut the door and activated layered wards that shimmered faintly over the walls. "All right. Tell me exactly what happened in there."

Elias met her gaze. "The DMA thinks I'm compromised," Elias repeated when Lindsey pressed him. "Their proposal is constant monitoring and restricted access.

Lindsey folded her arms. "And what proof are they offering for that conclusion?"

"Based on my magical abilities exceeding their expectations, and my connection to the artifacts being too precise for what they consider normal memory work." Elias' voice grew quieter. "They think repeated exposure might already be affecting my judgment."

Lindsey studied him carefully. "And what do you think?"

Elias hesitated, then said, "I think they could be right."

The admission caught Rivera off guard. She'd expected him to push back, not agree. "You really believe you're compromised?"

"I think the visions I've been having feel too real. The way the ancient magic reacts to me, how easily I can slip into those memories. It doesn't feel like ordinary memory magic anymore."

Alex leaned forward. "So what if your abilities are stronger than they expected? That makes you more valuable, not more dangerous."

"Or it makes me the perfect target if Edward's network was built to manipulate investigators like me," Elias replied. "If artifact exposure is bending my perception without me realizing it, then leaving me on this case risks all of us."

Lindsey's mouth tightened. "What are they recommending?"

"Stay partnered with Alex, but restrict my role in artifact analysis. They want someone else taking point on magical contact with Edward's network."

"This is ridiculous," Rivera protested. "They can't do this."

"My memory magic might also be what's affecting it," Elias said quietly.

Before anyone could answer, emergency alerts flared through the building. Sirens blared overhead, and the hallway filled with hurried footsteps. Agent Martinez appeared in the doorway, urgency written across his face.

"Multiple incidents across the city," he said. "Coordinated attacks. We need everyone."

Downtown Chicago—12:30 PM

The afternoon crowd along Michigan Avenue moved in a steady winter rhythm, shoppers and commuters wrapped in coats against the lake wind. Then the streetlight at the intersection of Monroe turned green, and the world shifted.

Every registered magic user in the intersection—six in total, from a teen delivery cyclist to a middle-aged woman carrying dry cleaning—stopped mid-step. Their eyes lost focus.

The first wave hit without warning. A wall of wind howled between the skyscrapers, ripping shopping bags from hands and shoving pedestrians into parked cars. Traffic lights exploded in showers of glass. The delivery bike folded like paper under an unseen force, skidding across asphalt as its rider stood frozen, arms rigid.

Panic erupted. Mundane bystanders screamed, scrambling for cover as gusts lifted trash cans into the air and sent metal newspaper racks tumbling down the block. Magic users who hadn't frozen tried to shield civilians, but each spell twisted in their grasp. Healing spells ignited into fire, shields fractured into razor ice that sliced through bus stop shelters.

Elias felt it from three blocks away, the artifact's cold pulse threading through minds, bending intentions into chaos. "Someone is testing control range," he muttered, pushing past fleeing pedestrians with Alex on his heels.

By the time they reached the intersection, CPD had cordoned off the street. The targeted magic users collapsed all at once, as if someone had cut their strings. No one was dead, but broken glass and overturned cars turned the block into a scene from a riot.

Phones were already out, livestreams spreading across platforms. By evening, the footage would loop on every news channel. Proof to anyone watching that magic could turn a busy street into a war zone without spilling a drop of blood.

Grant Park—3:15 PM

The second attack came during the winter festival in Grant Park, where families crowded between holiday displays, food stalls, and the ice rink.

It began when three registered magic users scattered through the park froze mid-motion. A street performer's levitating snowflakes twisted into glittering shards of ice, then shot outward in a spinning cloud that shattered against food stalls and benches. On the rink, a water shaper forced the frozen surface into sudden ridges and fissures, sending skaters sprawling. At the north end, a wind artist's gentle currents turned violent, overturning vendor tents and sending hot drink stands crashing into the crowd.

The magic was precise, designed to maximize panic without leaving bodies behind. Parents dragged screaming children behind barricades as debris skidded across the paths. Festival music cut off under the rising noise of shouts and splintering wood.

Park security moved quickly, but the three magic users fought with a focus and coordination that was not their own. Every attempt to restrain one left another free to unleash another burst of magic, forcing officers to fall back and regroup.

Then, as abruptly as it started, the control ended. The wind dropped. Ice ridges collapsed back into the rink. The three stood blinking in confusion, with no memory of what they had done.

Eight people were treated for cuts, bruises, and sprains. No one was killed. But footage of spinning ice shards over children's heads and tents collapsing onto stroller lines spread online within minutes, the kind of images that outlasted the panic itself. By evening, talk shows and street interviews repeated the same refrain. If magic could be turned like that, no one was safe.

◇◇◇

FBI Chicago Division—6:00 PM

"Systematic escalation," Lindsey said during the emergency briefing, crime scene photos and casualty reports spread across the conference table. "Edward's network is moving beyond individual targets into mass casualty events."

Rivera scanned preliminary reports from both sites. "They're not testing our response anymore. They're showing that magical terrorism can overwhelm emergency services faster than we can contain it."

"And feeding public fear that will push political over-reach," Alex added, seeing patterns of planning rather than random violence.

Elias stayed quiet at first, his expression troubled as he processed intelligence that painted Edward's network as more deliberate and more dangerous than they had realized.

"The psychological manipulation in Grant Park," he said at last. "It wasn't random. The targets were chosen to maximize emotional damage."

"How so?" Lindsey asked.

"Parents turning on each other while children watched. Security officers attacking the families they were supposed to protect." Elias' voice was flat. "It was designed for cruelty. Trauma that lingers."

"Which drives demand for tighter restrictions on magical civil liberties," Rivera said.

"And positions Edward's network as the alternative to democratic failure," Alex finished.

The briefing ran for another hour, tactical updates filling the silence. But Alex kept glancing at Elias, who retreated further into himself with each new detail about Edward's capabilities.

◇✧◇

Michigan Avenue—8:30 PM

The protests began that evening, crowds gathering throughout downtown Chicago as news of the attacks spread. Instead of unified outrage against terrorism, the demonstrations revealed deep divisions over how magical abilities should be regulated.

Outside the federal building, magical rights activists demanded protection from government overreach while non-magical protesters called for immediate restrictions on anyone with supernatural abilities. The two groups faced each other across police barriers, their chants clashing in words that reflected the tensions Edward's attacks were meant to inflame.

"Magical registration now!" shouted voices from one side.

"Civil rights for all!" came the response from the other.

Alex and Elias watched from Lindsey's office windows as Chicago police struggled to hold the line between increasingly hostile crowds. The protests were still peaceful, but the emotional charge suggested violence could erupt with only the smallest spark.

"This is what Edward wanted," Elias said quietly, studying the crowd. "Turn ordinary citizens against each other while positioning his network as the rational alternative."

"Creating conditions where people will accept authoritarian governance rather than chaos," Alex agreed.

Lindsey's attention was already elsewhere. "I just got off a call with Washington. Congress is scheduling emergency hearings on magical oversight. The President is considering executive action on registration requirements."

"How extensive?" Rivera asked.

"Real time monitoring, restricted movement, mandatory

reporting of magical activities." Lindsey's expression was grim. "Basically treating every magical citizen as a suspect."

Outside, the protests grew louder. More police arrived. Emergency barriers went up. News crews angled for the best shot of whatever violence might erupt.

"Edward's network doesn't need to conquer America," Elias observed. His voice carried a trace of admiration. "They only need to make democracy unravel through fear and overreach."

Alex glanced at his partner, unsettled by the tone. "You sound like you think he's brilliant."

"I think he understands human psychology better than anyone gives him credit for," Elias replied quickly. "Look at what he's done with minimal resources. He's made an entire country question whether magical citizens can be trusted."

The accuracy of the observation was undeniable, but Alex heard something else beneath it. Less professional analysis and more personal sympathy.

December 10—Early Morning

The call came early. Director Rowan had ordered new protocols without room for debate.

"Enhanced monitoring for Agent Sinclair is now in effect. Agent Sutton, you will maintain partnership status but with modified responsibilities regarding artifact analysis."

Lindsey relayed the decision to Alex and Elias, both of whom had been expecting it after the chaos in Chicago. The coordinated attacks and the footage spreading through every news outlet had given Washington all the justification it needed to turn earlier recommendations into hard orders.

"They are restricting your access to artifact evidence," she told Elias. "No direct contact with Edward's magical signatures. No independent analysis."

"What about field work?" Elias asked.

"You continue with Alex, but DMA oversight will be present whenever artifact magic is involved." Lindsey's voice made clear what she thought of the order. "They want specialists handling anything that might be influenced by unconscious exposure."

Alex kept his anger in check but not hidden. "This is insane. He is our best investigator."

"He is also potentially compromised," Lindsey replied. "The DMA thinks his connection to the ancient magic is affecting his judgment."

"My judgment is fine," Elias said quietly.

"Is it?" Lindsey asked. "Yesterday you sounded almost impressed by Edward's tactics. Like you were sympathizing with him."

The words lingered. Elias did not deny them right away, which made his response sound defensive.

"I can recognize sophisticated strategy without endorsing terrorism," he said.

"Can you?" Lindsey's tone was calm but edged with concern. "Because the way you describe Edward's network does not sound like simple analysis."

Alex wanted to push back, but he had noticed the same thing. Elias' insights were starting to carry undertones of admiration.

"What do you think?" Lindsey asked Elias directly. "Do you think Edward's methods are justified?"

Elias hesitated, his expression thoughtful. "I think he has identified real problems with how magical citizens are treated. The fear, the discrimination, the assumption that abilities make someone dangerous."

"That does not justify terrorism," Alex said.

"No, it doesn't," Elias agreed. "But it explains why people follow him. Why some magic users might listen when he talks about rational governance."

Lindsey and Alex exchanged glances. Sympathy for Edward's message was exactly what the DMA feared.

"You are on modified duties," Lindsey said. "You are not suspended, but artifact analysis goes through DMA specialists. No independent investigation."

"And if those restrictions make us less effective?" Elias asked.

"Then we adapt," Lindsey replied. "The DMA has authority over anyone whose abilities might be compromised. That includes you."

Elias nodded slowly, resignation settling over him. "I understand."

Chicago Streets—December 10, 6:00 PM

The protests had spread throughout the city by the second day, demonstrations in every major neighborhood as Chicago's population divided along the lines Edward's psychological warfare had been designed to create. Magical citizens demanded protection from government overreach while non-magical residents called for immediate restrictions on super-natural abilities.

Alex and Elias drove through streets where peaceful demonstrations teetered on violent confrontation, noting the way ordinary neighborhoods had become battlegrounds for fundamental questions about civil liberties and public safety.

"Look at what he has set in motion," Elias said, watching the protesters shout at each other.

"Two attacks and he's forced an entire city to question whether magical integration can survive."

"He's made them afraid," Alex replied, keeping his voice steady while studying his partner's expression.

"Fear and rational concern are not always different," Elias

said quietly. "Some of these non-magical protesters have reasons to be uneasy about people like us."

Alex felt genuine alarm. "People like us?"

"People with abilities that can override human consciousness, manipulate reality, influence behavior without consent." Elias' tone was calm, almost reflective. "If I can make an entire room experience false memories, what stops me from using that power for personal gain?"

"Professional ethics. Legal constraints. Personal morality."

"All of which assume I remain stable and motivated by ethics," Elias replied. "But what if prolonged contact with ancient magic erodes that? What if the artifacts were designed to shift how magic users think until they start to see non-magical humans as lesser?"

The words unsettled Alex, too close to sounding like sympathy for Edward's worldview.

"You are starting to sound like you agree with him," Alex said.

Elias kept his eyes on the protesters through the windshield. "I am starting to understand why people might find his arguments convincing."

◇✧◇

The morning briefing painted a picture of a city on the edge of breakdown. Overnight incidents included three separate clashes between magical and non-magical protesters, two attacks on businesses owned by magic users, and one healer assaulted outside her clinic.

"We're watching the city begin to unravel," Rivera reported, scanning the summaries. "Edward's attacks created the kind of fear and division that makes real policy discussion impossible."

Cross nodded over casualty reports. "People are taking sides on raw emotion. The magical community feels under siege, while non-magical citizens feel threatened by powers they cannot control."

"And Edward's network gains something from both reactions," Lindsey said. "Fear drives people toward authoritarian answers, while discrimination pushes more magic users into sympathy with his movement."

Alex listened, but his focus kept drifting to Elias. His partner's face showed a troubling respect for how well Edward's tactics worked.

"The targeting has been precise," Elias said. "Infrastructure attacks that prove emergency services cannot handle magical terrorism. Psychological manipulation that turns civilians into weapons. Each event engineered to create maximum trauma with minimum effort."

"You sound impressed," Rivera said, hearing the same tone Alex had noticed.

"I am impressed by the results," Elias admitted. "Edward's network has achieved in three incidents what most groups fail to accomplish in years. He understands that people crave simple explanations and someone to blame. He is giving them both."

Lindsey's eyes narrowed. "And you believe that makes his methods justified?"

"I believe it explains why they are effective," Elias said. "Democracy assumes that citizens will make rational choices if they are given facts. But what happens when fear overrides reason?"

The question cut into the foundation of their work.

"Are you suggesting democracy cannot manage magical integration?" Rivera asked.

"I am suggesting Edward may be right that democratic systems are not built to handle the kind of power gap magic creates," Elias replied quietly. "Perhaps rational governance by capable people is the only alternative to chaos."

The room fell silent. The unease was unmistakable. Alex watched his partner closely, recognizing that Elias was not only analyzing Edward's tactics anymore—he was voicing the exact questions that Edward wanted the world to ask.

Outside the windows, Chicago kept sliding further into unrest while Edward's network positioned itself as the only answer to a failing system.

18

The Decisions That Define Us

The highest duty of the citizen is to resist when the government is wrong
　　—Thomas Jefferson

FBI Chicago Division—December 12, 8:30 AM

The phone rang on Elias' desk while he was reviewing camera footage from the previous night's protests. He picked up, already sensing this call wasn't routine. The caller ID showed a blocked number, but something about the timing made him answer.

"Agent Sinclair."

"Hello, son."

Elias froze. Around him, the bullpen kept moving—the rustle of papers, muted conversations, keyboards clicking. Rivera was at her desk with Agent Martinez, going over witness statements from the protests. Alex, on the far side of their shared space, was on the phone with the crime lab.

"You're not my father," Elias said quietly.

Alex's gaze shifted toward him at the change in tone. He ended his call and moved closer, his focus sharpening.

"Twenty years, Elias." Edward's voice was calm, deliberate, each word weighed.

"Twenty years I've watched from a distance, knowing that one day you'd begin to understand why your magic doesn't behave like everyone else's. Why it answers to forces older than anything the DMA teaches."

"You abandoned me," Elias replied, his voice low but sharp.

"You let me think you were dead while you built your terrorist network."

"I gave you the chance to grow without interference," Edward said evenly.

"To find your limits by your own effort instead of being pushed into them. And you've exceeded even my expectations."

Alex closed the distance, silent but steady at Elias' side, watching the tension coil in his partner's shoulders.

"I'm a federal agent," Elias said. "I hunt people like you."

"You're a man with extraordinary abilities working for a system that will never trust you because of those same abilities," Edward countered.

"You've seen it since Grant Park. They've already started pulling you from field work, haven't they? Restricting your access. Questioning your judgment."

"It's always the same with them. The Service Requirement is proof. They don't see you as a man, Elias. They see you as an asset to be trained, shelved, and kept in reserve. Superior, but never free."

Elias gripped the handset tighter, pulse quickening. The observation was too close to the truth.

"The DMA knows you're different," Edward went on. "They know your tie to the artifacts cannot be explained by training or procedure. That frightens them."

"My connection to the artifacts comes from investigating your murders," Elias said.

"No. It comes from blood." Edward's tone softened. "You carry the same bloodline that forged those artifacts thousands of years ago. The magic recognizes you as one of its own."

Alex leaned closer, listening without interruption.

"The visions you've experienced aren't random psychic traces," Edward said. "They're ancestral memories carried in your bloodline from those who first bound magic into form. They understood how magic was meant to be used, without the limits of democratic compromise."

"You're lying."

"I'm offering the truth your colleagues will never admit. Why your abilities exceed their models. Why the artifacts answer you with such precision. Why they already treat you as a threat."

Through the bullpen windows, protesters still gathered outside. Some signs demanded magical registration; others called for protections. The chants drifted faintly through the glass.

"Look at what your democracy has built," Edward said, his voice tightening. "Fear. Division. Demands for control over people like us. The system will betray you, starting with those they cannot contain."

"So your solution is terrorism?" Elias asked.

"My solution," Edward replied, "is governance by the capable. People who understand power and how to wield it. You've seen what happens when magic is ruled by those without it — restrictions, suspicion, persecution."

His voice dropped lower. "How long before they separate you from the only partner who's ever understood you? They've already begun questioning your loyalty, restricting your role. How long before they remove you from the field entirely?"

"That won't happen."

"It's happening now. You're off my case. Barred from artifact evidence. Reduced to scraps while others take the lead."

Elias didn't answer. Alex's expression stayed guarded but alert.

"I can give you a place where your abilities are valued, not feared," Edward said. "Where policy is shaped by those who know what you can accomplish. You're my son. You belong with people who see your worth."

"I belong here."

"Do you?" Edward asked softly. "Even as they strip your access and prepare to cut you loose the moment you frighten them?"

Elias stared at the desk.

"Think about it," Edward said finally. "When you're ready to know the truth of your heritage, I'll be waiting."

The line went dead. Elias lowered the handset slowly, staring at it for a long moment.

"Wrong number," he said when Rivera glanced up.

"Sounded intense for a wrong number," she replied.

Alex said nothing and went back to his desk.

ASAC Lindsey's Office—10:00 AM

Lindsey's tone was brisk. "DMA intel puts Edward's suspected base at the Aurora Industrial Complex, forty miles west. Abandoned for three years. Now we've got intercepts, personnel movements, and supply runs. They've turned it into a command center."

Rivera frowned. "How solid is the intel?"

"Confirmed," Lindsey said. "The deployment window is under twenty-four hours. SWAT and the DMA's magical specialists will hit it. SWAT handles the tactical breach, DMA neutralizes artifact defenses."

Alex studied the satellite photos. Wide access roads, multiple structures, clean lines of sight. "Civilian risk?"

"Minimal. It's isolated. Main concern is artifact-based countermeasures. DMA teams will take point on magical suppression."

They moved into discussions about entry points, comms overlap, and staging. Elias' chair stayed empty.

The bullpen hummed with low conversation and the shuffle of files. Rivera glanced toward Elias' desk and saw him leaning close to Alex, their voices too quiet to make out. Both men looked tense.

"You can't be seriously considering this," Alex said under his breath, sharp enough to carry across the aisle.

"He's my father. I need to hear him out in person."

Rivera froze, pretending to focus on her paperwork, but her attention stayed on them. Elias turned to his monitor, hand moving quickly with the mouse.

A set of schematic diagrams filled his screen. Rivera caught the heading at the top: *Aurora Industrial Complex*. DMA had flagged those facilities yesterday, and Elias wasn't supposed to be anywhere near restricted files tied to Edward.

"What are you doing, Elias?" Rivera asked, keeping her tone even.

He didn't look up. "It's a registration audit. Lindsey asked me to cross-check registration records."

"That doesn't look like the registration database," Rivera said carefully.

"It is," Elias replied, his voice calm, but the file vanished from the screen with a click. "And I'm done."

Rivera looked to Alex for some sign. He met her eyes with

a quick grin, but it came too fast, too practiced. She turned back to her paperwork, unconvinced. A decision was already forming in her mind—something she would raise with Lindsey before the day was out.

Before she could press further, Agent Martinez walked up with a stack of reports. "Rivera, you still need those witness statements from the South Side protests?" he asked. His tone was casual, the kind of bullpen check-in that happened a dozen times a day.

Rivera blinked, the interruption breaking the moment. "Yeah, put them here."

Martinez set the files on her desk with a quick nod before walking away.

Rivera's gaze drifted across the bullpen to Marcus' empty desk. His coffee mug still sat beside his keyboard, the handle turned the same way he'd always left it. Someone had cleared his active files, but his nameplate remained, along with the small desk calendar he'd used to track court dates and deadlines.

Friday was circled in red ink. Their dinner reservation.

She'd been looking forward to it more than she'd admitted, even to herself. Marcus had been persistent without being pushy, funny without trying too hard. The kind of steady presence that made the job's chaos feel manageable. She'd planned to wear the blue dress hanging in her closet, the one she'd bought weeks ago but never found an occasion for.

Now the calendar page mocked her caution. All those months of keeping things professional, of not mixing work with personal complications. For what? So she could sit here staring at his empty chair, wondering what might have been if she'd said yes to dinner sooner, if they'd had more time to figure out what they could have been to each other.

Rivera forced her attention back to her paperwork, but the regret sat heavy in her chest. Some opportunities didn't wait for you to be ready.

A short while later, she lifted her eyes from her reports. Her gaze landed on Elias and Alex. Elias was bent over his keyboard again, Alex standing close enough to block most of the screen. She could hear them talking in low tones, the same tense rhythm as before.

She gathered her folders and crossed the bullpen to Lindsey's office. A moment later, the door clicked shut behind her.

"Something you should know," Rivera said quietly. "Elias just accessed Aurora schematics. When I asked, he claimed you assigned him to review connections on another case. I don't believe him. And he and Alex are whispering like they don't want anyone to hear."

Lindsey's expression hardened. "You're sure?"

"I saw it on his screen," Rivera confirmed. "I think he closed it as soon as I asked. Whatever it was, he didn't want me seeing it."

Lindsey leaned back, troubled. "I hope Elias isn't making choices he'll regret later." She exhaled and shook her head.

"If the DMA asks about this, don't lie to them. But for now Nicole, keep this between us."

Rivera nodded and stepped back into the bullpen. Elias and Alex were still at their desks, quiet and focused, their expressions unreadable.

Alex found Elias at his desk, sifting through administrative files.

"How are you holding up?"

"I'm fine."

"That's not what I asked."

Elias hesitated. "Harder than I thought. Watching everyone else gear up while I'm stuck here. Edward was right about one thing. They don't trust me. Maybe they never did."

"You can't let him in your head."

"He's not," Elias said. "He's just saying what I already suspected."

Before Alex could answer, Rivera approached. "Lindsey wants to see us in the conference room. Now."

Conference Room

Lindsey sat at the conference table, her eyes fixed on the sheet of paper in front of her. The header had the seal of the Department of Magical Affairs, the language beneath it sharp with directives she had no authority to change. Elias' name appeared twice in bold.

Rowan stood against the far wall with Ryan and Hartford beside her, their postures formal, their expressions leaving no room for negotiation. Rivera hovered near the door, a file clutched to her chest, while Martinez made quiet notes at the side of the room.

"Agent Sinclair," Rowan said, her tone clipped. "We intercepted a call to you this morning. Edward Sinclair contacted you directly."

Lindsey's head snapped up. "What call?"

Ryan consulted his tablet. "The one you received at 8:30. Two minutes, thirty-seven seconds. He attempted recruitment."

Elias blinked, caught between shock and anger. "You've been monitoring my phone calls?"

Rowan's gaze was steady, unflinching. "You have also accessed restricted files on the Aurora industrial facility. Which has been identified as possible base of operation for Edward's network."

"That's false," Alex said flatly, his voice ringing against the office walls.

"Is it?" Rowan asked. Her eyes stayed fixed on Elias. "He's

been researching target sites, speaking directly to their leader, showing sympathy for his reasoning."

Elias forced his voice into control. "Someone claiming to be my father called. I told him I didn't have a father."

"After hearing him out," Ryan said, his tone sharp.

Lindsey looked between them, unsettled. "You're twisting this. Elias would never—"

Rowan cut her off without raising her voice. "He's been compromised. He will be taken into DMA custody as a potential accessory."

Rivera's grip on the file tightened. Martinez paused midnote, then continued writing without comment.

Alex's chair scraped back. Silver light pulsed along his hands, the pressure in the room shifting as his magic stirred. "Like hell he is. You'll have to go through me first."

Ryan stepped forward. "Agent Sutton, stand down."

The air cracked. Silver arcs locked into place around Alex and Elias, a perfect dome that hummed with compressed power. Files and loose pages tore from desks, slapping against the barrier. Hairs rose on end as the charge built.

"Nobody touches him. Not now, not ever," Alex said. His voice was firm and loud.

"Alex—" Lindsey began, but Rowan's sharper tone cut her off.

"Agent Sutton, you're interfering with a DMA arrest. Drop the barrier." Rowan said.

"Not happening."

Ryan moved closer. The barrier flared, heat shimmering across its surface, the air inside alive with the vibration of silver light. He stopped short, one hand flexing as if testing the edge.

Rivera took a step forward, her voice uncertain. "Director Rowan, maybe—"

"Hold your position," Rowan snapped.

Across the bullpen, agents had risen from their desks,

weapons half-drawn, eyes wide. Some whispered, others stared. The sight of Elias behind Alex's barrier was accusation enough.

Alex reached back, gripping Elias' arm, steady and unshakable. "We're leaving. Now."

They moved toward the door. The barrier swept a corridor open through the bullpen, the silver glow pushing desks and chairs aside with steady pressure. Agents froze rather than challenge it. Rivera stayed rooted where she was, uncertainty written on her face. Martinez simply closed his notebook, his expression steady and cautious.

Rowan shouted orders into her radio. "Seal the exits. They don't leave this building." Her voice was loud enough to silence the room.

The barrier didn't falter until Alex and Elias reached the stairwell. The heavy door banged open under the pressure of their escape.

Concrete steps spiraled downward, the sound of boots and shouted orders echoing from above. Radios crackled through the floors as agents scrambled to intercept.

Halfway down, Elias spoke, his voice low. "Alex, are you sure you want to do this?"

"I'm not sure about anything except that we're not separating and we need to get the hell out of here," Alex said. His grip on Elias' arm tightened. "We'll figure the rest out later."

Footsteps pounded across the floors above. They hurried down the stairs, taking them two at a time, and rushed out into the night.

19
Coalition of The Willing

It is not enough to fight. It is the spirit which we bring to the fight that decides the issue
—T.E. Lawrence (Lawrence of Arabia)

Safe House—Somewhere near Aurora

The room was quiet, blinds drawn against prying eyes. The apartment's second-floor windows overlooked a narrow street hemmed in by aging brickwork and frost-covered sills. Two bedrooms, modern furniture, nothing fancy but comfortable.

"The Bureau doesn't know about this place," Alex said. "We can lay low here."

Elias stood at the window, watching the street below where the corner grocery still glowed. Snow drifted down in lazy flakes, catching in the light of passing cars. His reflection looked back at him from the glass, pale and worn, as if studying a stranger. He hadn't said much since they left headquarters.

"Get some rest. It's very late," Alex told him. "You need it."

Elias shook his head. "I won't sleep."

"You should try." Alex leaned on the counter, eyes steady. "We'll need clear heads for whatever comes next."

Silence stretched before Elias turned. "I need to talk to him."

Alex frowned. "Your father."

"Yes. I need to get close to him. Look him in the eyes. Have him explain to me what his plan is."

"What you're doing is dangerous, Elias," Alex said. "You're going to get yourself killed."

"Maybe. But I need to try."

Alex rubbed a hand across his jaw, torn between anger and worry. "Get some sleep first. Tomorrow we'll figure out how to find him."

Elias finally sat on the edge of the bed, shoulders tight. Then his magic flickered, a ripple that made him go still. "Something else out there," he said quietly. "Not him. Fae. Just passing through."

Alex's jaw tightened. "And you're sure?"

"Yes. But it isn't aimed at us." Elias lay back, closing his eyes. "Right now it's my father we need to worry about."

Alex stood in the doorway, watching him, uneasy. Elias seemed calm on the surface, but Alex knew the toll the preceding days had taken. He knew the risks of letting him walk straight toward Edward.

He closed the door partway and stayed awake in the living room, listening to the city outside, the hum of the fridge filling the silence between distant sirens. Wondering if, when the time came, he would have the strength to pull Elias back before he lost him to Edward and the artifacts.

◇✧◇

The last schematic hit the table, drone images spread out beside it.

"Everything we can control is in place," Lindsey said, tapping the map with the blunt end of her pen. "The rest, we'll handle on the ground."

Rowan gave the table one last look, her expression unreadable. Then she closed the folder with a decisive snap.

"Gear up. We move now."

Aurora Industrial Complex—5:00 PM

The Aurora Industrial Complex stood at the edge of the frozen landscape, its concrete walls blotting out half the horizon. Once a hub of manufacturing, it now loomed abandoned, the wind slipping through broken windows and across skeletal towers that bristled against the pale winter sky. The long warehouse roofs were dusted with snow, their ridges sharp as blades in the flat light.

Across the frozen lot, Bureau SUVs and DMA response vehicles were parked in staggered rows, engines off, their windows frosting over in the cold. A few unmarked vans idled along the side road, headlights dimmed, each waiting like a blade not yet drawn. SWAT teams waited inside, checking weapons in silence, the air around them thick with the weight of what was coming.

Magical suppression units clustered near the lead vehicles, unit patches on their jackets catching the glow from dash lights. Hands rested on suppression rigs, eyes trained on the warehouse fence. The quiet was worse than noise, heavy with anticipation. This was a team waiting for a single order to unleash violence.

Inside one of the parked command vans, it was warmer, but the tension in the air was palpable. Maps and schematics covered the folding table that ran the length of the vehicle. A wall of monitors streamed live perimeter feeds, each screen showing a different angle of the complex.

Rowan stood at the head of the table, posture controlled, shoulders stiff with the strain of waiting. Lindsey was to her right, speaking in low tones with a tactical coordinator, one gloved finger tracing the main access corridor. Rivera leaned over a smaller screen, fingers tapping quick commands as she cycled between aerial imagery and live intelligence.

Ryan bent over the southern approach, his eyes flicking between the schematic and the service entrance feed. Across from him, Hartford studied the interior routes, her gloved hand tracing fallback points with precision.

"This perimeter is locked down," Lindsey said at last, tapping three points on the schematic. Her voice cut through the background murmur of radio checks.

"Strike teams don't move until I give the order," Rowan stated.

Hartford didn't look up. "How will you know when to move to neutralize them?"

Rowan's eyes settled on her. "I'm not sure." The words came quiet, absolute.

Hartford studied her for a moment, then gave a short nod. Ryan looked at Rowan like he wanted to ask a question, but stayed silent.

Outside, the wind continued to howl.

◇✦◇

Aurora Industrial Complex—Edward's Command Center

The complex's core wasn't a single command post but a web of positions spread across the reinforced interior. Edward had designed it to withstand both magical and conventional assault, each corridor layered with choke points, overlapping fields of fire, and fallback routes that turned every approach into a gauntlet.

Dr. Pierce moved with practiced precision, crossing from one station to the next. Six memory specialists held their sectors, each gripping an artifact close enough to feel the pulse in their hands. The current of power was visible in their posture, the rigid focus of people braced against the weight of something far greater than their own strength.

In the west corner, a woman in a dark tactical coat leaned against a reinforced column. She balanced her artifact in one palm, the other hand hovering above it as she tested the weave of her spells, adjusting the pull with small, exact movements. Across the open floor, a man in a high-collared jacket stood watch near a barricaded stairwell, his artifact glowing faintly in the half-light.

The other four specialists covered the remaining choke points: one on the upper catwalks, two guarding separate entrances, and one positioned near the freight elevator shaft. Their distribution meant that any breach would be met from multiple angles at once, each defender amplified enough to hold far longer than an ordinary magic user could hope to.

The seventh artifact sat in a secured case near Edward's position. He had not touched it. His eyes moved instead from one specialist to the next, weighing their readiness in silence.

The hum of active magic filled the room, blending with the metallic echo of shifting machinery deeper in the complex. Overhead lamps struck the artifacts at broken angles. Reflections shifted along the walls.

"Positions are locked," Pierce reported. His voice steady.

Edward's gaze lingered on the northern catwalk. "Good. Stay sharp. They'll come sooner than they think."

"Martinez confirms the DMA and FBI are staged outside," the aide said, speaking quietly. "Alex Sutton and Elias Sinclair are fugitives."

Edward lifted the handset calmly, his expression steady, unreadable. "They'll come to me," he said, almost under his breath.

He turned away from the table. With his back to the room, he keyed in a number from memory. The faint clicks of the dial pad barely rose above the artifacts' hum.

The aide withdrew, leaving Edward alone as the call's first ring sounded.

Safe House

They'd spent the day in the safe house after both finally catching up on sleep. The air smelled of fresh coffee.

The faint hum of the wards Alex had worked into the doorframes and windows vibrated just at the edge of perception, a taut reminder that anyone trying to cross without permission would meet resistance.

Elias stood at the window, two fingers lifting the curtain just enough to watch the street. The glass was icy under his touch, frost etched in sharp white veins across its surface. Outside, the stillness felt false. The street was quiet, but it put him on edge. His phone buzzed in his hand. The display showed "Unknown."

He answered anyway. "Sinclair."

"Hello, son." Edward's voice was as clear as if he stood in the room. No static, no distance, just the familiar weight Elias had long tried to forget.

Elias said nothing.

"They'll come for me soon," Edward went on, his tone measured. "Before they do, I want you here. Face to face."

"I told you before, I don't agree with your methods." Elias kept his voice even, though tension edged every word.

"I think you're closer to understanding me than you admit." Edward's words were slow and deliberate. "You've been thinking about what I told you. You know there's truth in it."

Elias' eyes flicked to the wards glowing faintly in the corners. His grip on the phone tightened. "Maybe."

"I'll give you safe passage inside, alone if you wish. But you will come now."

The pause that followed stretched until Elias finally said, "Send the details."

The line went dead.

The front door opened with a muted click, letting in a cool draft. Alex stepped inside, setting a bag on the floor and bottles of water on the desk before shutting the door quickly. His eyes locked on Elias almost at once.

"Who was that?" His voice was clipped.

"Edward," Elias said. "He wants to meet before the DMA hits the complex."

"You're actually going through with this." Alex moved deeper into the room, concern etched across his face.

Elias met his gaze. "I'm going."

Alex studied him, eyes narrowing. "Then we should move."

But neither reached for the door. Elias turned back to the window, pulling the curtain just enough to glimpse the street again. Frost coated the parked cars, ice tracing pale patterns across the glass. The sky hung a flat gray, the kind of winter light that made every sound outside sharper than it should be.

Alex came to stand beside him, their reflections caught side by side in the cold pane. For a long moment they watched the empty street, nothing moving except a single scrap of paper twisting in the wind.

When Alex finally spoke, his voice was quiet but firm. "No matter how this turns out, the only regret I have is letting you keep your distance for eighteen months." His breath clouded the glass before fading.

Elias turned his head slightly, studying him.

"I'll stand with you," Alex said, leaving no room for doubt. "No matter what you decide to do."

Elias' expression stayed unreadable, but his grip on the curtain slackened. He let the fabric fall back into place.

Without another word, he reached for his jacket. Alex was already pulling on his gloves, his movements steady, the bag still at his feet. They looked at each other with an unspoken question. Neither knew what would happen tonight.

Aurora Industrial Complex Perimeter

The wind had picked up, rattling against the sides of the command vehicle. The steady rumble of idling engines outside filled the cold air.

Inside, Rowan moved from station to station with ease, her coat brushing the edge of the maps spread across the central table bolted to the floor. She leaned in to study the southern sector feed, every movement measured. Lindsey tracked her across the narrow space, waiting for a break to update her on comms from the outer perimeter.

Ryan stood braced beside one of the monitors, one hand gripping the back of a fixed chair, the other tapping against his thigh. His gaze shifted between the live perimeter feed and the printed schematics taped to the wall, mapping routes in his head, matching choke points to the intel on Edward's defenses. The glow of the screens caught in his eyes, sharpening them to a pale gleam.

Beside him, Eleanor Hartford had stripped one glove off. Her bare fingertip traced the blueprint of the southern wall, lips moving faintly as she rehearsed sequences under her breath. Timing, placement, fallback paths if the breach stalled.

"Units Alpha and Bravo will take primary," she said without looking up. "Charlie Team holds until contact is confirmed."

"Contact meaning Sinclair's specialists," Ryan replied.

Hartford nodded once, eyes still on the plan. "The moment Rowan gives the order, we go. No delay."

From behind them, Martinez spoke just loud enough to reach. "South entrance is clear of exterior patrols. Interior thermal shows minimal movement." His eyes stayed on the drone feed, but his thumb brushed the comms panel with a practiced ease.

Rowan stepped closer. "Interior movement?"

Martinez toggled a new view, pulling up a grainy camera from deep inside the complex. "Three heat signatures moving west to east. Could be a patrol rotation. Could be nothing."

Rowan's eyes narrowed. "Or maybe their preparing for their next move. Keep them tagged."

Martinez inclined his head. "Yes, ma'am." He returned the feed to the exterior, but not before noting the hallway camera number for himself.

Outside, boots crunched in the snow and weapons clicked as operators checked them. A short burst of laughter cut off when a sergeant walked past. Cold slipped through the thin walls.

Hartford pulled her glove back on. "Teams will be ready in ninety seconds once the order comes."

Ryan glanced at Rowan. "How long will we have?"

Rowan's reply came quiet, even. "No way to know." No

estimate, no guesswork. They had never faced anything like this, and she wasn't about to bluff.

She was already moving toward Lindsey at the far end of the table before another question could follow.

Martinez's eyes tracked her for a moment, then slid back to the monitors. His finger tapped twice against the comms panel before flipping to an encrypted channel. The angle of his body kept it hidden from most of the occupants. A faint, almost inaudible tone confirmed the transmission.

Aurora Industrial Complex—Edward's Operations Room 6:00 PM

Edward listened as the faint voice came through the secure line, its words masked under the cover of static. His expression didn't change, but the corner of his mouth twitched in something that might have been approval.

"Understood," he said, then ended the transmission.

The cold bit at exposed skin in the open yard of the Aurora complex. Concrete underfoot still held patches of ice from the last storm, and the wind cut between the warehouse walls, carrying the metallic tang of machinery.

Edward stood near the center of the yard, hands clasped loosely behind his back. Around him, the six memory specialists held their artifacts, each one positioned to cover a different angle of approach. Their breath rose in steady clouds, their eyes fixed on the edges of the compound where the first sign of movement might come.

Dr. Pierce moved from one to the next, speaking in a voice pitched just loud enough to carry over the wind. "North approach clear. West approach holding. South guard has full line of sight on the service road."

When he returned to Edward's side, Pierce's expression was calm. "They're ready."

"They may have visitors before the DMA is ready to breach," Edward said, scanning the perimeter. "Make sure they're prepared to adapt."

Pierce nodded and raised his voice just enough for all six to hear. "Hold your ground. Keep your focus on your artifacts. Nothing gets past you."

One by one, the specialists gave a short nod in return, their postures tightening against the cold.

From somewhere deep within the complex, a metallic clang rang out. It traveled through the concrete and carried into the yard, a sharp echo that drew every gaze toward the walls. The sound faded quickly, but the silence that followed pressed heavier than before, as if the outside world had edged closer to their threshold.

Safe House—6:00 PM

Elias buttoned his jacket and slid a hand into the inside pocket. His eyes swept the room one last time, checking the wards. The low hum in the walls felt steady, unchanged.

Alex waited at the door, holding it open, shoulders set. "Ready?"

Elias gave a short nod. They said nothing more as they stepped into the hallway. The air smelled faintly of stale heat and old plaster. Their boots struck the worn wooden steps, the sound carrying in the narrow stairwell.

Outside, the cold hit at once. The air was sharp enough to sting, each breath leaving a pale cloud. Frost laced the windshields of parked cars along the curb. In the distance, a siren rose and faded.

They moved toward the car without hurry but with purpose. Alex unlocked it. The quiet click sounded loud in the evening stillness. They stepped inside. The interior was freezing, but the heater began to hum as the engine turned over. Neither looked at the other as Alex pulled into the street.

Elias closed his eyes and drew in a long breath, steadying himself.

The staging area had shifted. Vehicles that had idled in neat lines earlier were now dispersed to cover approaches. Magical suppression units adjusted their positions, slipping into the narrow gaps between warehouse outbuildings and heavy equipment.

Hartford was with her team near the southern sector, giving final instructions in a clipped tone. "Stay low, move only on my signal, and keep the channel clear." She scanned their faces, confirming they were ready. "We go when we're told, not before."

Ryan passed behind her, checking a comms link with Alpha Team. The feed in his earpiece crackled as he verified their positions. His gaze kept darting to the south entrance camera, its grainy view holding his attention.

Inside one of the armored command vehicles, Rowan stood with Lindsey over a central display. Drone feeds flickered across mounted monitors, showing the complex from multiple angles, the images shifting as operators adjusted camera positions to cut glare off the snow. The low thrum of idling engines bled through the metal floor, mixing with the static of radio traffic.

"Southern approach has increased thermal signatures," one tech reported, eyes on his screen.

Rowan leaned in. "Mark them."

The markers appeared on the display, small red outlines that pulsed faintly. She studied them for a long moment. "Hold positions."

Aurora Industrial Complex—Edward's Operations Room 6:20 PM

Edward stepped to the wall where a large tactical display had been mounted. The screen pulled from the internal camera network, each feed showing a different stretch of the complex. He tapped through the angles until the south service entrance filled the frame.

"Pierce," he said without looking back.

"Yes?"

"Our guests are close. Prepare the specialists."

Across the open yard, the six memory specialists shifted their stance, drawing slow, deliberate breaths. They formed a wide perimeter, each gripping an artifact in gloved hands. Breath misted in the cold air, rising and fading while their focus moved between the compound's edges and Edward's steady figure.

Pierce made his circuit with slowly, pausing at each station. He bent close to speak a few words that only the specialist could hear, then moved on, coat snapping faintly as the wind cut through the yard. The wards along the walls gave off a low vibration, the sensation brushing against him like pressure on the skin.

By the time Pierce returned to Edward's side, the formation had settled, postures rigid, artifacts steady in their grasp.

Aurora Perimeter—6:22 PM

Martinez spoke just loud enough for Rowan to hear. "Two signatures, moving toward the south entrance."

Rowan's eyes locked on the feed. The figures appeared small against the looming steel doors, their outlines sharp against the snow in the fading light.

"Hold," she said.

She didn't look away from the screen. "Sutton and Sinclair. Get ready to engage targets."

Acknowledgments came back in quiet voices over the channels.

"Do we wait for your signal?" Hartford asked.

"Affirmative. No movement until my mark."

South Approach—6:25 PM

Alex and Elias moved steadily toward the complex. Their boots crunched over the snow, the sound carrying across the empty lot. The steel doors ahead caught the thin light, their surface scarred by years of use.

Alex's gaze swept the edges of the yard. Nothing moved, but he felt watched. Magic hummed faint in the air.

Elias kept his focus forward, hands loose at his sides but ready.

They took the last few steps into the shadow of the building. The air grew warmer here, the massive walls breaking the wind.

The steel doors began to open with a low groan.

Edward emerged from the dim interior. The weak light caught the edges of his coat as he stepped forward, movements calculated. Behind him, the faint hum of the artifacts pressed outward.

Elias stopped a few paces short and his shoulders stiffened.

Alex's gaze shifted between them. His breath rose in short clouds as the cold numbed his face and stung his lungs. He steadied himself for what came next.

No one spoke.

20

A Paradise of Ashes

The supreme art of war is to subdue the enemy without fighting.
—*Sun Tzu*

Edward's gaze swept over them both. "You came."

His voice was steady, almost quiet, but it was easily heard in the open space. "I understand now. What you were trying to tell me before. The world is broken, and magic is the only fix."

Alex's head snapped toward him, disbelief flashing in his eyes. "Elias?" His voice was low, edged with something between shock and warning.

Elias kept his eyes on Edward. "You're right. No government built on fear will ever protect us. We have to rebuild it ourselves."

Edward's expression shifted, the corners of his mouth lifting in the faintest smile. "And now you see there's no fixing it within their rules."

Elias gave a single, short nod. "No, there's not."

Alex took a step closer, boots crunching in the packed snow. "Elias."

This time Elias turned to look at him. For a moment, something unspoken passed between them, too quick for anyone watching to decipher.

Alex's hand came up, resting on his partner's shoulder. "Elias?"

The pause that followed was sharp enough to cut.

Edward's gaze moved between them, his satisfaction deepening. "When the DMA and FBI breach, we'll break them. With you at my side, their best won't survive the hour."

"They won't," Elias said.

Alex frowned. "No. You can't do this, Elias."

Edward's voice hardened. "Pierce."

From the shadows inside, Dr. Pierce stepped forward, the artifact in his grip pulsing faintly. His free hand began to shape the weave of a spell, the air around him growing taut.

"Stop him."

Magic flared between Pierce's hands, a cold blue shimmer that lit the dark of the entryway. Alex was already moving, silver-white energy curling around his arms, condensing into a shield as the first bolt of force struck. The impact cracked the air like a whip, the shockwave shoving Elias back a half-step.

Alex caught himself and drove forward, his own magic slamming into Pierce's defenses. Sparks of silver and blue scattered across the ground, hissing where they touched snow. Pierce's jaw tightened as he pushed, power arcing between them, the air bending with heat and pressure.

Edward's attention shifted for a moment. A flicker of light appeared to his right, quick as the strike of a match. He turned sharply toward it, but there was nothing. Only the wall of the complex and the faint shimmer of frost on the concrete.

When he looked back, Alex had broken through Pierce's outer defense. The older man staggered a step, but his counterstrike hit home. Alex's shield held long enough for him to slam a palm against Pierce's chest and release a burst of silver light. The blast hurled Pierce backward into the steel frame of the doorway.

Alex swayed on his feet, blood seeping through a tear in the side of his coat. He dropped to one knee, breath ragged.

From beyond the gates came the deep concussion of explosives. The DMA and FBI were making their breach.

Edward straightened, his voice cutting through the gathering noise. "Hold your positions. Don't let them past you."

The specialists shifted into their arcs of fire, spells building in their hands, the yard filling with the glow of concentrated magic.

The first wave of suppression units poured through the breached fence, shields raised, weapons ready. The instant they crossed into range, the air erupted with force.

Bolts of power and elemental strikes tore into the front ranks, dropping half a dozen before they could return fire. Two DMA snipers on the outer perimeter answered, one round slamming into the chest of a memory specialist. The amplified magic flickered once before the body hit the ground.

Elias turned sharply toward the fallen specialist, something unreadable crossing his face.

Edward's hand clenched at his side. "Focus. Close the gap and break them."

The yard broke into chaos. Suppression units advanced in staggered formations, forcing the specialists to divide their attention. Elemental counterstrikes ripped into snow and asphalt, throwing agents off their feet.

Alex tried to rise, teeth bared against the pain, but Elias' grip tightened. "Stay down."

"I'm not—"

"Stay down." The weight in Elias' voice froze him in place.

A sniper round cracked through the air, striking Elias in the side. His breath left him in a sharp exhale. For an instant he stayed upright, then the impact drove him forward, pulling Alex with him as they hit the ground together.

Above the clash, Edward watched, calm and commanding. The artifacts burned brighter, and the tide began to turn.

Snow swirled low across the yard, catching in the glare of active magic. Alex and Elias lay motionless in the churned frost near the breach, their bodies half-hidden by the spray of debris from the last blast. No one moved to check them; the battle had surged past, and in the chaos, stillness meant nothing good.

Edward didn't spare them more than a glance. The fight was still in front of him. Five specialists held the line, each a fixed point in the storm. Their artifacts pulsed in sequence, faint hums overlapping into a single, resonant vibration that threaded through the air.

The first DMA suppression agent to get close enough to try a grab was lost in an instant. His stance faltered, shoulders slackening before his rifle lifted toward his own team. The shot cracked out, dropping the point man of Alpha Squad. The others hesitated, and that heartbeat of a pause let a wave of heat roll in from the west choke point, hurling two agents off their feet into the snow.

Edward's eyes tracked the fight the way a chess master reads a board. The specialists weren't wasting power on wild attacks. They were precise, each strike measured, seizing control of one opponent at a time until the assault began to fray.

"Shift your positions," he called, voice calm over the noise. "Make them doubt their flanks."

On the upper catwalk, the youngest of the specialists, a wiry man with close-cropped hair, adjusted his stance. His artifact glowed with a deep amber light as he fixed his gaze on the far end of the yard. Below, a suppression officer broke from cover to reposition. The specialist's magic rippled outward, invisible to most eyes, but Edward felt it in the air like a subtle pull.

The officer's stride faltered. His weapon rose, not toward the defenders, but toward a teammate crouched behind a snow-dusted supply crate. One clean shot, and the crate's cover was gone along with its occupant.

Panic moved faster than orders. The unit scrambled for new cover, each shaken by the knowledge that any one of them could be turned against the others.

From the east entrance, Pierce's voice came. "The western approach is holding. They're bottling themselves in the center."

Another team pushed from the south. Hartford led them, the hard edge of her magic visible in the shimmer around her outstretched hands. Edward recognized the type, disciplined, trained for suppression rather than destruction. She was fast, her unit moving in tight formation, shields locked against incoming fire.

The woman guarding the south gap let them come within twenty feet before she moved. The artifact in her grasp blazed, throwing her face into stark relief. She didn't aim at Hartford. She picked the agent to her right.

He stiffened mid-step, then pivoted, weapon snapping toward Hartford. She caught the movement in time, a suppression ward flashing into place. The shot hammered the barrier in a burst of heat and force, shoving her back a step. She forced her forward line into cover, their lost momentum breaking the push. DMA strikes answered, elemental bursts tearing asphalt and spraying snow and grit into the air.

From the north barricade, five more agents fell, one caught in crossfire between teammates, another tackled by her own partner before either could make sense of it.

The FBI sniper teams on the ridge adjusted their aim, but

the specialists moved like shadows between anchor points, never lingering long enough for a clean shot.

Edward felt the rhythm deepen. Each hostile mind seized became another weapon turned inward. He glanced at Pierce, who was reading the pattern too. "They're breaking," Edward said.

Pierce allowed himself the faintest smile. "They'll be broken within five minutes."

At the far end of the yard, the snow churned with boot prints and the crumpled forms of DMA and FBI agents, some struck down, others turned on each other until they were dragged clear. The hum of the artifacts stayed steady, unwavering.

From somewhere near the breach, Rowan's voice shouted orders, but distance and the roar of magic swallowed her words.

Edward's satisfaction grew. This wasn't just holding ground. It was dismantling the assault piece by piece, forcing them to destroy themselves.

And Alex and Elias, two of the FBI's best, lay in the snow at his feet, unmoving.

Edward stood rooted, every thought aligned to the unfolding pattern as the six memory specialists held their positions across the yard, each anchored behind cover in the sprawl of rusted machinery, cargo crates, and snow-dusted loading bays. Their artifacts pulsed in rhythm, the overlapping hum threading through the clatter of weapons and shouted commands.

Pierce stood at his shoulder, reading the field with the same precision he might apply to an equation. "The south push is slowing. Hartford's pinned behind a forklift stack. West side is losing ground."

Edward allowed himself a small, cold smile. "Good. Keep them where they are. The longer they hesitate, the easier they are to turn."

Near the south side, one of Hartford's agents broke from cover, sprinting low between a pair of storage containers. The specialist covering that sector adjusted her stance and fixed on him. A faint ripple moved through the air, barely visible in the falling snow. The agent's steps faltered. He pivoted without warning and fired at his own team leader.

Hartford caught the movement in time, a suppression ward flaring into place. The impact slammed the barrier, driving her backward into a crouch. She forced her forward line deeper into cover, the sudden disruption breaking the momentum of their advance.

On the west approach, a pair of FBI agents moved in tandem toward an abandoned lift truck. The specialist stationed there tightened his grip on his artifact. One of the agents froze mid-step, then turned on his partner, tackling him hard onto the frozen ground.

"They're unraveling," Pierce said, his tone calm but edged with satisfaction.

Edward's gaze tracked the chaos. "Not quickly enough. Signal the south to press harder. Break their formation and the rest will collapse."

Pierce relayed the command. The specialist in the south brightened her artifact to full power. Another ripple of magic rolled out, stronger this time, reaching a cluster of agents sheltering behind a stack of steel drums. Two turned at once, opening fire on the agents beside them.

The effect spread quickly. Return fire came from both sides of the DMA line as friend and foe blurred in the confusion. Snow churned under rushing boots, and the sharp cracks of gunfire mixed with the heavier roar of amplified magic.

Edward folded his hands behind his back, the wind tugging at his coat. "This is almost over."

Pierce scanned the yard taking in the bodies scattered in the frost. "It is over. They just do not see it yet."

Aurora Industrial Complex—7:15 PM

The fight was over. Snow lay churned into a slurry of ice, mud, and debris. The air still shimmered faintly with the residue of amplified magic, each pulse from the artifacts sinking into the cold like a fading heartbeat.

DMA agents lay where they had fallen, some unconscious, others dragging themselves toward what little cover remained. The FBI had pulled back to the far edge of the yard, those still standing holding their weapons but making no move to advance.

The six memory specialists stayed in position, artifacts cradled in their grip. The hum they produced had softened, no longer the hard thrum of battle but steady enough to keep the survivors wary.

Edward stood at the center, frost clinging to the edge of his coat where the wind had caught it. He turned slowly, surveying the yard. Every remaining sound felt small: the labored breathing of men in the snow, the crackle of cooling metal, the clatter of a dropped weapon.

Pierce approached, boots crunching through the icy mix. His expression was calm, composed, the look of a man who had known from the start how this would end. "They are in full retreat," he said. "Hartford's unit broke first. Rowan was pulled out two minutes later. Ryan fell back when the left flank collapsed."

Edward's gaze drifted toward the breach where the battle had begun. Beyond the bodies and debris, two figures lay still in the snow. Alex and Elias had not moved since the first minutes of the assault.

Pierce followed his glance. "Do you want them buried?"

"Burn them," Edward said without hesitation. "They no longer matter."

One of the specialists shifted, artifact flaring in a controlled pulse. Edward gave him a nod of acknowledgment. "Well done. All of you."

No one spoke. The specialists held their posts, eyes sweeping the edges of the yard for the chance of a second wave. The air felt heavy, the stillness that follows a decisive victory.

Pierce stepped closer. "Orders?"

Edward let his eyes pass over the yard one last time before turning toward the shadowed interior of the complex. "We go inside. There is work to be done."

Aurora Industrial Complex—2 Days After The Battle

Snowmelt pooled in the uneven stretches of the south yard, the water thin enough to refreeze in the cold wind. The scorched patches of asphalt still held the faint smell of burned magic, a metallic tang that clung to the air long after the fighting had ended. Broken wards crackled weakly along the fence line, their shimmer dim and unfocused now that their casters were gone.

Inside the central building, Edward stood at the wide windows that overlooked the yard. His reflection was faint in the glass, pale against the gray daylight. Beyond the glass, teams of magic users in heavy coats were moving between supply trucks and the makeshift checkpoints that had gone up overnight. No one shouted orders; the work had settled into a rhythm that came from the workers themselves. They knew what was expected. They had chosen to be here.

Pierce entered from the side, the sound of his boots loud

in the open space. He carried no clipboard this time, just a folded map with a few marks in red ink. He set it on the nearest table and smoothed it out.

"Southern districts are secure," Pierce said. "The north is slower—more mundanes, fewer of our people willing to step into authority."

"Then we make them willing," Edward replied.

"They are not refusing outright," Pierce added quickly. "They are watching, waiting to see if the change holds."

Edward finally turned, walking toward the map. "And it will. Because we will not let it fail."

He tapped the northern edge of the map where the pale yellow lines met the river. "Who controls the docks?"

"Two of the local combat users volunteered to take command there," Pierce replied. "They have small teams with them. Enough to hold until more arrive."

"Keep them supplied," Edward said. "If the docks are steady, the rest of the north will follow."

A moment passed in silence before Pierce said, "Word from the east markets is not as smooth. Prices are fluctuating. Some traders are holding back stock to negotiate for more favorable exchanges."

"Stop them," Edward said flatly.

Pierce hesitated. "That could drive them underground."

"Then they will be dealt with underground," Edward said. "No one controls the flow of goods except us."

From the yard below came the sound of a door slamming and a sharp exchange of voices. Edward stepped closer to the window again. Two magic users were in the street beside a supply cart, one leaning in, the other pulling away. The argument was too far to hear clearly, but the stance of the men told the story. Just a disagreement, not disloyalty. Not yet.

Pierce followed his gaze. "There are going to be disputes. People have their own ideas about how this should be run."

"Then they will learn," Edward said. "Unity is not an option. It is survival."

He moved back to the table and set his hands on either side of the map. "The mundanes will resist in small ways. Refusals, slow work, hoarding. They are not the threat. Our people are."

Pierce gave a short nod. "Factions?"

"They will form," Edward said. "It is only a matter of time. Combat users will think they should lead because they can win battles. Memory users will think they should lead because they can outthink them. Elementals will think the land itself is theirs to command. And all of them will be wrong."

"Because only you can lead," Pierce said.

Edward's eyes met his, steady and cold. "Because only I have the vision to keep them from tearing each other apart."

From the far end of the hall, the rumble of voices swelled as a group of new arrivals came in from the cold. Boots scraped the floor, coats were shaken free of snow, and the scent of wind and ice swept into the room. One of the arrivals, a tall woman with frost still caught in her hair, stepped forward.

"West gate is quiet," she reported. "No trouble since dawn."

Edward gave a single nod. "Good. Keep it that way."

She hesitated before speaking again. "Some of the mundanes are saying the DMA will come back. That they will take the city back."

"They will not," Edward said. His voice was calm, certain. "The DMA is gone. The FBI is gone. This is all that remains."

The woman nodded once and stepped back, her expression tightening as if she had braced herself against the truth.

Edward let the silence settle before he spoke again. "Pierce, post magical oversight at every supply depot. Every shipment in or out is counted. No exceptions."

"That will slow distribution," Pierce said.

"That will prevent disorder," Edward replied. "We control the supply lines, we control the city."

He turned back toward the window, his reflection once again overlaid on the snow and the movement below. "This," he said, almost to himself, "is how the world begins again."

The command center was alive with movement, the kind of ordered chaos Edward found satisfying. Uniformed teams checked in from patrols, others rotated through the communications banks, and the large digital map on the far wall showed every district in steady green.

From where he stood, it looked like victory.

Yet the voices had an edge that had not been there the day before. Elemental users gathered near the logistics station, their jackets marked with the crest Edward had given them. They spoke in low tones to one another, heads bent over a tablet showing supply routes. A few feet away, a pair of combat specialists leaned against the wall, arms crossed, watching the conversation with undisguised irritation.

"They have no idea how to run security," one of the combat agents muttered, just loud enough for his partner to hear.

"They think pushing freight around with wind and ice makes them tacticians," the other replied.

Across the room, an illusionist adjusted a display on the map, shifting boundaries to show projected influence zones. "If we were handling this, the civilian districts would fall in line without a single shot fired," she said to the memory user beside her.

The memory specialist gave a small, knowing smile. "Or you could let us in. We can persuade them to cooperate permanently."

The illusionist's gaze flicked to Edward, gauging his reaction. He gave none.

◇✦◇

Edward stood in front of the glass wall overlooking the vehicle yard. Trucks rolled in and out, their trailers sealed with the elemental faction's mark. Edward watched as a driver presented clearance papers to a uniformed elemental at the gate. After a moment's inspection, the truck was waved through to the northern warehouses.

Pierce stepped up beside him. "Reports from South Shore. Shelves in three markets are empty. The locals are complaining, saying nothing has been delivered in four days."

Edward's eyes stayed on the yard. "We have supply runs scheduled."

"They are being intercepted," Pierce said. "Elementals are prioritizing their own zones. Anything marked for South Shore gets rerouted north before it leaves the yard."

"They're using it as an excuse to build influence in the north," Pierce said.

"Then remind them every district answers to me," Edward replied. "Reassign half their convoy schedule south."

When Pierce left, Edward crossed the floor toward the logistics table. Four faction leaders stood around it, each marked by the subtle cues of their discipline. The combat leader was speaking, voice tight. "And without us, you lose the streets those trucks have to drive through. My teams secure the convoys, not yours."

The illusionist leader gave a short laugh. "Security is nothing if the public refuses to open their doors. You want compliance, you need subtlety. We can make them believe the shortages are their own fault."

The memory specialist across from her leaned on the table. "Or we can make them remember a time when cooperation was natural. Force is a blunt instrument. Memories are sharper."

Edward let the exchange go on just long enough to see the

postures shift. Each was standing a little taller, voices tightening, the space between them charged with more than magic.

By evening, the first real signs of fracture were spreading beyond the command floor. At the north warehouse, a combat team refused to clear a departing truck because the manifest listed a southern drop. A guard with elemental magic at the gate argued loud enough to be heard over the idling engines.

In South Shore, residents gathered outside a shuttered grocery, demanding answers from the patrol stationed there. The officer in charge claimed the next shipment was coming in two days, but the crowd had heard the same promise twice before.

The illusionists began running targeted projections in those areas, trying to dampen public anger. It worked for a few hours at a time, but when the glamour faded the shelves were still empty.

Edward walked the perimeter of the command center late that night. The corridors were quieter, but the tension had settled like a weight on the air. Passing the break room, he caught the end of a conversation.

"If we had the distribution, it would already be fixed."

"Elementals are hoarding. Everyone knows it."

Moments later in the yard, he watched another truck bound north roll past unchecked.

Pierce had already briefed him on the growing unrest. Mundane citizens were refusing curfews, sabotaging power substations, blocking main roads with burning vehicles, and ambushing smaller patrols before vanishing into the side streets. Armed groups were raiding warehouses and distribution hubs, stripping them clean before magical reinforcements could arrive. Sporadic gunfire echoed in multiple districts each night, and the skyline was marked by columns of smoke where fires still burned unchecked. Intelligence reports confirmed that federal and state forces were mobilizing outside the city, preparing a coordinated push to retake Chicago by force.

The office was still, insulated from the noise of the command floor below. A single folder lay open on the desk between Edward and Dr. Pierce, the paper inside creased from being handled too many times.

Pierce's voice was low. "The shortages are severe. South Side has gone six days without a full delivery. Smaller stores are empty. Most of the warehouses in that district have been stripped."

Edward's eyes stayed on him. "And?"

Pierce hesitated, glancing at the page again as if the words might change. "They have... resorted to... extreme measures."

"My perfect society is eating itself," Edward said.

Edward's eyes drifted back to the folder, but something in the air shifted. It was subtle at first, like the room had drawn in a breath. Then he heard it—faint, distant, a voice he almost recognized.

"Elias. Elias!"

No. That was impossible.

The sound came again, closer this time, urgent enough to ripple the edges of the space around him. The walls seemed to bend with it, and the light overhead wavered.

Pierce turned his head sharply, scanning the corners. "What is that?"

The voice cut through again, sharper now, almost inside Edward's skull. "Elias! Let it go!"

The room flickered. One moment it was the command office, the next it was something else—the open space from earlier, agents positioned in a wide perimeter, the winter air biting through. The images stuttered between the two until the office finally dissolved completely.

Edward was standing in the middle of a ring of DMA and FBI agents. A shield shimmered into place around him, locking him in with an invisible wall. His magic slid against it uselessly, like water on glass.

On the ground a few feet away, Elias lay propped against

Alex's chest, his head tilted back against Alex's shoulder. His breathing was unsteady but measured. Alex held him firmly, one arm across his chest, the other bracing him upright, the exhaustion clear on his face.

Rowan and Lindsey stepped forward. Rowan's gaze stayed on Edward. "It's over, Edward. You've been defeated by your own son."

Edward shook his head slightly, as if that could clear the impossible from his vision. "How?" His voice was hoarse. "How did you do that? What was that?" His eyes stayed locked on Elias.

Elias' reply was quiet but cut through the cold air. "Thirty minutes."

Edward's brow furrowed. "What?"

"You've been in there thirty minutes," Elias said.

"Long enough to eliminate your memory specialists."

A slow, deliberate smile curved Elias' mouth. "Long enough for you to watch your perfect society eat itself."

Every agent in the ring turned to look at Elias. Rowan's expression tightened. Lindsey's brows rose slightly. Even Pierce, standing just behind Edward, looked from Elias to the agents as if to confirm he had heard correctly.

Alex's hold on him didn't change, but his gaze shifted down to Elias. A disbelieving shake of his head made it clear he knew exactly what Elias had done. *I can't believe you went there*, his expression said—yet in his eyes flickered with the faint satisfaction of knowing it had worked.

Edward's mouth opened, then closed, no answer coming. Silence settled like frost.

Rowan moved toward them without a word. As she knelt beside Elias, her eyes fell to his right hand. Resting against his palm was a golden artifact, its surface alive with shifting bands of color that shimmered more brightly than any Edward had ever seen. It pulsed faintly, as if still holding the echo of what it had just done.

Rowan's hands were steady as she eased it from Elias' grip. She stood and crossed to Lindsey, who was already holding the small lead-lined box. The lid opened with a muted click, and Rowan lowered the artifact inside. When the latch snapped shut, the light in the air seemed to dim.

She turned back to Alex. "How is he?"

Alex met her eyes, his own face drawn with fatigue. "He'll be okay. We just need to rest and get warm."

Rowan gave a short nod, then signaled to the agents.

Pierce still stood rooted behind Edward, his expression one of raw disbelief. Edward himself said nothing, the question of how still burning in his eyes even as the agents closed in to move them toward the waiting transport.

A Bureau healer broke through the ring and crouched beside Alex and Elias. Her hand went to the clasp of her field pack, fingers brushing the glass vials inside. "Does he need help?"

She reached toward Elias, but before she could touch him both men answered at once, voices rough but certain.

"Not!"

The word cracked through the cold, final and unyielding.

Lindsey stepped in then, steadying Elias on one side while Alex kept hold of the other. Together they pulled him to his feet, the three of them moving unsteadily but with purpose as they crossed the battered yard.

21

Where Memories Lie

We are bound to our ancestors by the most sacred of ties
—Cicero

FBI Chicago Division—The Day After Aurora

Alex found Elias staring out the window at the street below. A small group of protesters had gathered across from the federal building, their signs visible even from the third floor.

"Still out there," Alex observed, joining him at the window.

"Every day this week," Elias replied. "Same faces, mostly. That woman with the 'Protect Our Children' sign was here yesterday too."

Alex counted maybe thirty people, far fewer than the crowds during Edward's attacks, but their chants held the same edge. "At least the numbers are dropping."

"Are they though? Rivera mentioned three more businesses posted 'No Magic' policies this week." Elias' voice was flat. "The coffee shop on Monroe hung a sign that says 'No magic use allowed.' Whatever that means."

"It means they're scared."

"It means Edward won." Elias turned from the window. "Not the way he planned, but he got what he wanted. People questioning whether magic and democracy can coexist."

Alex watched a mother pull her child closer when a man with visible wards walked past the protesters. "City Council gets dozens of calls a day about 'suspicious magical activity.'" Yesterday someone reported a street magician in Millennium Park."

"And?"

"Turned out to be a guy doing card tricks for tips."

Elias almost smiled. "The emergency hotline?"

"It's still active and still busy." Alex shook his head. "Maybe it'll fade. People forget."

"Or maybe this is just what it looks like now. The new normal Edward created." Elias picked up his coffee and took a sip. "Ready for Lindsey's debrief?"

"Ready as I'll ever be. She's pissed at us for keeping her in the dark."

The afternoon sun shined bright through the windows of Conference Room 4A as the last of the debriefing team filtered in. Alex sat beside Elias, and glanced down at his partner's hands, folded carefully in his lap to hide the slight tremor that hadn't quite faded yet. The magical exhaustion from maintaining the construct for thirty minutes straight wasn't something that healed overnight.

ASAC Lindsey sat at the head of the table, still trying to reconcile how two of her agents had gone off-script, and somehow ended up arresting the country's most wanted terrorist. Deputy Director Rowan sat beside her, flanked by

Agent Hartford and Agent Ryan. Rivera sat across from Alex and Elias, looking like she'd spent three sleepless nights trying to piece together a puzzle where half the pieces had been deliberately hidden from her.

"Before we start, I want the truth. Because what I saw in this building the other day looked like two agents defying a DMA arrest order and forcing their way out. And then suddenly you were running your own operation with zero communication. I need to know what actually happened. All of it."

Deputy Director Rowan stepped forward, her auburn hair catching the afternoon light. "Agent Lindsey, what you witnessed was not agents going rogue. It was a carefully coordinated operation designed to position Agent Sinclair where he could deploy his magic most effectively."

Lindsey stared at Rowan, her expression tightening as the truth sank in. "You knew? While I was coordinating with DMA tactical teams, while you were reporting Elias as a wanted man, you already knew Alex and Elias were acting under your direction?"

"Yes, under our direction," Agent Hartford interjected. "In coordination with a DMA operation that required absolute operational security. Especially from the FBI."

"Agent Martinez was arrested immediately after the final operation," Agent Ryan reported. "He'd been feeding information to Edward's network since the warehouse incident eighteen months ago. He's been charged with espionage, conspiracy, and treason. He'll spend the rest of his life in federal prison."

"That doesn't explain why my agents weren't informed about the scope of this operation," Lindsey said, her anger barely controlled.

Rowan's expression grew more serious. "Because operational security required that Edward Sinclair believe he was successfully recruiting a disaffected federal agent. Any hint that Agent Sinclair was operating undercover would have compromised the entire mission. He needed to believe that he had a chance at recruiting his son or he wouldn't have let him into the compound. And Agent Sinclair needed to be within close proximity of Edward and his specialists in order for him to use his special abilities."

Lindsey was having none of it. "I don't care what the DMA calls operational security, I call it gambling with my agents' lives."

"What special abilities? What exactly did he do? I for one still don't understand?" Rivera asked.

Elias looked up for the first time since the meeting began. "Memory magic on a scale that's never been attempted before. Creating and maintaining a fake memory construct complex enough to convince someone like Edward that he was experiencing reality when he was actually trapped in an artificial environment."

"When I saw how Agent Sinclair's magic reacted to the artifact during the briefing," Rowan said, "I realized there was something unusual about the way he connected to it. It wasn't a reaction I had ever seen before."

"And when he created that stone circle memory that the entire room of federal agents could see, I started to suspect he might be able to construct something sophisticated enough to fool Edward."

Rowan continued, her gaze fixed on Elias with something close to admiration. "That wasn't a known ability. None of us expected he could do anything like that."

Rivera stared at Elias with a smile. "You made Edward think he'd won. You trapped him in a fantasy where his revolution succeeded, then let him watch it destroy itself."

"For thirty minutes," Ryan added shaking his head in disbelief. "He sustained an incredibly elaborate magical construct that required concentration and a level of magic beyond anything in DMA records."

Rivera looked between Alex and Elias. "That's why you needed to work together. Alex was providing magical support while Elias maintained the construct. When I saw you huddled together, you weren't arguing with him or questioning his beliefs. You were already planning this?"

Combat magic can enhance and stabilize memory magic when properly used," Alex explained. "But the level of control needed for what Director Rowan proposed would only have a chance of working between two people who've spent years learning to weave their magic together.

"Which is why the 'going rogue' element was necessary," Rowan said. "Edward would never have allowed Alex and Elias to get close unless he believed he was recruiting someone who'd genuinely turned against the system."

Alex found himself remembering the moment in the safe house when Ryan had passed him the small bag while he'd been buying water at the corner bodega. A casual contact that had transferred the DMA artifact to his possession, giving Elias the magical amplification he'd need for what they were planning.

"Agent Ryan made contact while Alex was purchasing supplies," Rowan continued, following Alex's line of thought. "The artifact transfer was preplanned and coordinated inside the grocery store."

"And you carried it through the entire operation," Rivera said to Elias, finally understanding how they pulled it off. "You used the ancient magic to support the construct that convinced Edward he was experiencing victory while he was being captured."

"Damn," Rivera muttered. "Moments like this make me wish I had the gift of magic."

Elias nodded slowly, fatigue evident in his expression. "It was a gamble. We had no way of knowing if Edward would fall for the illusion, or how long I could maintain something that complex."

"The plan called for fifteen minutes maximum. Based on what Agent Sinclair told us, that was longer than any construct he'd ever created," Rowan admitted. "We'd calculated that anything longer would risk magical exhaustion that could permanently damage Agent Sinclair's abilities."

"But you held it for thirty," Hartford observed, looking at Elias with amazement. "Twice as long as anyone thought was possible."

"And quite a bit more elaborate than we'd discussed," Alex added, his tone carrying both pride and gentle reproach. "Having Edward's people turn on each other and his perfect society eat itself? That was your creative addition."

A ghost of a smile crossed Elias' face. "I thought it would be more convincing if his ideology revealed its natural flaws rather than being attacked from outside."

"It was also more psychologically devastating," Rowan noted. "Edward didn't just lose. He watched everything he'd worked for collapse on itself from internal strife."

"Which was the point," Hartford said. "We needed him broken as well as captured. Someone with his level of magical knowledge and ideology couldn't be allowed to maintain hope for an eventual escape or rescue."

Rivera consulted her notes, pieces of the operation finally falling into place. "The DMA agents positioned around the complex weren't just backup. They were specifically targeting Edward's memory specialists."

"The moment Dr. Pierce tried to attack Agent Sutton, Agent Sinclair began the construct. Edward and Pierce went still for too long to be hesitation. It was clear they were caught by something the rest of us couldn't see. That was the clue Agent Sinclair had engaged the construct. Using that distraction our tactical teams eliminated every one of Edward's operatives," Ryan confirmed.

"For a moment it looked like Edward might have sensed something, but he was so distracted by Pierce trying to kill

Agent Sutton that he never realized the artifacts were no longer functional because their wielders were dead."

"Coordinated timing that required split-second precision," Hartford added. "If Edward's people had been allowed to use their artifacts during the construct, they would have overwhelmed Agent Sinclair's abilities and broken the illusion."

"How could you coordinate something that complex without informing me and the FBI agents whose lives were placed in danger?" Lindsey asked with anger in her voice.

"Because we couldn't risk Edward finding out and by then we already suspected we had a mole in the department," Alex replied. "The entire operation relied on us making contact at the right moment and trusting that Elias could maintain the construct long enough for backup to eliminate the external threats."

Lindsey leaned forward, her anger building as she stared at Rowan. "So you let my agents operate without knowing that one of their colleagues was a mole?"

"Martinez was identified as the potential security risk only hours before the final operation," Rowan replied.

"Which brings us to the part that still doesn't make complete sense," Rivera said, her analytical mind working through the details. "How did you know Edward would call Elias directly? How did you know he'd want a face to face meeting?"

"Because we'd been monitoring Edward's communications for months," Rowan said finally. "We knew he'd been attempting to recruit Agent Sinclair since the artifacts were first deployed."

Lindsey's voice was cold. "What if Elias had refused? If they'd reported the contact immediately instead of going along with your plan?"

"Then we would have proceeded with conventional tactical assault and accepted a much lower probability of success," Rowan admitted.

The room fell quiet as everyone processed the scope of what had been accomplished and the risks that had been taken to achieve it.

"Edward?" Rivera asked. "Where is he now?"

"The federal supermax prison in Florence, Colorado," Ryan replied. "Solitary confinement in the facility's magical containment unit. He'll never see daylight again."

"And Pierce?"

"He's in the same location but separate wings. The entire network has been dismantled, the artifacts secured, and their operational capabilities eliminated."

Rivera consulted her tablet, scrolling through classified updates. "What about the registration requirements? The emergency protocols that were implemented after the attacks?"

Rowan's expression grew more serious. "The immediate crisis has passed, but the political effects will be long-term. Public trust in magical integration has been damaged in ways that will take years to repair."

"Congress will probably roll back the most restrictive measures," Hartford added. "But the emergency registration protocols established during the crisis have created databases and surveillance capabilities that weren't possible before."

"It turns a static registry into a live incident feed that links incident time and location to registered user IDs and shares it with partner agencies."

"Meaning the government has more tools to surveil magical citizens than ever before," Alex observed.

"And more justification for using them," Lindsey agreed grimly. "Edward's network succeeded in creating exactly the kind of fear based overreach they claimed to be fighting against."

◇✧◇

The afternoon sunlight had faded to evening by the time the debriefing concluded. As the room emptied, Alex and Elias remained in their seats, both processing not just the operation they'd completed but the previous weeks that had led to it.

Lindsey lingered as well, her expression still marked by anger at being kept in the dark.

"I have one more question," Elias said, looking directly at Rowan as she prepared to leave.

She paused, her expression becoming more guarded.

"At the SCIF briefing, when you first saw me. You looked at me like you already knew who I was. Not from my file, or from my reputation. Like you knew me personally."

Rowan was quiet for a long moment, her green eyes holding Elias' gaze with something that might have been recognition or regret.

"Your mother," she said finally. "Margaret Sinclair. She and I were friends at university, before she met your father. Before everything went wrong."

"You knew my parents?"

"I knew your mother. I knew what Edward was becoming, and I tried to warn her. She didn't listen, or couldn't listen, or..." Rowan's voice cut off. "I've regretted not trying harder ever since."

"Is that why you recruited me for this operation?"

"I recruited you because you are your mother's son. She was a Llewellyn, same as you are. I suspected you had inherited her type of memory magic. A type of magic only direct line descendants possess. We've traced the Llewellyn line, and it links not just to the Celtic artifacts we recovered but to other, more classified gifts as well."

"Knowing who your parents were, knowing what Edward did to your family... yes, that made it personal and I should've told you. But you were already under so much pressure that I decided to wait to tell you until the operation was over."

Elias stared at her. "My mother's ancestors created those artifacts?"

"We believe so. The Llewellyn line descends from the original Celtic practitioners who forged them. That's why your memory magic responds to them with such precision. It recognizes you."

For a moment, Elias didn't speak. The connection was more than academic now. It was in his blood, written into the same magic he'd spent his life learning to control.

Elias absorbed that, his mind flashing back to the mill and the moment the air itself had answered him, when fire and wind had bent to his will in ways he had never commanded before. He'd told himself it was adrenaline, desperation. Now he wasn't so sure.

"You think the elemental surge…" he began to ask but stopped.

Rowan nodded. "The Llewellyn line wasn't limited to memory magic. The original forgers channeled multiple disciplines through the artifacts. That kind of power across disciplines is almost unheard of now. But in you, the potential still exists, with or without the artifact. She paused. "It's why, after the incident at the mill, I insisted you re-register. I wanted it on record that you aren't just a memory specialist and that you're also a natural elemental specialist. I didn't want anyone in the future thinking that you were hiding an artifact."

Elias stared at her, the weight of her words settling heavier than he expected. For a moment all he could summon were fragments—his mother bent over the kitchen table with a notebook, hair falling loose as she scribbled; the smell of lavender perfume when she kissed his forehead goodnight; the way she had tried, gently but insistently, to steer him away from his father's darker moods. He had never connected those ordinary moments to anything larger than a mother's protective nature.

Now Rowan was telling him that every instinct, every flare

of memory magic that had come so naturally to him, was rooted in her bloodline. The artifacts at Aberdeen, his powerful memory magic, even the surge of elemental power he couldn't explain, were suddenly no longer just coincidence or aberrations. They were symbolic of something far older, something his mother had carried and passed on without ever having the chance to tell him.

The revelation was both a relief and disorienting. It wasn't just Edward's shadow shaping him. It was her, too, and that realization steadied him in a way he hadn't felt in months.

But Rowan's words lingered. *Other, more classified gifts.* He started to ask, but Rowan's attention shifted to Alex instead.

"You should ask your parents what they haven't told you," she said quietly. "The Sutton family history is more complicated than it looks on paper. Some bloodlines were meant to cross, and some connections between magic users aren't coincidental."

Alex frowned, caught off guard. "What are you talking about?"

Rowan didn't answer directly. "Another time. For now, it's enough to know your role in Elias' life isn't a minor one. Take care of each other." She smiled at them as she turned and walked away.

After the DMA officials left, Lindsey, Alex, and Elias sat in the empty conference room as evening settled over Chicago. The city's lights began to twinkle outside the windows, winter darkness settling over the buildings.

"How are you feeling?" she asked Elias, noting the way exhaustion still clung to him.

"Drained, confused. Relieved that it's over." Elias rubbed his temples, the gesture betraying the headache that had been his constant companion since Aurora.

The truth was worse than the word *"drained"* suggested. His ears still rang faintly, as if the construct's hum had settled into his skull and refused to fade. His hands trembled if he held them out too long, the fine tremor hidden only by keeping his fingers laced together in his lap. Even his vision sometimes blurred at the edges, a reminder that thirty minutes of forcing another man's reality into shape had pushed him past anything he'd thought possible.

He remembered the moment the construct collapsed, the backlash of silence like pressure popping in his chest. Since then every breath held a trace of that strain. He'd walked away, but it felt like he'd left pieces of himself in that artificial world.

"And angry that so much of my life has been shaped by Edward's manipulation."

"But not all of it," Alex said firmly. "Your career, your magic, our friendship. Those were real."

"Were they? Or were they just the result of planning by people who needed me to become exactly who I am?"

Alex studied his partner's profile, seeing the doubt tugging at everything Elias had accomplished.

"Does it matter?" he asked finally.

Elias looked up, surprised by the question.

"I mean, does it change why you became an FBI agent, or all the good work you've done? Does it change the fact that you've helped solve dozens of cases and probably saved hundreds of lives?"

"I suppose not."

"And does it change the fact that when it mattered most, when you had to choose between Edward's revolution and protecting innocent people, you chose to stop him?"

Elias was quiet for a moment, considering the perspective Alex was offering.

"The construct you built," Alex continued, "that wasn't the result of manipulation or positioning. That was you using your abilities to protect people from someone who would have destroyed everything decent about the world."

"Even if the world doesn't know it?"

"Especially because the world doesn't know it. True heroism doesn't need recognition."

A small smile crossed Elias' face. "When did you become so philosophical?"

"About three days ago, when I watched my partner take on the most dangerous magical terrorist in the country using nothing but memory magic and determination."

Lindsey watched the exchange. "You two are going to be insufferable now, aren't you?"

"Probably," Alex admitted.

"Definitely," Elias agreed.

"So what now?" Alex asked.

"Now Elias comes back to counterterrorism where he belongs," Lindsey replied. "And you get back to the work of stopping people who threaten innocent civilians."

He reached for his phone, noting the accumulated text messages from his mother. "My parents are expecting us for Christmas dinner. Mom's been planning the menu since we had Thanksgiving there."

Alex looked up from his phone. "What do you think? Ready for another Sutton family holiday?"

Elias' smile became more genuine. "That sounds perfect."

"That's what I was hoping you'd say."

As they gathered their files and prepared to leave, Alex found himself thinking about Agent Cross, and how he would have loved seeing him and Elias working together again.

"One more thing," Alex said as they reached the door. "The construct you built for Edward. The part where his people turned on each other and his perfect society ate itself. That was…"

"Poetic justice?" Elias suggested.

"I was going to say a little over the top, but poetic justice works too."

Elias laughed for the first time since Aurora, the sound echoing off the conference room walls. "You should have seen his face when he realized what was happening. That moment when he understood that everything he'd worked for was destroying itself from internal contradictions."

"I did see his face. I was there for the real confrontation, remember?"

"Right. Sometimes the construct and reality blur together in my memory."

They moved toward the door together, then stopped when Lindsey spoke again.

"Alex, Elias," she said quietly. "Whatever happens next, whatever cases we work, whatever operations the DMA might want to coordinate. I need to know. I can't protect my agents from threats I don't understand."

"Understood," Alex replied.

"And I need to know that you trust me enough to keep me informed, even when other agencies prefer operational secrecy."

"You have our word," Elias said.

"And make sure you get your timesheets in on time this week. If I have to deal with another 'late timesheets' email from accounting, I'm going to lose it."

"Yes, ma'am," Alex replied for both of them.

Lindsey gave them both a look that landed somewhere between exasperation and relief, then stayed behind at the conference table, the weight of too many secrets still on her mind.

The two agents walked on toward the elevator, their steps in sync, the tension of the past days finally easing. Outside, Chicago's winter evening pressed close against the glass, the city waiting as it always did for what came next.

Later, driving through the downtown traffic toward their

apartments, they both felt the satisfaction of finishing the most important case of their careers. Edward's network was dismantled, the artifacts secured, and the threat ended. But more than that, they had rebuilt what had been broken for eighteen months—not just their partnership, but the friendship that made it possible.

Christmas lights strung across the streets glowed against the winter dark. In a few days they would be with Alex's family again, something wonderfully normal after everything they had faced.

Epilogue

The bond that links your true family is not one of blood, but of respect and joy in each other's life
    —Richard Bach

The Sutton Family Home—Christmas Morning

Snow had fallen overnight, covering the wooded property in white. Alex woke to the smell of cinnamon rolls and coffee, and the sound of his father and Elias arguing good-naturedly about proper snow-removal technique outside his bedroom window.

"Morning, sunshine," Colleen called from the kitchen as Alex came downstairs. "Those two have been up since six, debating military strategy for sidewalk maintenance."

The morning unfolded in comfortable chaos. James managed breakfast with military precision while Colleen orchestrated gift distribution around the tree. Elias moved through it all with the ease of someone who'd finally found where he belonged.

"Before we start with presents," James said, standing with his characteristic bearing, "I have something for Elias." He handed over a small wrapped box containing a house key and a metal plate engraved with Elias' name. "We had it made for the front door. So you never have to knock again. This is your home, son. Always."

Elias stared at the key in his palm longer than he meant to. It was just a piece of metal, light enough to disappear in a pocket, but it weighed more than any artifact he'd handled in the past year. He had lived in a foster home, rented apartments, hotel rooms that blurred together after too many cases —but none of those had ever felt like his. Doors he passed through, doors he locked out of habit, but never doors he belonged behind.

James's voice was steady, but the meaning underneath it left Elias momentarily unable to speak. *So you never have to knock again. This is your home.*

He thought of his childhood house, a place he had almost no memory of. He thought of the dorms at Quantico, where walls were thin and temporary. And then he looked around the Sutton living room—the tree lit with familiar ornaments, the smell of cinnamon rolls still drifting from the kitchen, Colleen's expression openly hopeful—and realized this key was more than permission. It was acceptance.

When he finally managed a "Thank you," his voice was quiet, not for lack of feeling but because the weight behind it was more than he could put into words.

Alex watched Elias turning the key over in his hand, gratitude written across his face. For a moment Alex thought of Rowan's cryptic words in the conference room—*ask your parents what they haven't told you.* The reminder lingered in the back of his mind. Christmas morning wasn't the time to bring it up, but he knew sooner or later he'd have to ask his mother and father what she meant.

When the gift exchange began, Alex handed Elias a

leather-bound journal. "For case notes, or whatever you want to keep private. It's warded against magical interference."

Elias opened it to find the first page inscribed:

For the memories worth protecting
– A.S.

"Thank you," Elias said, recognizing the inscription's meaning. "I'll use it well."

"My turn," Elias said, pulling a small box from beneath the tree. Alex unwrapped it to find a silver disc about the size of a quarter, etched with Celtic knotwork, set into a sturdy keychain ring.

"It's not just decorative," Elias explained. "Director Rowan gave me a tracking spell to embed in it. If we're ever separated again, or if something happens and you can't find me, just touch the symbol and it will lead you to me. No matter where I am."

Alex turned it over in his palm, the weight solid, practical. The design caught the glow from the tree, throwing pale reflections across the floor. "So I can always bring you home."

"Exactly."

Alex clipped it to his keys, the gesture instinctive, like checking gear before heading out on a case. "Best backup tool I've ever gotten."

Christmas dinner was James's perfectly roasted turkey and Colleen's stuffing that lived up to its reputation. They argued over board games until Colleen threatened to confiscate the dice, watched old movies in the glow of the tree, and let the afternoon fade into relaxation and laughter.

That night, as they packed for the drive back to Chicago, the spell of the day lingered. Elias glanced at Alex and his parents and felt how close he had come to losing this. For the last year he'd felt alone, doubting his gift, almost convinced he was nothing more than a pawn in his father's game. Now he knew better. His magic was his, his life was his, and he was not alone. Family was Alex and his parents, and with them he had a home he would hold on to, no matter what.

FBI Chicago Division—December 27

Agent Nicole Rivera met them at the entrance, a folder tucked under her arm. She had just been officially transferred from Major Crimes to Counterterrorism, her energy and excitement unchanged.

"Interpol notified us about two strange cases overseas," she said, handing the file to Elias. "A Royal Army officer in the UK and an Austrian skier. Both assaulted, both missing very specific memories. The soldier has no recall of a mission in the Middle East where he lost men. The skier doesn't remember an Olympic win. No other apparent connection between them. Interpol suspects there are more victims, and they believe whoever's behind it may have crossed into the States."

She gave Elias a look. "With our luck, Chicago's where it lands. Sounds like your kind of weird, Elias."

He flipped open the file, scanned a page, then closed it with a snap. The corner of his mouth tugged upward. "After preventing a magical civil war, this sounds almost relaxing."

After Rivera left them with the Interpol notice, Lindsey walked over and set a sealed envelope on Alex's desk.

"The Bureau has completed reassignments. Both of you are being transferred to Boston. Report date is the end of February. You've got sixty days to close things out here and prepare for your move."

Alex let out a low whistle and looked at Elias. "Boston."

Elias nodded, a genuine smile breaking through. "A fresh start."

Alex laughed. "I've got a feeling something interesting is waiting for us there."

The end for now…

The story concludes in book two of the Inheritance Duology —>

"All That Was Written"

Nine months after surviving the chaos in Chicago, FBI agents Alex and Elias are now settled in Boston, building a life with their girlfriends, Emily and Abby.

Everything changes when they open a chest of ancient family journals warded by an unfamiliar magic. One of those journals has been waiting for them for two hundred and fifty years.

But it isn't the only thing that's been waiting.

Unsealing them sends a magical pulse across the city that draws a fae woman into their lives. She talks of Seelie Courts and werewolves, things that exist only in fairytales. They don't believe her.

They should have.

She transports them to the past. Now stranded in the middle of a war, Alex and Elias must decide if they're willing to risk their future to help a long-forgotten people.

In the present, Abby and Emily take matters into their own hands. As an unseen hand writes new passages into the journal, they must decipher a prophecy to bring the men home— all while managing the dangerous fae woman who stayed behind.

Thank You for Reading

Thank you for reading *Where Memories Lie*. If you enjoyed it, please consider leaving a review on Amazon or Goodreads. Reviews help other readers discover my story and supports future releases.

ABOUT THE AUTHOR

An Alaska based author, Irene has been immersed in fantasy since childhood. She writes stories where the supernatural weaves through everyday life. Her travels around the world and her experience as a pilgrim on the Camino de Santiago convinced her that magic lingers in every city. She continues to explore new places with her husband and believes that airports are just poorly operated portals to new worlds.

instagram.com/ireneleeauthor

facebook.com/authorirenelee

tiktok.com/@authorirenelee

Acknowledgments

Writing *Where Memories Lie* has been a long journey. For months I worked evenings after long days on the job, and spent full weekends writing. I could never have finished it without the people who encouraged me.

To my husband—for listening to me endlessly talk about this book, for not getting annoyed when I worked on it even while on vacation in Spain, and for letting me use one of his art pieces as a key element in the cover design.

A special thank you to my beta readers: Catrin, who gave me invaluable edits, suggestions, and encouragement; and my old friend Donna, whose feedback early on led to a large rewrite of key elements of the story. It was a magical coincidence that my characters shared their names with your Alex and Eli.

To my boss, Lindsey C., who has her own secret magical abilities. I created and named the character of ASAC Lindsey for her.

Thank you all for believing in me and providing words of encouragement.